W9-CCG-894

The ABANDONED WOOD *Monique Saint-Hélier*

In a style that is precise, delicate, and haunting, Monique Saint-Hélier tells the story of the end of a family. Only two of the Aléracs, once the proudest and wealthiest family in the whole region, are left to taste the bitterness, the melancholy that poverty and the loss of great properties inevitably mean. These two are the grandfather Guillaume, who is still as haughty and witty as he ever was, and Carolle, the lovely girl whose mother had died in giving birth to this illegitimate child.

There are two other principal characters in the story. One is the ineffectual, lonely dressmaker, Mlle. Huguenin. The other is Jonathan Graew, now substantial farmer, whose encroachments upon the land and the wealth of the Aléracs are responsible for their defeat. All of these characters are completely drawn. "Madame Saint-Hélier's treatment of a character," writes Edmond Jaloux, leading French critic, "is like the lifting of a veil; we get a complete revelation; his reaction to the physical world; how the physical world has directed his course through the spiritual; his experiences and impressions; his memories; the secret tragedies of his life; fragments of his day-dreaming . . . In Madame Saint-Hélier's magic world everything trembles with life."

Altogether this is an unusual and fine novel, perhaps one of the best that has come from France in many years. James Whitall, well-known translator and author of "English Years," has done an excellent translation.

THE ABANDONED WOOD

MONIQUE SAINT-HÉLIER

The Abandoned Wood

TRANSLATED FROM THE FRENCH BY JAMES WHITALL

HARCOURT, BRACE AND COMPANY

NEW YORK

Published in France as "Bois-Mort"

COPYRIGHT, 1936, BY
HARCOURT, BRACE AND COMPANY, INC.

*All rights reserved, including
the right to reproduce this book
or portions thereof in any form.*

first edition

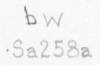

Typography by Robert Josephy
PRINTED IN THE UNITED STATES OF AMERICA
BY QUINN & BODEN COMPANY, INC., RAHWAY, N. J.

TO THE DEAREST OF FATHERS

MAY 26 '36

CONTENTS

PART ONE

An Evening at the Aléracs'

CHAPTER ONE

*J*ONATHAN GRAEW's footsteps died away. If Mlle Huguenin had leaned from the window—a thing she never did—she might have caught sight of his tall, bent figure before he reached the Aléracs', where the road turned sharply towards the village. She sat in her chair with a hand on the windowpane, watching the wet leaves swirl in the wind; one cluster of red berries clung to the rain-blackened rowan tree. She sat quietly and her lips parted slowly in a thin smile, showing a little gold filling in one of her teeth.

People still ordered waistcoats from her, brown or grey; and the brown days alternated with the grey days, making her year striped like a zebra. Brown half-wool, grey half-wool; cutting, measuring, trimming, sewing. But that wasn't all of it. One could play tricks with the gloomiest existence. There had been happy days at first and she remembered them so well that she could, as it were, take them out to pasture; she would go out driving her whole flock of happy memories before her —memories of her eighteenth year, of her twentieth, of a wide-brimmed hat—all jumping about awkwardly,

3

licking her, nibbling at her, and rubbing their rough little heads against her hips like lambs who hadn't learned how to use their eyes. For her, happiness was like that: white wool, eyes that wandered, and the need to put out her arms.

On the morning of her betrothal she had been happy. It was Easter and all the windows were open; the jonquils were coming up and the sky was washed clean. It was at the third window where she now sat with her sewing that he talked to her. He told her that he loved her. She was sitting with her profile to the window and could see both the room and the street. He told her that he loved her and at that moment Jonathan Graew had walked past.

Until the day of her death she would see those pink *immortelles* in a basket tied with ribbon that was too pink and a little crumpled; and her fiancé's face, severe and too triumphant; and the odour of lilacs, new leaves, and florist's paper that crackled when one touched it; but more clearly than anything she would see that white thread on her fiancé's knee, just at the break in his trousers. It was about seven inches long and she couldn't help seeing it, couldn't take her eyes from it. Impossible to explain the embarrassment it caused her— she couldn't have done so herself. She had blushed on seeing it and she blushed now when she remembered it.

4

Her fiancé looked at her more and more triumphantly and, when he told her how much he loved her, she was merely disturbed at seeing the white thread move and twist about. She wondered whether she should speak to him about it, interrupt him, tell him he had a white thread on his knee, or whether she should show it to him, or just take it off herself—but she dared not, for one does not touch a man's trousers.

Oh, it had been so like her! The only time a man had ever told her he loved her, she had scarcely heard him because her mind was distracted by a little white thread.

Today was a brown day. She was working with "half-wool," a stuff of the colour and almost the thickness of a ham-rind. She leaned over her work, gravely pre-occupied: measuring, applying the pattern to the material, cutting here, trimming there, marking each measurement with quick movements. At the edge of the table a piece of yellow chalk shone with unpolished brilliance, greedily. All was accurately done; she raised her head and started to smile, but the smile suddenly left her face. Good gracious! Had she made a mistake? Twelve and a half inch armholes? Surely Henry Cazard did not have such big arms. The scissors, the lining, and the basting thread shook miserably in her hands; her thoughts flew to her red leather notebook which she ran through twice before finding page 19 bearing the measurements of Henry Cazard of Haute Maison: shoulders 15¼ inches, back 22½ inches, arm-holes 12½ inches. Of course his armholes were 12½ inches! How stupid she was to get into such a state over measurements that she knew by heart. There wasn't a man in the parish whom she could meet without thinking: armholes 11, waist 33, or whatever they were. Would she always be like a little frightened girl? Her myopic eyes blinked rapidly and she repeated almost aloud: "Henry Cazard of Haute Maison, armholes 12½ inches"; then lower, like an echo: "armholes 12½ inches"; then in a soft dream-like voice: "almost an inch larger than Jonathan Graew's." She bent over her work again with a smile that one would have liked to touch and her mind filled with sweet forbidden thoughts that made her beautiful.

The light from the window fell upon her scissors and they became transparent, the colour of frost. She looked closely and saw reflected in them a woman thinner than a knitting needle with a long yellow nose.

Attractive! She laughed almost soundlessly, but the vastness of the room for such a tiny laugh frightened her and she was silent. . . . It was time to light the lamp; she could not see to work and the wind blew dismally. She got up, walked to the mirror, and stood there surprised to find how nice she looked. Her long scissors were in one hand; with the other she fluffed up her hair, arranged her collar, and flicked several threads from her dress. "I do look nice, but it's because there isn't much light." She smiled drearily and did not light the lamp. In the darkening room she stood for a moment, uncertain, frowning. Then she went to the chest and looked into a vase of asters, raising their heads with both hands and slowly letting them fall again. For the thousandth time she wondered whether or not to burn the *immortelles*. Those straw flowers made her feel sick. Again she saw that too triumphant smile; again it was Easter; again she smelt the odour of new leaves. . . .

She had once received flowers from a man; he chose *immortelles* because he loved her. This had happened to her, to the woman by the window who hadn't the strength even to draw the curtains. And now there was nothing left of her betrothal but a little basket of flowers that smelt of furniture polish, a bowler hat raised in greeting, a child's voice questioning: "Daddy, do you

7

know that lady?"—and she hadn't even heard the answer. The dried blossoms looked up at her with their dreadful constancy; they did not seem to be asking for mercy. They weren't called *immortelles* for nothing. They were always there, in basket or wreath, the keepers of memories that had faded.

If Carolle were here, thought Mlle Huguenin, she would make short work of them. "Do they go or don't they, dear? They go." She could see her grasping the poker and making a bright spot among the embers, then the basket on the embers, the nozzle of the bellows under the basket . . . and her betrothal vanishing in little flames.

Suddenly Mlle Huguenin turned from the window and replaced the basket on the Louis-Philippe table in whose smooth surface one could follow the intricate golden veins of the tree. She surprised herself by speaking aloud: "What an idiot I am!" A dim light came in at the window, not nearly enough to work by; but the metal trimmings on the furniture and the eyes of the portrait on the wall gleamed. All was so still that her life seemed to come close about her like the water of her bath; she could feel it. The fire subsided, leaving only a bed of ashes, and the room began to smell like the garden outside. There was only a little bunch of asters, but all was so still and dark that one could imagine oneself surrounded by flower beds, and what could be seen of the floor shone like a pool of water.

Mlle Huguenin bent over the asters, breathing quickly and shivering a little. How she loved their perfume! What had she to do with brown or grey woollen stuff, or No. 3 silk, or No. 2 cotton? Oh, she wasn't what everyone thought. "Enough of all this! Enough of chairs and white curtains." She looked at her furniture: heavy, handsome, patient, and reserved. She put out her arms to defend herself: "Enough!" but already her voice was softer. She was the village saint; people called her in for births, illnesses, and deaths. When men say, "She's a saint," it means that one is done for. Men don't marry saints; they don't clasp saints in their strong arms. They put them in church in niches, to wear coloured robes, or in a stained-glass window picturing a sky full of miracles. And when a woman in a forsaken village is called a "saint," she is doomed to loneliness.

She pressed her face against the windowpane and gazed out into the empty street. The earth was a place of wind, rain, and falling leaves; it no longer belonged to men. She remained for a long time at the window, and the darkness finally enveloped her. She did not realize that she was weeping.

Mlle Huguenin worked quickly, for she had lost a great deal of time. The waistcoat had to be delivered tomorrow and she was dining with the Aléracs that evening. She plied her needle quickly and regularly, carefully watching the shape of her buttonhole and pushing the stitches together with her fingernail. Her buttonholes were masterpieces. In her big chair near the fire, the one that Carolle had christened "the silk house" because of its soft cushions and gentle curves and its smell of orris root, she evoked dreams of the past. The lamp light was like a huge yellow flower and Henry Cazard's waistcoat looked so ugly that it was indecent.

She hated herself for having wept, and was possessed by the fear of becoming a sour old maid, unable to combat her tormenting loneliness. There must be some other way for her to live; there must be! Did marriage bring contentment to women? She could hardly believe it. They had children, but there were certainly some women who did not like children. No, it couldn't be children, for then the matrons of orphanages would all be happy. What was it that she lacked? Certainly not memories. No one could take her memories from her. . . . It wasn't that, nor was it the solitude or the silence. It was the dreadful feeling of emptiness, of having noth-

10

ing behind her—a wall of glass. She had never possessed the courage to change her course—always a tiny link in the slowly moving chain.

All the Huguenins seemed to crowd around her in the empty house, accusing her: "Why did you never marry? Why haven't you any children? Why are you leaving us all without descendants, hanging year after year like rusty well-chains? You have betrayed us. What is to become of our lands? To whom will you give our house? Who will care for our graves? For whom will the cherries ripen, and whose horses will be in the stable?" She was drawing her thread too tightly; it had broken twice already. Pushing the needle into the stuff, she took the spool in her left hand, the thread in her right, and gently pulled out a needleful while the spool spun round with a sound like fluttering wings. She cut the thread neatly and the spool fell noiselessly into her lap. Then Mlle Huguenin breathed into her thimble to make it stay on her finger. For a moment she closed her eyes and sat, saint-like, with her big hands motionless; then she pulled out the needle with blinking eyes and half-open mouth, put the end of the thread into the eye, pulled it through, and without raising her head finished the sixth and last buttonhole.

2

"May I come in?"

There must have been singers in that family; the voice was extraordinary, a delight to hear, without thought of the words spoken. Its tones were drawling and melodious, husky only occasionally, and the sounds enveloped one intimately. The lantern had gone out and the voice which came from the end of the corridor seemed perfectly in tune with the surrounding darkness.

"I'm taking off my galoshes—oh, my hands are frozen. Don't get up; I'm coming."

She had pushed the door open, looking at first like a huge bunch of autumn leaves. To judge by the perfume, they were plane tree and beech. The bunch moved forward, enormous, yellow, and rain-soaked. Behind it something beige, then brown shoes which the firelight, with embarrassing exactitude, showed to be a little worn.

The wind rattled the windows terribly, like a headless demon with a hundred arms.

"Aren't they marvellous, dearie?"

Mlle Huguenin looked up, and the bunch was lowered gracefully till it concealed her head.

"Carolle, you're suffocating me. Gracious, be careful of the lamp!"

They both laughed and Carolle stamped her feet to warm them. Mlle Huguenin tried to extricate herself, complaining because the leaves were wet, because she couldn't see, and because Henry Cazard's beautiful waistcoat . . . but Carolle was not to be deflected. It was fun to see Mlle Huguenin struggling with the leaves in the ordered stillness of that room.

"It's too bad of you, Carolle. Really, at your age!"

"A little patience, Madame: 32, 33, 34, all right. Again: 32, 33, 34. Yes, you're a little deaf on the right side, just as I thought." She had spoken close to Mlle Huguenin's ears, keeping her head encased in leaves. Mlle Huguenin was making goat-like motions to shake them off when Carolle suddenly let the whole bunch fall into her lap, covering her with yellow, green, and red leaves that smelt of the trees and the watery skies. The whole earth was there on her knees, and its perfume, potent with age and destruction, enveloped them both.

Henry Cazard's waistcoat had slipped onto the polished floor, as well as the scissors and the spools of silk; and the thimble had rolled out of sight. In the end they were both laughing again; Carolle kissed her friend, sat at her feet, threw her beret into a corner and began to run her hands through the leaves; they were soft and had only a thin line of green at the edges which looked white in the lamp light.

To Mlle Huguenin, Carolle seemed very like her mother, but suddenly the girl looked at her with wide grey eyes and in that moment the cool forceful expression had nothing of her mother in it. Still . . . It was then that Carolle announced, casually, and as though the fact were of no importance: "I've sold my beets, you know."

"You've what?" Mlle Huguenin exclaimed in a startled voice. "Carolle, you're making fun of me. Did you sell them to Jonathan Graew? Tell me quickly."

"I have no dealings with Jonathan Graew." Her voice sounded dull and disinterested. Mlle Huguenin watched her face. Could it be that she had not let Jonathan Graew have her beets? If she had not, there would be trouble. The whole countryside would be talking.

"I thought—that is, I've been told that Jonathan Graew is the one who . . ."

". . . holds the beet concession in this district. That's true."

"Well?"

"I sold mine to a stranger."

"You wouldn't dare, Carolle; that would offend everyone."

"Then everyone will be offended."

"You enjoy doing that?"

"Yes, I do, in a way." She held an aspen leaf to the light, looking through its delicate network of veins and its thin supporting flesh.

"And where did you find your buyer?"

Carolle raised her eyelids slowly and answered:

"At the *Petit Monaco,* yesterday afternoon."

"You were seen?"

"Certainly; the place was full. One knew the Frenchman was coming to buy beets and that there would be trouble on account of Jonathan Graew and the factory in the Meuses wood. You know what a factory there means for us?"

Mlle Huguenin nodded.

"It means dispossession, doesn't it? And we've owned the Meuses wood for Heaven knows how long."

Mlle Huguenin did not answer; she looked weary.

"You want details, reasons? I went in and saw Graew with his crowd in the corner. There was an infernal racket, but after I had taken three steps the noise stopped."

"Then?"

"Nothing. I made my sale, that's all."

"Was the other man there?" Mlle Huguenin's voice trembled like the flame of a guttering candle.

"Of course he was there."

"You knew it beforehand?"

"Oh, darling—it's such a job managing the Aléracs, isn't it?" She took Mlle Huguenin's hands and kissed them one after the other. ". . . the stinker!"

"Who? Graew?"

"No—the other man."

"What words you use, Carolle!" She was about to say, "Your mother would not have allowed it." But when a child has no mother, it is a little too easy to say that she would or would not have allowed something, but all the same Carolle should not have used a word like that.

"All right; twenty sous for your charities. Your money-box is empty" (it was their custom that Carolle's bad words should bring help to the poor at Christmas), "but is 'stinker' worth twenty sous? It's not such a dreadful word when you consider what I might have said."

"Put in ten sous then, but tell me everything."

Carolle took them out of an old purse which looked absurd in her—it was not enough to say lovely hands, for they were more like wings.

"If only you could have seen me in the rain, out there in the fields with that creature! We measured everything and verified the boundaries, though the mist and rain made it very hard to see at all. Heavens, it was thick! I thought of you, dear, sitting by your lamp, sewing. Naturally he tried to cheat me. Did he know what a beet was or not? And Jesus-Marie-Joseph, was he to learn his business from a girl? It was obvious that my beets had the blight and were hardly worth the buying, that they would not produce sugar, but pepper. All the Saints were called upon, but I was as hard as a stone. He wanted to know what a fragile young thing like me had to do with beets. Well, the fragile young thing stood there in the mud and rain, and she told him that if her beets had the rust, his pigs had the wheal-worm. I held on to every sou, right up to the end."

She laughed mirthlessly, and when Mlle Huguenin asked her whether she had not been frightened alone in the fields with that man, she replied simply with a changed expression on her face: "Yes, I was."

"There was a moment when I thought the deal was off. He began to hesitate, to argue. What about cartage? His horses could not be fed on air. Perhaps I would like to lend him a truck and some gasoline. He leaned very close to me and I felt his breath on my neck."

"What did you do then?"

"I put up my price. I felt perfectly calm and determined, and nothing on earth would have made me take a sou less. He wrote me out a check at the edge of the Anges field and I examined it carefully with my electric torch. Once it was in my hand, all I wanted to do was to throw it in his face and the beets and everything. I'm not a horse-trader."

She stood up suddenly; her narrow face and her eager young body made one think of a colt.

"Oh, Carolle, do be careful of the lamp!"

"Don't worry, dearie, it won't budge. That lamp is as steady as Pharos itself."

The hoarseness of her voice prevented Mlle Huguenin from noticing that it was trembling.

"Is your throat sore? Have you caught cold?" Carolle listened to a multiplication of familiar questions, realizing that she would have to yield, get down on her knees, open her mouth; that the shade would be removed from the lamp, and that she would be blinded by its light—all because ten years ago she had had diphtheria. Mlle Huguenin forgot all about the leaves as she took off the shade. The thin yellow flame looked like a tongue of fire and she thought of Pentecost.

Carolle put her tongue out; their two silhouettes on the wall played a game, full of bows and politeness. A tile, clattering down from the roof, sounded like a dinner plate, and the wind rattled the windows.

"Open your mouth—wider; now turn your head to the left—now to the right . . . there's nothing the matter with you." She dismissed her with a pat on the cheek.

How she adored these moments when Carolle yielded to her, when she became again the little trusting girl they had brought her years before. She looked at Carolle now with all the old tenderness. She remembered her scrambling about with a pile of picture books, toy trains, pails; ink was spilled, taps were turned on. . . . Mlle Huguenin spoke now just as she had done in the past: "You're the loveliest little girl in the world." Her arms clasped her and she went on softly: "maybe not the best-behaved"; then even more softly: "but it doesn't matter." She was smiling at her as few mothers can smile.

Carolle soon disengaged herself; when anything moved her she felt awkward and peevish. She began to sing:

> *Il était haut comme un champignon,*
> *Frêle, petit, délicat, mignon.*

Her deep voice sounded cross:

> *Et jaune et vert, comme un perroquet,*
> *Avait bon caquet.*
> *Jean de la lune, Jean de la lune.*

19

Then she gathered up the leaves and ran off towards
the kitchen, still singing. Now and then a word or
two vibrated in the room where Mlle Huguenin stood
arranging her dishevelled hair. She could follow
Carolle's movements by the sound of the voice. She
heard a clatter of vases, a tap turned on full. "She'll
flood the kitchen—what *is* she doing? Gracious, she'll
upset the kitchen lamp! . . . I'll drive her mad with
my fussing about lamps, poor little thing." Again Mlle
Huguenin felt like weeping and she picked up Henry
Cazard's waistcoat and folded it carefully. She was one
of those women who often think about dying. "What
if I should die tonight?" For her, death was neither
an accident nor an illness. It was an exacting house-
wife who must find everything neat when she came.
Mlle Huguenin put her spools of silk in their box,
her scissors in their place, flicked the sewing machine
with a linen cloth, wiped the wheel with some cotton
waste (there was always a bit of oil there) and inspected
the belt. All this was done with dream-like movements,
but nevertheless with the utmost care.

She always seemed particularly anxious to remove
the traces of her passage through this world, to leave
nothing of herself, so that anyone entering the room
could go about his affairs without a thought or a question about her. She wanted silence, oblivion. "You will

find no evidence of me anywhere." . . . Noiselessly
and expertly, she replaced the wooden cover; beneath a
thick blue Indian shawl and a carefully placed photo-
graph, the sewing machine became one of those strange
pieces of furniture found in country sitting rooms.

Abraham and Isabelle Huguenin could have been
sitting at their card table. The cards and the perfume
of verbena tea were not there, and she could not hear
their voices saying: "trumps"; "hearts"; "diamonds";
or "will you cut, my dear?" But she had only to imagine that infusion of verbena and they were with her:
her father with his pipe, and her mother in her im-
maculate lace kerchief and the gold brooch that now
lay in the right-hand corner of the top drawer of the
chest, beside the violets. Strange—she kept a brooch and
a pipe, but the people who had really existed, whose
voices had sounded in the room, she could not keep.
There was no chest large enough. "What an idiot I
am. No chest large enough!" The chests that were
large enough were brought into the house. They were
coffins.

Carolle was coming now. "Quick, some powder
around my eyes—there. My ring, my lorgnette, my
knitting; am I ready?"

Mlle Huguenin was sure the kitchen had been
turned upside down, but Carolle said there was noth-

ing serious: "You'll see—only a little water; your tap squirts. There was no vase for the leaves, so I tried the butter-crock."

"The butter-crock!"

"Yes, dearie. But it wouldn't do."

"And where did you put the butter?"

"In a bowl. Where else? Don't worry about butter when I've been creating a masterpiece for you. Look!"

She pushed the door open to display the big, black, three-legged potato pot sumptuously extravagant with colour: green thorn and autumn foliage of a beauty so poignant and so eloquent as to be almost immodest. One felt drawn to sit down close to it and wait, silently.

But after the fashion of clocks which always come to the aid of family life, Mlle Huguenin's struck six. Carolle lit the lantern and knelt before the fire; a few large embers had to be carried in a shovel up to the bedroom stove. The faint odour of soot, ashes, smoke, and burning wood enveloped her as she climbed the stairs, followed by the cat. When she came down, she covered the fire, put up the screen and threw some apple peelings upon the ashes. Then a little powdered sugar on top—a thing she had seen done as long as she could remember. The lamp was turned down, matches put out, and Mlle Huguenin wrapped herself in her old cloak. Its colour had gone but it was indispensable.

It had been named *la Gloire de Don Ramire*. Many had used it during the long twilights in the garden and it was often left on the garden bench, covered with dew, uncomplaining, unwearied. It faded like the grass in the meadows, but, like the grass, it always reappeared. It was an old friend, without whom it seemed disloyal to spend an evening out.

When they opened the door a gust of wind flattened them against the wall, and *Gloire de Don Ramire* tried to take flight. The lantern's beam caught the figure of Jonathan Graew returning from his errands. Their hands met above the lantern.

"Good-night, Jonathan Graew." Carolle was glad she had spoken to him as though he were a farmer and had not said "Mr." Her heartbeats quickened with her hatred of him.

"Good-night, Jonathan." Mlle Huguenin's words were sent through the wind clearly and graciously as though she were offering a gift. But Jonathan Graew said to himself: "Patience, that young Alérac won't always be putting on such airs." He smiled at them both, and the three stood there in the fury of the wind, wondering if it was going to snow. They shook hands awkwardly and though one could not see their faces one knew that they all wore expressions of distress,

23

that for some reason they had not the courage to sepa-
rate.

Then Carolle leaned down and picked up the lantern,
swinging it to and fro like a station master. Were they
going to wait in the rain like this until Judgment Day?
After all, they each had their place; his was down there,
theirs was up here. Each was distressed and that was
enough. But they were distressed in different ways.

In the lantern light everything was distorted: Jonathan Graew looked first like a pumpkin, then a tree-
trunk. Mlle Huguenin was an angry signal post: green,
yellow, and black, twisted with exasperation at Carolle's
impertinence. The light in Carolle's hand seemed as
unreal as a luminous star on a Christmas tree.

Jonathan Graew's steps could still be heard, for he
had walked up into the wind. The others made the
best speed they could, the lantern showing inky pools
around them in which stones shone like lacquered
frogs; from the ruts in the road a pleasant odour of
decay rose acridly to their nostrils. The hedge concen-
trated the force of the wind upon their heads; then it
flattened itself out like a big hand placed between their
shoulders. When it slackened they had the sensation of
falling backwards towards the wet mud. Then it would
be at their skirts, sending them hurrying along, their
faces plastered with damp leaves. The few hundred

yards that remained seemed a long journey filled with unexpected obstacles. The lantern light was confusing: a plane tree became a colt, the hedge a nameless, galloping animal. The water in the pond slapped, and the wind, leaping upon the earth, made the creaking branches of the trees fling down little bundles of leaves. There was a faint perfume of asters, dahlias, and daisies that would soon be dead, broken off by the strength of the wind. In her flapping cloak, Mlle Huguenin looked like one of those melancholy angels in a graveyard.

Carolle Alérac, her lantern clasped firmly in her hand, her lips parted and her nostrils dilated, was very happy. She would have liked to stay there till the end of the world.

CHAPTER TWO

GUILLAUME ALÉRAC opened the door and went out into the hall, thinking he had heard the sound of footsteps. The yellow flame of the taper he was holding danced on the white walls; in the room behind him there was a blazing fire which diffused a golden glow. He was surprised all over again by the proportions of the hall illuminated by the fitful flame he was holding above his head; it seemed to him enormous, a cavern of shadows. One could just make out a staircase and benches. The faint yellow light from the taper fell on the chin of an ancestor upon the wall; the faceless and bodyless chin vanished suddenly, and one saw a ringed finger, a lace collar. Then the flame was still for a moment and the gilt frame of the portrait gleamed softly through the shadows.

Footsteps were now distinctly audible. Guillaume Alérac, seen from a distance, looked very tall and straight, and the light upon his hands made them seem more than usually beautiful. He was not at all like Liberty Lighting the World, but full of reserve and austerity, as though there were very few people upon

whom he cared to shed his light. His gestures were ter-
rifyingly aristocratic and commanding, but one could
not help being drawn to him, and to respect him was
easy, for respect was his due. There were some who
adored him completely and this was evident merely
from the way he held his taper as he stood upon his
threshold waiting for his granddaughter.

"He looks like a Rembrandt, doesn't he, Carolle?"

"Yes—a Rembrandt . . ." but she was thinking
something quite different. To her, he was an extraordinary being; she felt that there was something super-
natural about him; he seemed to her to be gazing eagerly
at death.

He greeted them with a wave of his hand; the taper-
flame danced and the shadows leapt on the white walls.
"Quickly, let me pass; I'll explain later." It was Mlle
Huguenin's muffled voice from behind her sleeve.
Carolle's laugh came from inside her scarf. She kissed
her grandfather with lips that were so stiff from the
cold that they felt like pieces of bread against her teeth.

"What a storm! Marvellous, isn't it?" Guillaume
Alérac's voice had that peculiar tragic quality so noticeable in his granddaughter's. It was a voice to be listened
to with one's whole body. He was tall and rugged—a
beech tree on a hilltop in winter. Much more like a
tree than a man, and like a tree the storm suited him.

The wind blew right into his body, into his blood-stream, bringing a smile to his face. In the firelight one could see that he was old—and magnificent. He walked up to Mlle Huguenin with his beautiful hands outstretched and she put the tips of her fingers in them quickly, as though she were a Catholic about to cross herself. Both of them smiled sadly.

There was no illumination but the fire, and the pink and violet lights behind them with which it had banished the night made the room strangely beautiful. The woodwork had turned geranium pink and a golden gleam touched the sea-charts on the walls. The Aleutian Islands were yellow, then green; then they disappeared altogether. Presently, at the end of the room, out of range of the fire, one could see a long loaf of bread and a carafe upon a tablecloth that was like a square of moonlight.

Carolle threw herself into the "seal" (her favourite leather chair) which was close to the fire's warmth. "Careful; you'll get chilblains, Carolle." She did not move and her hands were too cold to remove her gloves or make any sign whatever. The sudden warmth of the fire after the cold wind was killing her, but she adored that kind of death; she was drifting, drifting. . . . Now only a little round cold spot at the end of her nose. That enormous foot did not belong to her; it never had. Before a huge fire it had come to life; it was probably the foot of a young obelisk. It showed promise, that foot; it would go far. She thought of the *Arc de Triomphe* and laughed with her eyes closed. "I'm the mother of the *Arc de Triomphe*." She moved the massive foot and found that it was only a little one in a yellow leather shoe. "Oh, look at that hole in my sole!" She began to see the shoe with a pile of others in the village bootmaker's shop—the smell of wax and leather, shoe-strings hanging on the wall; tapping, hammering by the light of a steady shaded flame. What a dismal end for the *Arc de Triomphe!*

She jumped up, tore off a glove, and put a cold hand down her companion's neck (Mlle Huguenin, who was arranging her hair, gave a little scream of annoyance); then she took her grandfather by the shoulder and made them both play "pease porridge hot." Mlle Huguenin screamed again because her chignon had collapsed and her fingers were numb. Carolle grasped her hands and there was a good deal of laughing mingled with the screaming; a ring rolled on the floor. Motionless by the stove in the corner, Gottlieb sat watching them, his peculiar lifeless smile scarcely reaching down to his mouth. He looked like a Chinaman, or rather a Japanese, and his extraordinary eyes lay beneath his lashes like flowers just lifted from water.

Dear Gottlieb would say: "I am the village idiot, Madame, the village idiot." And he would speak as though asking to be forgiven for something.

Some rubbing with eau de cologne brought the game to a close. Gracious, what hands! So cold! Relenting a little, Guillaume Alérac bent over them, held them in a way that made it clear how well he understood women, that his knowledge of them was exact and his attitude towards them inflexible, but that he loved them. In his laughter at their cries it was possible now and then to detect a youthful note, and suddenly one had the impression that his youth had not lasted long enough.

"Heavens, they are cold! Why are your hands cold, Carolle? Tell me?"

"But, Grandfather, there's a dreadful storm outside!"

"A storm? You don't call this little breeze nosing round the windows a storm!"

"We could hardly walk in it."

"Nor breathe," said Mlle Huguenin.

"I thought my lantern was going over the hedge."

"I was afraid I'd lose my cloak."

"We looked like angels with spreading wings."

"And we met Jonathan Graew."

"Looking like an angel with spreading wings?"

Four different kinds of breathing could be heard in the silence of the room, but no words. Then the conversation sprang up; words perched here and there and were scattered like feathers in an aviary. Upon the walls, hands merged into heads and heads into arms. These silhouettes made Gottlieb laugh and frightened him too. He raised his hand and a gigantic arm signalled to him from the wall, but the shadow of the teakettle diverted his attention.

Guillaume Alérac stood up with such a tender smile upon his austere features that Carolle jumped from her chair and ran to him.

"You are the most magnificent thing in the whole world!" She threw her arms about him. His slender body, his silvery hair, and the melancholy ease of his graceful gestures were irresistible. "You're like a beautiful tall tree." She took his head in her hands and held it firmly. He merely looked at her, but there was something in his expression which made one feel like weeping.

"You see," he said, "how she makes me realize that I'm only an old tree-stump."

"What?" Carolle tried to spring away from him, but he held her by the wrists. She struggled, looking at him with wide eyes in a pale little face. "You an old tree-stump? Never!" An expression of terror, almost electric, passed over her face; she actually glowed with anger. She would not have it that he was old; his years were his endowment; they had nothing to do with getting old. She would have liked to trample on death so that nothing could interfere.

But presently Carolle began to laugh, and her laughter was so quick, so young, and so lovely that it penetrated all the shadowy corners of the old house, transforming it into a new green and white one on a sunny hill-top surrounded by elder hedges and a white fence, with a corn-loft and everything that one could wish.

Guillaume Alérac was still holding his granddaughter by the wrists. She was very like a spirited young animal, prancing about to test its own strength and that of its tamer. The latter was leaning towards her affectionately in the glowing fire light, and Mlle Huguenin smiled as she watched them—a tall jonquil rising out of her wicker armchair.

Brilliante sur sa tige et l'honneur du jardin. . . .

"The Principality will now partake of dinner." Gottlieb made his announcement and began to occupy himself with the soup-tureen.

"What Principality, for Heaven's sake?" It didn't matter; the idea amused them.

The atmosphere trembled a little near the fireplace, because of the excessive heat. The hands of the Aléracs wavered slightly; Mlle Huguenin's calm features looked as though a very thin curtain of silk veiled them, and the outlines of the chairs were uncertain. When the candles were placed on the table one could see three vases of flowers, two bottles; and on the wall a tiny pointed shadow like a nose: the Penelope's flag fluttered at half-mast over Formosa. At least half of the sea-charts were invisible on the walls: America gone; the Falklands, the Fijis, where were they?

If one stood close to the sea-charts one could see that they were yellow and flimsy with age, and full of tiny holes. Someone must have followed the courses of the ships with a needle; probably a woman, but she evidently knew what courses they sailed. No sailor could have found fault with her knowledge. "I'm writing you from an island on the way to Hongkong where there are many parrots." She had reached the island with her needle-point . . . prick . . . prick . . . Cuba, San Domingo . . . prick . . . prick . . . such a tiny hole to mark that monsoon from the northeast—two or three Aléracs lost in more than a hundred fathoms, there in a little needle-hole. Yes, Penelope, there was no time to shift the helm; one minute and they were food for the fishes. That's how it happened.

Ils étaient cinq marins. . . .

Leaning close to the chart she had again found the spot where they had perished and had stuck the flag there, to remain fixed in the sea under the motionless stars . . . it was always dusted with infinite care.

To those who have once been rich, is it a consolation to know where their lost fortunes have gone? Carolle was amused to think that she could put her finger upon the very spot, beneath that flag (a hundred fathoms down, it was true), where casks of dollars and Spanish duros were lying, and enough tea to fill all the cups in England, when actually she was obliged to count her twenty-sou pieces with the utmost care.

The disaster at Formosa had been a bitter blow for the Aléracs—an armada of coffee, sugar, gold watches, and singing birds—those miraculous little gem-encrusted birds that perched on golden sticks and sang. Within their breasts were mechanisms so tiny and so delicate that it took weeks to assemble the parts of the minute movements. Kings and Island Governors had bought them. Louis XVI had had his.

An Alérac had once told how a slave-dealer wept when he heard the song of one of those little jewelled birds; it had sounded to him so fragile, so celestial.

34

The Aléracs had made a fortune in these singing birds, and in gold watches which the ladies of those days insisted should be round and sensual, thick with diamonds, and decorated with Louis XV and Louis XVI knots, butterflies, or even pastoral scenes. The Aléracs had covered the Islands with watches; they had ships, factories, and sons whom they sent to the Islands. Their sons bought slaves, plantations of sugar-cane, and long, low Creole houses. That traffic implied many voyages and it brought in a great deal of money. The Aléracs were held in high esteem; hats were raised to them; banks were put at their disposal; balls were given in their honour; gauze ball-gowns swished softly on warm nights. With gold-headed sticks and ceremonial gloves, the Aléracs went into churches and saw lovely names of young girls written in the registers beside their own; and at home, on the other side of the world, the new names, perhaps a little too unfamiliar, fluttered aimlessly through the great rooms like butterflies at sunset: Pepita, Jeffa, Dolores—and once, inexplicably, the Swedish name Ingrid.

It was a custom with the Aléracs to take their wives to the Islands (one of the conditions of marriage) for, having become a powerful family, they were afraid of getting involved with native women and having illegiti-

mate children; there must be no little coloured Aléracs.
The wives came home to complain bitterly of the cold.
Fur wraps were purchased; houses were filled with foot-
warmers, beds with hot bottles, and boudoirs with
curling-irons. In the town they were called "Spaniards."
They didn't often have babies.

Fortunes are subject to a malady that culminates once
a century. It can cause swellings: one is suddenly rich;
then slowly the money disappears: anaemia—or quickly:
galloping consumption. The Alérac fortune was reaching the point of non-existence. The family had now
learned economy. They tried to forget the exasperating
times when a handkerchief costing thirty francs could
never be enjoyed because those thirty francs had, as it
were, soiled it beyond washing. Debts had grown alarm-
ingly; creditors walked up the tree-lined drive followed
by the dog who didn't growl any more because he knew
them too well. It was hateful to have the butcher and
the grocer bringing their accounts for the twentieth
time when one knew them by heart—always spotted
with grease or blood or marked by dirty fingers.
Awful to have people talk about the dead bodies of
beasts the way they did, or of lumps of sugar or little
green lentils at many times their value. Oh, money,
money, money! Let all there was in the world be thrown

in their faces. Sometimes Carolle thought she would go mad with her poverty.

The big reception room with six windows was closed; also the music room which smelt of raspberries. Furniture polish and firewood were expensive. It was difficult to decide about the other rooms. Guillaume Alérac loved his house, but not because it was noble or beautiful—he didn't care in the least about that, or for what it might contain in the way of fine pictures and furniture; one did not take things of that sort out of this world. It was for the memories it contained that he loved his house, for its soul, its spirit which would comfort him at the portals of death. "In my Father's house are many mansions . . ." If only his own house could be one of those mansions!

Everyone was familiar with his slow stroll from room to room, his pipe in his hand and the cat walking in front of him. When his cool grey eyes met those of an ancestor in lace collar or jabot and he stopped before the high gilt frame, one left the two of them together, knowing they would have things to say to each other. The centuries that separated them became as nothing —perhaps a few moments of awkwardness, no more than the time necessary to exchange greetings and go off together. For Guillaume Alérac, time was not a fleeting thing, but a fixed point upon the verdant path of life.

2

The winter was going to be a hard one: "A good one for wolves" . . . "There'll be plenty of boars" . . . "Be careful of your fowls. Henry Cazard of Haute Maison saw a fox" . . . "At the Parsonage they say there are plenty of martins." These bits of news were shouted from milk cart to milk cart in the early morning. Brakes creaked in the dry cold air and cautious hands held the reins.

"It reminds me of the winter of '70, Carolle." Guillaume Alérac had consulted his barometer. The garden looked as though a blight had come upon it; the nasturtiums were black and the earth was like stale chocolate with cracks in it. The fence was grey with frost and the sun that shone upon it was a toy sun made of spun glass. That afternoon Guillaume Alérac had ordered the gardener to put straw around the urns and sand on the paths. Then he walked out the front door, bare-headed, to throw bread crumbs to the birds. From all directions they came; it was as though the leaves of the trees had become little curved, feathered stomachs, chirping and hopping about on legs. When he came in, his face looked like grey blotting paper. Carolle said nothing; she was one of those people who know what infusion to prepare before asking: "Are you ill?" She began to cut the twigs from a bundle of wood, whistling several bars of Mozart to which her grandfather beat time unconsciously with his foot. Then she made a fire, and it was a fire that the Aléracs were going to remember. The bellows were weak; she tore a finger-nail; her hair became impregnated with smoke. The operation terminated in a camomile shampoo and a bath, but the fire had been made.

"Is your grandfather to be roasted on a spit or burnt at the stake?" He smiled his slow smile at her over the *Times;* she smiled back and it seemed to her that their smiles clasped as perfectly as two little hands on an old-fashioned ring. He did not draw up to the fire or even uncross his legs, but as she listened to the silken hissing of the flames she heard him discreetly rubbing his hands together. He wanted desperately to take her in his arms and tell her that she was everything to him, his most precious possession, but instead of indulging in such a demonstration he merely continued to smile at her.

She had taken the dogs out that afternoon for their daily run; not by the pond, but farther afield, past the wood-sheds. It was odd that some things so closely connected with a house in the country could go wrong. It was difficult, for instance, to imagine a shortage of wood on a place covered with trees. The Aléracs were short of wood already, and it wasn't even Christmas. She ran and leapt about with the dogs, but her eyes were upon the fagots; they counted the logs and measured the peat. Guillaume Alérac, hearing her laughter and the cracking of her whip, was pleased to think that there were still moments of enjoyment for his granddaughter. Again he was surprised to find himself hoping . . . What was he hoping? Idiotic of him at his age! What was there to hope for? Absolutely nothing and it was just as well to realize it and not waste time uselessly. Things had to be faced, and it was impossible . . . or else . . . but that was impossible too. A smile full of sadness passed over his face; he had never given in, never, and he would not do so now. In the past his answer had been *no,* and for the future it would be *no.* His old hands tightened round the gold-headed stick at his back. At the edge of the orchard he halted to gaze with unseeing eyes at an espaliered pear tree against an old wall. What did it all amount to? There were more important things to be considered than just living. . . . With the end of his stick he raised the bent head of a dahlia.

The pear tree against the wall had turned red and

yellow in the cold. He leaned close to look at the trunk, which had drawn the life out of its family of branches; its bark had burst, revealing the yellow wood, and the branches stretched out like arms. "You too," thought Guillaume Alérac, laying his long hand upon the trunk, "crucified . . . all of us . . . but why?"

He ran a finger along the split bark which was warm in the sun. It was three o'clock in the afternoon. "Ah, well—as long as there is earth under one's feet." He raised his head and looked over the orchard wall at the soft yellowish sky. The wind plucked the leaves from the trees by ones, twos, and threes, almost imperceptibly—an absent-minded wind; though it had so many things to do, so many leaves and petals to pick, it loitered. Much better not to force things; it didn't matter how they were picked . . . that red dahlia in disorder against the wall had never learned to comb itself . . . it was an odd wind, like a stable-boy idling while his master slept.

Guillaume Alérac removed his hand from the pear tree and stood for a while looking at the ground with the head of his stick under his chin—a familiar attitude when something was on his mind. Then he walked up the path between the gooseberry and black currant bushes, with blue shadows beneath its bordering hedges of box.

41

How good it was to hear that laugh! How reassuring to hear her with the dogs, to hear her whip snapping and imagine her splendid active body in the autumn sunlight. What a magnificent child she was! And what a woman she was going to be! Suddenly the smile left his face. Give her . . . to whom? What man in this forsaken place? He thought of Rivière, the banker, who had a son; of Rochedieu who also had a son; of de W—— who had one too. He wrinkled his nose as though an unpleasant smell assailed his nostrils; then he started to laugh—what a fool he was! When one is poor, isn't one obliged to keep one's daughters? She couldn't marry a peasant. An Alérac? An A-lé-rac: the familiar syllables of the old name quickened his heartbeats. And to have her trained so that she could be a governess, or the Lord knew what, in some English manor house was unthinkable. Good God, an Alérac!

3

Late in the afternoon when she knew that all the farm people would be sitting before their fires, her grandfather in his leather chair with two fingers resting against his temple and a pile of religious books by the Arnaulds in his lap, she had started off over the bare fields. A cart passed down the road and she stopped to wait, motionless as a tree, for it to pass. Her steps were rapid, like Gottlieb's, and too long for a woman's. She knew what was underfoot: young corn here (she must skirt this field); the potatoes had been earthed up (oh, smell the leaf tops!); and more of that cammoc! Clover would have to be sown there next year.

The reek of wood smoke and dead leaves was everywhere—in the misty greyness a tree, three trees, another field, boundary walls; then into the forest arched with branches—dead ferns lying round the tree trunks, mosses sucking up the water, big greasy toadstools smelling of decay, too large for the time of year, holding stagnant rain water like yellow rubber bowls.

She made her way quickly, bending over, almost creeping, listening to every noise. She did not want anyone to know—she did not want anyone in the village to say: "Those Aléracs go out to pick up firewood."

In winter it was always bitterly cold—ice everywhere. Down in the court the cistern was like a flat white eye at the bottom of a hole. The pipes were treated like ailing children, all wrapped in wool and flannel. Old stockings muffled the taps; and the pump, in its padding of sacks, resembled a paralyzed kangaroo.

With her soldering-lamp Carolle visited all the bathrooms in the house, where, in spite of old socks, stockings, cravats, and every sort of encouragement, there was not a tap that would run. Charms of the country in winter. Through the windows, the crows, sombrely ironical, watched her at work, and when she turned her sputtering lamp towards them they only raised their wings a little and clapped them back on their sinister bodies to resume a pose of such perfect immobility that one could imagine them carved out of ebony.

Carolle had turned the house upside down without consulting anyone. In the old kitchen, a vast room panelled right up to the ceiling, she had made their winter den. It was warm and comfortable, and the panelling had been polished till it shone like chestnuts. Through the window one could see the red maple, and the heath beyond, where some colts were running about, was dotted with yellow gentians.

It was amusing to be among pots and kettles; books had been brought: the Bible, *Robinson Crusoe,* and some sea-charts. No more poverty; no more economizing. One felt very Jules Verne: red books with gilt edges. The Captain's cabin, safe from shipwreck. Upon the long, low walnut table, honey-coloured with pink reflections—a piece of furniture never to part with—had been placed the Captain's little brass model of the capstan, his globe, and his three pipes.

44

The grill in the corner had been brought from the stable. A grill had been needed, or a screen (it didn't matter) to hide the sink—not a town sink, the very sight of which made one ill, but a granite trough resting on two supports. In summer it was filled with forget-me-nots and it would have been marvellous in winter with pink azaleas, but there were neither azaleas nor the money to buy them, so its ugly emptiness had to be concealed. Green plants were not popular with the Aléracs. Carolle had gone rummaging, and it had taken a whole day to clean off the grill with sandpaper. Carolle and her helpers were covered with powdered rust; faces, hands, shoes were yellow with it, and their eyes gleamed behind heavy red lids like the narrow eyes of idols. But the grill was at last smooth and clean. Later they put gold leaf on the pointed ends and stretched a piece of rep—no, it was some heavier material—anyhow they stretched it behind the grill, which now gave the impression of barring the way to some place of mystery.

All was cozy and comfortable in that kitchen; the leather chairs had lost their stuffing, but one was happy in them. The big armchair was very old and authentic. With pieces of furniture, unlike people, the more patine, the more beautiful; their decrepitude is like an unassailable and sweeter youth. Even the old wax-grey

45

flagstones were luxurious. Masha, the cook, would never set foot upon them without crossing herself; she was certain they had been stolen from a cemetery and she felt as though she were walking on dead people . . . but then she was a little mad.

CHAPTER THREE

*A*T THE end of the table he stood watching them eat. He was happy, a thing one could not say of many people. But at that moment it was true of him. He was like a bit of country before sunrise—untouched, alone, and smiling; and it was all the more true of him because everything was going to change abruptly, as it did each evening. The people he was watching knew it and were ready to help him. But there was nothing to be done for Gottlieb then. One had to wait, in frightened silence, for his return from a difficult journey.

He was so handsome, looking at them from the end of the table: a little too intently, perhaps a little too immovably. He followed every one of their gestures, glad they were hungry, delighted when they drank. With his increasing pleasure his expression became more and more intent, until suddenly, like a person who is going blind, he fixed a terror-stricken gaze upon each of them in succession; then he began to sway drunkenly, making desperate efforts to keep his balance by clinging to the edge of the table. One could touch him and speak

47

to him, but he could neither feel nor hear, for he had been summoned to another realm.

The pallor of his face was something more than pallor; it was the visual evidence of a ghastly fatigue in some terrible struggle. But of what use was it to hope that he would win a victory? His soul hovered, seeking to escape a tragedy in which it could not endure to participate. One got the impression that he was on the point of death, that his huge empty body would collapse with a horrible noise; and though the Aléracs lived through the same experience every evening it was always heart-breaking. Masha stood just behind him, watching closely, ready to catch him in her arms and carry him away.

An appalling change of some sort seemed about to occur in him. Was he losing his human attributes? He had been Gottlieb and now he was not Gottlieb at all. If only one could have helped him in that desperate struggle, through the long tormenting transformation! He seemed to be spreading his wings out over the Aléracs like a brooding hen, with neck stretched forward. It was as though he could feel them beneath his curving wings, against his warm feathered body. He half closed his eyes and one could almost hear heart-beats in the room. . . . Suddenly he made a clucking noise and Carolle, who had been waiting for it, spoke in a slow, scarcely audible voice: "Some bread, please, Gottlieb," and she held out her hand for it.

It only required a word or two to reinstate him in the world of people. He passed the bread at once with dream-like movements, smiling. The attack was over.

Poor Gottlieb! There was nothing that could be done for him. Every evening the Aléracs had to endure this horrible thing, after which they wanted to shake themselves like dogs who have been too long in the rain. Gottlieb remembered nothing; he rubbed his right temple with his middle finger three times and went on serving the dinner.

That evening he produced a fantastically arranged duck with olives. He had placed it on the oldest, most battered of all the dishes in the house. For that dish he had a weakness which could not be cured, and he always brought it in triumphantly whenever a dish of its size was required. In the end they had given it to him: "Keep it, Gottlieb. It's for you; take it to your room." But it reappeared in its place between the samovar and the apothecary's jar, and he still persisted in using it on certain mysteriously recurring days of which no one knew the significance, days that were called "anniversaries of the dish." One soon became used to them.

49

The duck was surrounded by a flotilla of olives, with a piece of holly at its prow, a green candle stuck into an orange at its stern and an encircling bulwark of chestnuts. The arrangement was fantastic and it amused them. He carried it like a royal bouquet, carefully watching the flame which flickered dangerously in spite of his cautious movements; then, sliding the dish across the white sea-way of the tablecloth to its place, he bent over to sharpen the knife and left the room smiling oddly and without raising his eyes.

He killed the birds he cooked quite willingly—even with a certain enjoyment. He did it quickly because he hated blood, but it was pleasant to hold them by the wings and press their noisy throats, while their feet clutched at the air, especially hens' yellow feet. How he would laugh then! He had chased those crazy birds that would always make one last plunge for a grain of corn and then fly from him like a sheet of writing-paper, this way and that. "I've got you now . . . didn't want to come in, eh? Wanted to flap and jump about some more, what?"

But when he saw them in the dish, deprived of their feathers and their arrogant combs, so naked, so fallen, he was filled with tenderness for them and sang a little song to them, gently. He did his best to encourage them, and when he abandoned them upon the tablecloth, almost skinless and sometimes headless, their feet lying on the kitchen table, he often wept.

What was the meaning of his strangely garnished duck this evening? It wasn't Christmas, so why the green candle with its softly gleaming flame? The table was too empty; its wide expanse of white signified something, but what was it? He was always looking at the tablecloth and perhaps its old-fashioned pattern had produced the orange, the duck, and the holly. Or was it simply a funeral wreath for his duck? Who could tell?

A duck gliding over the water is a lovely sight, but a roasted duck on a platter, without its feathers, its beak, and its rapidly paddling feet of yellow rubber, is rather saddening. Perhaps he was thinking this when he sorted out the olives, and the wreath of chestnuts may have formed itself naturally; then the sprig of holly was added and he may have said a prayer. But one felt somehow that an orange and a green candle were not right for a duck's tomb. The fantasy came from some more distant quarter, a thousand leagues beyond the world of ducks. "Something more complicated, something . . ." Carolle was making gestures like a blind person.

"What do you think, Carolle?"

"I don't know. I'm searching. I've got my rod out."

"And what is Cinderella's godmother fishing for?"

"She wasn't fishing; she was tapping the pumpkin that changed into a coach. I am fishing for oranges and ducks, and I've got . . ."

"A sprig of holly." Her grandfather made fun of her; he adored her passionate desire to understand everything, that exacting conscience of hers which gave her no peace, especially concerning Gottlieb whose case interested her vastly.

"Perhaps there is nothing to understand?" Mlle Huguenin spoke gently, but Carolle was exasperated. As if there existed anyone about whom there was nothing to understand! We were all full of confusion, obscurity, and the waste of forgotten worlds. Our minds were ragbags of crazy ideas.

"We are also called the children of God," murmured Mlle Huguenin, turning to look at Gottlieb who had just placed a bowl of salad at her left.

"I believe," continued Carolle obstinately, "that the orange, the candle, and the flame have some special meaning for him. Wait! The colour may be important. A green candle like that would have been hard to find in the village. He must have looked a long time for it."

"Perhaps he had it already," suggested Guillaume

Alérac. "He couldn't have bought it at Mme Campiche's, not a fluted candle of that colour. I wonder how long he's had it. Let's see." He pared off a thin shaving of wax with his fingernail and Carolle shut her eyes; for some reason she could not bear the sight of her grandfather touching that candle.

"The wax is dry; see how it flakes—almost like borate. That candle is an old one."

"Ten years?" asked Mlle Huguenin.

"More than that. Twenty or twenty-five."

"Older than I am, then?" Carolle examined her senior carefully.

"What struck me particularly," Guillaume Alérac continued, pouring out some wine, "was the way he carried that duck, his seriousness. What a strange expression he had! He reminded me of someone I met in Tibet."

"A priest?"

"No. An archaeologist. The grave radiance of his gaze when he found a stone he wanted was like Gottlieb's just now. Didn't you notice his face?" He had turned to Mlle Huguenin.

"I thought he looked handsome," she replied; then she blushed, believing that no spinster should admit that she found a man handsome, even the village idiot.

The narrow flame of the little green candle burned steadily. "It must not be put out," Carolle's low voice besought them, but when she saw that they were surprised at her seriousness she went on jokingly: "It's mine, isn't it?"

"As you like."

They were enveloped by the odour of duck and olives and the soft light of the candelabra. If Guillaume Alérac had put out his arm he could have touched Hongkong on the chart. The fruit bowl in front of Carolle seemed filled with opals and Mlle Huguenin's wine glass glowed like a ruby.

2

When Guillaume Alérac poured out the next wine, Carolle asked him about the Graews. She wanted to know whether they drank or not. Her question was put in a slightly unnatural voice, a tissue-paper voice, giving a false impression of softness. Her heart was beating rapidly. She was afraid of the answer and would have liked to put her hands over Mlle Huguenin's ears and tell her not to listen, and at the same time she wanted to cry out: "Listen and you will learn that your hero, your Buckingham in wool, takes after his forebears."

Mlle Huguenin tried to help herself to some duck.

"I am going to faint," she thought; "Carolle knows—when did she find out? Does everyone know?" Her breathing must have sounded like a pump—her heart would surely leap out of her body! She put a slice of duck on her plate and heard Guillaume Alérac's reply, but so faintly: "You mean, were the Graews addicted to drink?" The palms of her hands perspired freely. How awkward she was with the duck! He took the spoon from her hand and put a pile of chestnuts on her plate, patted her wrist . . . how women's hands trembled sometimes! She was able to exclaim at the colour of the wine, its bouquet; and after the ceremonial silence following their first swallow she complimented Guillaume Alérac, but all the while she was thinking of Jonathan Graew's smile, a drooping smile that always seemed to be falling off his face (was that the way one smiled when one had been drinking?) . . . and when he opened his mouth, what was there on his breath? It was absinth, but she did not want to admit it to herself; no, she would not admit it! She gave him that absurd loophole; if she did not admit that his breath smelt of absinth, then it would be that he had not been drinking absinth. She put down her glass; Carolle held hers between her hands as though to warm it. The wine suddenly looked so cloudy in the candlelight that she wondered whether everything that men drank was cursed.

The sugary perfume of absinth clung to her body like an earwig that could not be shaken off. Carolle's unrelenting gaze was upon her and Guillaume Alérac began to speak again. Heavens, what was he going to say?

"I have known the Graews for a long time," he turned slowly to Mlle Huguenin and, bending his head a little, he picked out several more olives for her and filled her glass; his words were distinctly spoken, "and I only saw Jonathan Graew's father drunk once." He turned to Carolle. "And that 'once' was absolutely justified."

"Can we hear about it?"

"His two sons came down with influenza the same day, and twenty-four hours later they were both dead— pneumonia of the left inferior lobe. I was with them. You are too young for me to describe death to you." Carolle protested. "Our attitude towards the dead is indicated by our manner of speaking of them. We say 'dead body' just as we say 'seaweed' or 'shellfish.' We put it at once into its wide classification: human vertibrate. A prayer or two, a few memories, and all is over." He thought for a moment, his fork poised in the air, "It's as though one used charts, statistics, addingmachines. Those two Graews were twins, almost Siamese; one couldn't help confusing them. They were always called 'the Graews,' never Elie and Samuel. Even when encountered separately: 'I met the Graews.'

'Which one?' 'The Graews.' Well, the moment they were dead, they separated as quickly as they could, escaped from each other, as it were. A host of differences, which we had never been able to see, were noticeable immediately, altering them so much that it was difficult to imagine how they could ever have been thought to resemble one another. One was tall, with a tragic look, an obstinate nose, and full of insolence. The other was tall too, but effeminate; even his bones seemed flabby.

"One might say that forty-eight hours after his death a man shows the outward indications of his true self—the one no one knows about. And that is why the faces of the dead are so peculiarly upsetting. . . . 'My husband?' 'My brother?' 'My wife?'—'Who is this stranger?' "

Guillaume Alérac's voice was so low that his words seemed to lose themselves in the night, to be seeking some unseen listener. He sighed deeply and began again more clearly: "I saw Jonathan Graew's father grasp both his sons by the hand; he wanted to drag them back into life, to force them out into the fields. They were his sons, his labourers; the best he had because they did not have to be paid. He could not give up this profit and he fought unreasonably to keep it. There are those who struggle with angels; he was struggling with the

57

dead. . . . I lifted up little Jonathan—he was about five—and put him in his father's arms. The child barely escaped being beaten to death. He wanted strong men who could plough his fields. Pretty soon the mother and the child left him with his dead sons. He put a harrow and two scythes at his door; no one should take his sons from him."

"Did he love them?"

"In his own way, he did. Added together, his fields, his sons, and his wife made one, but it was a very large 'one.' His getting drunk made it possible to give them a decent burial. They were taken from him gently as he sat with his hands on his knees, looking at the floor (spotless even then) and repeated over and over again: 'The resurrection of the body, the resurrection of the body.' "

". . . and the potatoes." Gottlieb, who was passing the wine, made this contribution in an extraordinary bass voice. Carolle jumped, but Guillaume Alérac kept on talking, his hands motionless on the table.

"He did not follow the two coffins out of the house and through the fields, but Madame Graew walked after them, bent over as though she were carrying her two sons on her back."

"I saw them go past my window," said Mlle Huguenin; "I was very young, and Mother held back the curtains."

Even the wind seemed to be listening to Guillaume Alérac; it was blowing now very gently, close to the window. The fire's reflection was like a huge rose which grew smaller and smaller as the fire subsided. All was so still that when Mlle Huguenin took a swallow of wine one could hear it going down her throat. She choked and apologized; tiny tears no larger than grains of rice appeared in her eyes. The green candle was still burning.

"I can tell you definitely, Carolle, that Joshua Graew never touched another glass of alcohol. That was the only time. Each man suffers as he must, my dear. We're not really bad, any of us. Anyhow, it ended there absolutely."

"Finished, the mole, blind, greedy, dried up, under the earth." Gottlieb stood near the fireplace, seeing to the punch. He seemed to rise out of a bouquet of words. "Finished . . . the mole . . . blind . . . greedy . . . dried up."

"Do you think the old man was like a mole, Gottlieb?" asked Carolle, her elbows on the table and her chin in her hands.

"Finished, the mole—deep, deep—" With a grin he took up the punch-ladle and rapidly moved it through

59

the air, copying so exactly the peculiar movements of a
mole that Guillaume Alérac began to watch him at-
tentively. No detail of Gottlieb's behaviour should be
neglected. He made a mental note of the word "mole"
and speculated for a moment as to the possible value of
making a careful study of his reactions.

It was astonishing how professional Guillaume
Alérac's expression could be when focussed upon the
object of his interest. Its intensity was concealed behind
a mask of indifference, his eyes no longer revealed his
actual feelings, and one had the impression that they
had become two precise scientific instruments, that
nothing pertaining to the soul could escape their fatal,
almost mechanical, scrutiny.

"Couldn't one say, Grandfather, that his life is the
same as ours, but that he lives it on a different floor, to
which we have no key?"

"It would be more apt if you said that we have no
lift; the search is very fatiguing."

"But it's so full of interest, so exciting. One becomes
a hound, sniffing and scenting; one searches and finds
nothing; one comes upon something, draws near, and it
is nothing; one waits and fails utterly, or else one suc-
ceeds. Don't you think I might have been a good psy-
chiatrist, Grandfather? A trapper of souls?"

Mlle Huguenin laughed happily and naturally, disposing of the trapper idea with a fan-like gesture of her small hand; she was so out of date, so 1830, that one wanted to scold her for knowing so little of the realities of the world she lived in. Then one was overcome with pity, realizing that those colourless gestures were all she had to defend herself with.

At that moment Carolle had a vision of Jonathan Graew taking those fan-like gestures of hers and breaking them one by one, not out of unkindness, but because he had strong hands. She jumped up and grasped the back of her chair: "How I hate him, hate him!" Her words were more whispered than spoken, but Mlle Huguenin started. She knew of whom Carolle was thinking.

"What's the matter, Carolle?" Her grandfather put a hand on her shoulder; he had thought her rather nervous lately and he looked at her now closely. Perhaps it was that slight squint he had imagined he noticed the other day. He made her look up and down, right and left, and follow his finger, but dismissed her with a tap on the chin. No, he was mistaken; Carolle's eyes were perfect in every way.

"In every way, Grandfather?"

"In every way, Mademoiselle." He smiled at her with almost touching affection. He felt so old and she needed him so badly! She leaned over to rest her head against his shoulder, and felt herself borne away, far away to some safe refuge, slowly . . . slowly . . . "In my Father's house are many mansions . . ." Was she perhaps going to one of those mansions? . . . She opened her eyes and saw that Mlle Huguenin was lighting the rum pudding. The flames leapt up from the dish, scaled the soft sides of the pudding, and then went out with the tiny sound of a match being dipped in water.

Back to earth . . . everything before her . . . all the difficulties to face . . . but at least the earth smelt of rum pudding. Mlle Huguenin cut the helpings: a huge one for Gottlieb who adored rum pudding; a huge one for Carolle too, with the maximum quantity of rum (she loved it burning on her plate); Guillaume Alérac was also fond of it and Mlle Huguenin too, in spite of her anguish. There was no sound for several minutes save that of the spoons, but the smell of the rum was so strong that one could almost hear it too. It had come to sit with them at the table, cheerful and potent. Now it would be with them the whole evening. She was so glad!

CHAPTER FOUR

*E*VERYONE moved to the fireplace for coffee, and the odour of rum went with them. Cares fell away—the lions slept in the desert; it was that enchanted hour when angels enveloped themselves in mist and descended to the earth of men; when doors opened noiselessly and visitants hovered on the thresholds. Outside, every other street lamp had been extinguished.

"You know, don't you, Carolle, who saw the Graews arriving here fifty years ago?" She put down her cup without drinking, surprised that "the Graews," a topic she had "sown" in the conversation during the duck course, should crop up again. She wondered why it had. Her grandfather was scraping out his pipe, during which absorbing operation he continued to speak without raising his eyes. Carolle put a hand upon her friend's knee, palm upwards, and left it there. The hand seemed to be saying: "It isn't my fault that we are talking about the Graews this time—I don't have to be forgiven, do I?"

Mlle Huguenin looked up from her knitting and her smile was neither gay nor sad, but Carolle felt she would

63

give anything in the world to be able to put Jonathan Graew into her arms. . . . The wool of the pull-over was primrose-yellow, exactly the colour Carolle adored, and the clicking of Mlle Huguenin's needles was such a discreet clicking!

"I was standing under the silver poplar at the top of the main road." Guillaume Alérac opened his tobacco pouch. "I remember the air was like crystal," he began methodically to fill his pipe, "and I could see as far as Roches de la Mort over the grey-green fields; the oats were already standing high." He closed his pouch and the odour of English tobacco, its peculiar pungency almost grasping one by the hand, took each of them apart, as it were, and addressed them privately. Their sensibilities were sharpened, nostrils became flexible— as delicate as sweet peas and as still as sleeping butter-flies. The odour enveloped Guillaume Alérac's listeners, but they could not disregard his words, for they sounded with a distinctness that was somehow frightening.

"It was a magnificent arrival for the Graews. They took up the whole road" (Already! thought Carolle) "and I stood aside to let them pass, being thus able to see them from every angle: full faces, profiles, and backs. Two goats came first, then Joshua Graew, then his two sons carrying scythes, and finally his wife with a cage of birds. The men bowed politely, but she kept her eyes upon the horizon in front of her. Despite the fact that she was a peasant, she wore a hat and gloves, and, though I never saw it again, a large gold locket."

Guillaume Alérac crossed his legs and looked at Carolle who sat on the floor, chin in hand. "There was something very special about those Graews, a kind of machine-made dignity—even the goats walked stiffly. Yes, they were an unusual family . . . they turned into the Taillères road and eventually the whole company came to a halt at the Alérac portals. . . ."

"Someone should have set the dogs on them," said Carolle in a low voice.

"I can see those scythes, those goats, and the cage of birds now, and the tall woman blotting out the landscape. At that very moment your grandmother drove out into the road in her English barouche. The Graews were standing on the right and as she passed she waved to me with her whip, an enchanting gesture which made everyone gaze after her until the turn in the road hid her from our view. She was ravishingly beautiful. . . . Well, when she had gone all of us smiled. Strange people —impressive in some ways."

How could her grandfather say such things? Carolle was furious; she folded her arms and gritted her teeth. Guillaume Alérac could not help laughing: "The Aléracs' watchdog!" He patted her cheek affectionately.

What had the Graews done that one could admire?
Was it that, with two scythes, a woman and two goats,
they had dispossessed the farmers, taken their ploughed
fields from them? How soft Mlle Huguenin had been!
Hadn't she let them have her last acre? Couldn't one
hear the scythes under her very windows? Oh, nothing
escaped Jonathan Graew; he never wasted anything.
If grass had grown on her drawing-room floor, they'd
have brought the scythes right into the house. . . .
They hadn't stayed long at the farm on the Taillères
road, those moles. Night and day grubbing in the earth,
grovelling, scratching, cutting . . .

"For the first twenty years, Carolle, there wasn't a
single flower in their garden; nothing but vegetables,
some in cold frames, but all green, and among them
Madame Joshua Graew's grey skirt moved ceaselessly
like a huge bell. What a strange woman with her
servant's clothes and gloves to work in!"

Carolle had heard enough about those gloves; farmers,
pastor, midwife, everyone knew about them. What
idiots they were to remember her with reverence (of
course she had had to die sometime) because of those
gloves! "The greedy old mole! Why, she even econo-
mized in her screaming when she had a baby!"

"What's that? Carolle, what *are* you saying?" This
time it was Mlle Huguenin interrupting.

"It's true; the midwife told me. She turned and twisted on her bed for hours, but nothing happened. 'Scream, will you? Scream!' But she paid no attention to the midwife, kept as silent as a tomb, and finally it was the baby who screamed."

"She was a very handsome woman," continued Guillaume Alérac, "lovely eyes, tiny ears, and hands that—well, they were hands that never gave in. We men don't like that kind very much." He smiled a rare smile, his thoughts returning to his youth—little, soft, yielding hands in his.

"Do you remember her straw hat?" He turned to Mlle Huguenin.

"Oh, yes, the one with the big thistle in front! In the autumn if Mother saw her walking towards the quarries she would say: 'There goes Madame Joshua Graew to choose her thistle.' And I used to watch for her to come back. Once I saw her; she had the thistle in a basket and one of the prickles was sticking up above the edge." She laughed a thin colourless laugh. Guillaume Alérac laughed too. "How dreadful women were, prying into each other's affairs and criticizing . . . she *was* handsome and that flowerless garden of hers was extraordinary—a delight to the eye with its neat geometrical rows of carefully chosen vegetables. She was out with the first sunlight, tying things up with stakes and raffia, her big straw hat pulled down over those amazing dark green eyes. Your grandmother would often go and chat with her, and she always came back perplexed at finding Madame Graew clearly well-born, pottering about in a vegetable garden. She imagined all sorts of domestic dramas and her determination to get at the facts was incredible—but incredible!" He raised his eyebrows reminiscently. . . . "However, she was never able to discover anything."

"Were they fond of each other?" Carolle asked.

"Sometimes they were and sometimes not—you know how women are. It was the strangest combination; one often thought they detested one another, and then, no. The Negroes and the organ were a great bond of sympathy. The way women went on about converting the Negroes in those days was appalling. There were meetings, conferences, and Mission days; they talked about Mappopé and King Khama."

"Oh, yes, I remember!" Mlle Huguenin exclaimed. "Mother told me about it."

"Do you know, Carolle, that Madame Graew had one of the loveliest mezzo voices I've ever heard? Your grandmother adored music, and why the two of them didn't wear out the organ, I can't think. Music absorbed them completely and they came home from those meetings as pale as angels: one to her raffia and the other to her Aléracs. Then the organ would possess them again. It was like that all their lives and I must say it had its pathetic side: two women with absolutely nothing in common who were brought together by the singing of an 'F sharp' or a 'B flat' in unison."

Heavens, that quiet voice of her grandfather's, and the woman listening, listening . . . ! She was like a shadow-filled room whose door was being slowly opened. Her fields had been taken from her, but hadn't she been robbed of things more important than her fields: her dignity and her peace of mind? Oh, how old they were! When one is old one's defences are easily broken down. Father in Heaven, for whom did you intend sickness, earthquakes, and floods?

Anger burned in her cheeks until she began to imagine that the air about her face was being warmed by it. "Wasn't all the land owned by Aléracs for hundreds of years?" Carolle asked in a dull voice.

"Every acre as far as Roches de la Mort, but not the farmhouses. Still, if you were to look at the old records you would find that we owned them too, but that was so long ago—those deeds are very ancient. An Alérac returning from the Islands was often so pleased on his first day at home that he gave the farmers their houses— I suppose it happened that way—it's not important. The money came from the fields, not the houses. We held on

69

to our lands; it was in our blood to do it. Landed proprietor first; then . . ." She recognized him; he had come to her from among the dead.

"It was all the same: sugar-cane, the Islands—worn out with it all. When they'd had enough of it, they came home, sometimes only for long enough to look over the estates—then abscess of the liver (a colonial inheritance) and they were off to cluttter up the Alérac cemetery. It was their way of rejoining the family: Alexandre, Joachim, Amédée; a farmer here, a cousin there, and several charming sisters-in-law: Lolita, Mercédès, and Nathalie with 'she loved little white lambs' on her gravestone. So little to do with death, that epitaph! . . ." He leaned forward to fix the fire. "She was tall, slender and, I believe, delightful. When she died Joachim nearly went out of his mind. Haven't you noticed how the earth round her tomb is always marked by footprints? Well, they say those are Joachim's—he can't stay away from her."

"Is she the one in the red cloak with a little white fur collar?" Mlle Huguenin asked.

"Yes, she's the one. Wait a moment." He opened a little chest and took out a miniature.

"Was she happy?" asked Carolle.

"She was loved, and that's a good deal." Guillaume Alérac glanced quickly at his granddaughter with an expression of irritation on his face, half reproachful, half defensive. Carolle's heart began to beat rapidly. "I must be mad," she thought, "quite mad. It's this south wind that's upsetting me. Those two were hardly ever together. Still . . ." Then, aloud, she persisted: "I wanted to know whether her marriage was a happy one."

"No marriage is happy." His gaze rested upon her calmly now.

"Your grandfathers and great-grandfathers enjoyed being landlords: a harrow for this farmer; for that one a horse; for another, a new roof. Can't you see the parasols, and the gold-topped sticks slashing the grass? 'Take care, darling, this path is rough.' They were continually officiating at weddings and baptisms; church bells sounded. . . ."

He went over to one of the charts and tapped the Calm Zone with his finger: "Money was lost there, plenty of it . . . competition . . . Formosa . . ." He made a gesture of putting something away from him, and the shadow of his hand on the granite chimney-breast trembled slightly.

"We had just fitted out the Jason and the Céleste (no repairs on the estates that year!) and needed all the money we could lay our hands on, what with shipping competition and a disastrous tornado off Jamaica. The

Graews arrived at that point, Carolle; we sold them the
Taillères farm—at a good price, I must admit—and they
paid cash, which suited us admirably. So the Graews are
involved in my memory of all that: the Jason, the
Céleste, and the bad news from Jamaica; and also in
my vision of our blue hydrangeas which they gazed at
through the iron grill. It was impossible not to look at
those hydrangeas. Can you imagine how beautiful they
were—a hundred, perhaps two or three hundred blue
hydrangeas; the lawn was banked with them; then there
was the low grey house in the background with its ter-
race, its wild grapevines, and its faded shutters. And
beneath the trees, those tufts of creamy blue—your
grandmother was mad about them. The sun could not
leave them alone; even when the shadows darkened
under the trees it lingered, found some excuse to turn
those hydrangeas into globes of blue light. Your grandmother used to call them her 'well-beloved sons' and
would take them in her two hands to gaze into their
faces."

Guillaume Alérac began to laugh, and his laughter
made one think of summer gardens in soft sunlight;
one heard the liquid sound of sprinklers, saw the palms
in the fountain pools . . . and suddenly, in the obscurity caused by the fading fire, the hydrangeas were so
near that a hand stretched out could surely have touched

72

them as the dying Isaac touched the false Esau—could
have given them their birthright.

Mlle Huguenin's knitting lay in her lap like a sleeping rabbit. Her head rested on the soft back of the
chair and she was looking at the fire. But where was she
actually? Certainly far from the body that awaited her,
with the dove-grey dress and the ring with its blue stone.

One could scarcely see Carolle—just a bit of her cheek
—but one heard her breathing and knew that her mind
was filled by the story of the Graews. The hydrangeas
were dancing before her eyes and the course of her
breathing was uneven, a stumbling pace with occasional
halts, followed by quick leaps ahead. She gave no other
sign of her absorption in what her grandfather was saying. If she stretched out a silken foot towards the dying
fire, it seemed far more than in the case of Mlle Huguenin, to be part of a body that was waiting to be claimed
by a returning traveller.

2

"The Graews were lending money (the farmers always needed it) and when I discovered this . . ." He
got up and began to walk slowly and silently about the
room, like an animal in the dark; then he stopped in
front of Mlle Huguenin, who was still far away, and

wrinkled his brows as he looked down at her. Heavens, how lewd women looked when they were dreaming of fools! He would have liked to throw a scarf over her face. But they were all the same, even the most fastidious, and he thought dispassionately of what his own years and experience had taught him. "That money-lending of the Graews did not suit me at all. Not at all!" He spoke these last words with such force that Mlle Huguenin emerged from her dreams and took up her knitting. "When had they begun to lend money? How much? To whom? At what interest? Any investigation? None was made, and I was not alone here; I lived under the thumb of Uncle Jérome and he didn't want investigations. If the farmers borrowed elsewhere, so much the better; let them keep on doing it. If they smothered themselves in debts, so much the worse for them. The Graews left us alone and we them. What had become of Uncle Jérome's privateering blood? Swollen joints, yellow skin, riddled with liver pains, magnificent eyes, an injured shoulder and three wives—oh, not three at once; he was an upright man." Guillaume Alérac laughed. "A huge fortune, no children, and a hatred of the sea (possibly because my father had been drowned)—all our ships making faces at us in dry dock." He stretched out an arm in the darkness to tap one of the charts, and it was probably the exact spot where his father had perished. "What a life I had after that! I had been the prodigal son, but now I was going to end in poverty. The misery and sordidness of my predicted fate pleased Uncle Jérome. His smile broadened at the thought of it; the old prophet would have his fill of that vision; I was not allowed to imagine myself living out the parable. He took me by the lapel of my coat: 'No fatted calf for you. Understand? Read that Bible to me.' But he took the Holy Book himself, found the place and jeered: 'Will you listen to this story of an old rascal of a father taking back his lout of a son?' Line by line he read it, but when he came to the fatted calf his voice broke and I saw that he was weeping. Then his anger surged up again: he pounded the table with his fist; papers flew in every direction; he swept the back of his hand over the ledgers. Hadn't enough money been used up by that old harlot of a sea? Hadn't the Aléracs had enough *Canaques* and Chinese girls? Did they still want them? . . . He rubbed his sore joints. 'You say good-bye to your Chinese girls. No more sea risks; not even twenty sous' worth.' He slashed at the green cloth top of the conference table with his stick. 'What's an idiot like you going to do about those cargoes? Pay for them?' He leaned over me threateningly: 'Pay for them? Starboard to port, you know, every foot!' He went through the motions of measuring up a ship's cargo. 'And don't

75

bother me any more about that Alérac at the bottom of the sea!' He flung out his bony arm towards me, his skin turned a sulphurous yellow, and his hands were pressing against his sides; the crisis was upon him, the final one."

Guillaume Alérac put down the poker and was suddenly silent. An owl hooted outside, tentatively and shyly, but its hooting had a frightening sound.

"He had told me he would disinherit me, and he did it. The Aléracs keep their word." Guillaume Alérac seemed proud of the fact that Uncle Jérome had kept his, even in that. He liked everything about his relatives, but above all he valued their faults. "We'll die of hunger, but people with cancer are cured; consumptives in several hospitals have pure air to breathe; and prayers are said for 'our benefactor' and all is as it should be, but . . ." Guillaume Alérac straightened his shoulders, "when he died I killed the fatted calf."

"With what?" Gottlieb asked. He was flat on his stomach, lying on the flag-stones, roasting an apple on a spit over the embers.

"With sauterne."

"Sauterne?" Gottlieb's bewildered laughter seemed to slide along tracks and then come to a sudden halt. He pulled out the spit and the odour of roast apple enveloped the Aléracs like a cloak thrown over their shoulders. "Sauterne? What is sauterne? A little knife?" He saw the knife with its pearl handle; a tiny patch of moonlight in a leather case. A nice name, sauterne. Twice he called out: "Sauterne! Sauterne!" but no knife appeared. It couldn't be the knife. He smiled. And there was one thing in the house which was definitely not sauterne: the cat. "Sauterne!" The cat paid no attention; it walked over to Guillaume Alérac and jumped to his lap, then to his shoulders, curved itself there, licked its paws and slept. He tilted his head to one side so as not to disturb it. He started to open his pouch, but gave it up. His shoulder was weighed down and a huge tail hung to his elbow. There was a silky warmth at his neck and on his cheeks; a little heart was beating close to his chin. Whenever he made the slightest movement, the cat opened severely complaining eyes—wide, moon-green eyes indicative of its magnetic personality. It had come from Persia.

Mlle Huguenin knitted interminably, hundreds of pull-overs, it seemed, every hour. The world was full of pull-overs; one walked on sleeves, collars, and wrist-bands. "The poor ye have with you always." "Even with a hundred pull-overs an hour?" Carolle's legs were tingling right up to her knees, to her garters . . . oh, those miserable Graews scattering their money everywhere!

"The most extraordinary thing about the Graews was that they were in no hurry to be repaid. Far from it; the farmers borrowed and they lent. Roofs were renewed, new stables were built, new fences. Someone told Robert Lefort there was mineral ore on his property and he began to plough up his grazing land; one ploughshare cracked in two like a nut. He borrowed the money to buy another, then a second and a third and a fourth. There was no fifth because he was dead. Behind his fourth ploughshare he fell; it was a rupture. He owed the Graews for three ploughs and five ploughshares." (Item number one, thought Carolle.) "And those people at the Hermitage trying to drain their marshes: fires everywhere, flames dancing over the pools; it takes a lot of wood to drain a marsh. Who paid for it? The Graews, really." (Item number two.) Carolle's legs were still tingling; she stretched one of them out over the Hermitage marshes; it was silken and shiny, and, though it had an ill-tempered look about it, it was a pity there was no one to see it except an old man and Gottlieb who had no eyes for such treats. Sauterne? No, Carolle's leg was not sauterne.

3

The years that passed were all alike, piling up one after the other to make a high time-wall. But nothing had changed; the same apple trees were there, with or without apples; the same meadows; the same labour; everything except the fact that one was in debt to the Graews for one's house, and often for a little more than one's house. Impossible to understand how that could be when one worked and toiled continually. The sun and the moon shone one after the other; rains, frosts, and snows had come. Harvests were brought in, pigs were killed, lambs were born, burials, deaths, everything just the same, just the way it always was on this earth. Everything but the house which had belonged to one and which was not going to belong to one any longer. Suddenly it seemed to be part of oneself, and there seemed to be a trembling in its solid framework. Fool, it's not your house that quakes, it's your heart. Thirty pieces of silver for the potter's field; thirty pieces of silver to deliver up your house.

"That was how the Graews acquired . . ."

"Acquired? Stole, you mean!" Carolle's voice was so hoarse that her companions thought she was starting to have a sore throat. She moved closer to the fireplace; her

79

face was white and in her unseeing grey eyes were little points of yellow light.

". . . Grand-Combe, Fauconnière, and the lease of the Robert cattle," he counted the properties on his fingers; their names fell noiselessly upon the flagstones. Then the farmers had come to the Aléracs, looking greyer than stones and prepared to fight for their property. Guillaume went security for them and they retired but were soon back again. Further guarantees. The conflict was on: clod by clod, field by field. A bank failed, and the Aléracs were beaten. Then the Graews' reapers and haymakers were heard at their very gates. There should have been hay growing on the lake for them! Carolle smiled bitterly; Jonathan Graew would have died of joy over that. So they were to be admired for tempting the farmers with their money until they all bought reapers and haymakers; talked of cattle-raising, foaling, hunting. Why not racing, betting, and gambling? The word "return" was heard everywhere, but bankruptcy and dispossession were their only returns.

"It must at least be said for the Graews that the dispossessed were not obliged to leave their houses. They merely ceased to be proprietors and had to render accounts."

"Wasn't there one of those quaking fools who could

go out into his garden and pick up a sharp stone and fling it at the generous benefactor's head? Not even one?"

"It is written: 'Vengeance is mine.'" Mlle Huguenin's voice sounded as breathless as a little train in the country.

"Fortunately," Carolle thought, "it's not yours. What would you do with it? Make a pair of moccasins for Jonathan Graew or give him a soft chair for his declining years? She would be better dead, but one day if I have anything to . . ."

Mlle Huguenin was looking at her with frightened eyes. Oh, Carolle wanted to be done with this praising of the Graews! What would come next? Would she have to admire those ancestral portraits which had not appeared on their walls until after they had got their hands on the Alérac farms?

"There was something odd about their silence and secretiveness; such strong, splendid people—and I always felt that if one tapped them they would sound like empty tumblers. What was it that dwelt within them? What? Who? What memories? What remorse? . . . Money? No, why should that have troubled them? They had plenty of it—we knew that soon enough, alas."

Guillaume Alérac drummed on the windowpane with his fingers, paced the floor near the fireplace, and then went over to Mlle Huguenin whose eyes were following him everywhere. She was worn out by the story of the Graews—a sponge squeezed dry. "Have you never imagined that they received their punishment?" The words pressed heavily upon Mlle Huguenin. Carolle raised her head. Guillaume Alérac picked up a knitting needle which had fallen from Mlle Huguenin's lap, and though she took it from him it seemed to the others to be still rolling on the flagstones with a noise like spilled coins.

"You can't imagine how beautiful Jonathan Graew's mother's face looked when she was dead. It wore an expression of deliverance and of calm triumph: 'I have made my journey and I've kept my faith,' and one felt that she had indeed done well, that she had been happier than many another, in that she had got what she asked of life; but she was weary, weary. . . . Such pride and at the same time such humility! And how could one blame her for wanting her son to live an upright life and a better one than her own?"

"An upright and a better life! Oh, Grandfather!" Carolle's voice unfurled itself, swelled out like a big white peacock, flamboyant on a garden wall. "Jonathan Graew won't have that kind of life!"

"And why not, if you please?"

"Because he drinks." Carolle had turned towards Mlle Huguenin; she spoke the last word slowly and with extraordinary conviction; she saw it wave like a banderillo above her friend's face and she thought of bullfights, of things she had never seen—horrible, hot, and red. How easy it was to be cruel! Then her voice became gentler because she was sorry for Mlle Huguenin: "I've seen him drunk twice since Sunday; dead drunk—in the gutter. At first I thought it was Castagné," she drew a deep breath, "but I used my lantern, and it was Graew, Jonathan Graew."

"Well?" Mlle Huguenin wondered whether God was all-powerful or not.

"Well, that means he's finished, doesn't it? And since Catherine isn't a piece of land to be bought or sold, or to cultivate or drain like a peat-bog, he's finished even though he were to marry her."

Carolle's face was beautiful: her cheeks were very white, her lips soft and fragrant, and her body seemed to move with the grace and lightness of the air itself. Her breasts rose and fell quickly under her pull-over. She flung her words straight before her, above Mlle Huguenin, towards the window. She would have liked to open the window and cry out to the windy fields that everything would be changed, that an unconquerable spring would soon come to save the earth. All was well now that Jonathan Graew was ruined and finished.

4

Guillaume Alérac walked about silently, his hands clasped behind him, and his silhouette sliding along the walls. From the coldness and fixedness of his expression, one imagined him looking at some arid landscape. The last of the Graews dead drunk in a roadside ditch! . . . His hands opened and shut, his nails dug into his palms, and a cruel magnificent smile revealed his teeth. His heart beat rapidly. For a moment he rested his forehead against the windowpane and from the other end of the room could be heard the sound of Mlle Huguenin's knitting needles clicking faintly and pointlessly. Through the window he saw a laurel leaf shaped like an oval shaving bowl shining in the glow—from what? —perhaps the stable lantern. . . . Dead drunk! And these cold nights! Mightn't his luck turn this time? Dead drunk. . . . The properties were coming back, crowding each other a little shamefacedly between the hedgerows, hurrying back to the Aléracs. With what money were they to be kept? He laughed. Oh, that was nothing. Money would be found somehow. Suddenly he raised the window, clicked his lighter, and held it close to the thermometer. He closed the window with a sigh of relief (if the cold continued like that, there was a chance), but he found himself getting entangled with that phrase in the Bible about sparrows; it began, as it were, to drag at his feet—to open a trap door under him: "Not a sparrow shall fall to the ground. . . ." He was furious. What had this sparrow business to do with him? He was no bird-catcher! Oh, he was always getting caught up by something in the Bible. The Bible was always giving him shocks, but he loved it just the same. His arrogant hands would caress his worn Bible with more tenderness than any woman had ever received from him. He loved God in that way; he knew of no other. But this evening, no . . . no! The properties were coming back to him. Of course Jonathan Graew was of more importance than a sparrow, but . . . if it pleased Jonathan Graew to get drunk, let him get drunk. And if he was found at dawn lying dead in a ditch, well—he could be put in the Alérac cemetery. He would have his bit of turf, his verse from the Bible, and his flat stone. Guillaume Alérac composed an epitaph for him: "Happy is he who has a faithful servant." Or perhaps this would be more suitable for a Graew: "For ye know neither the day nor the hour . . ."

Why did the fool get drunk? Because of Catherine? Guillaume Alérac could see her now: pale, enigmatic, with her luxuriant hair and wandering smile. Let him marry her and leave them alone! Increase and multiply! Samuel, son of Joshua, son of Eli, son of Jonathan.

Graews everywhere, like a flock of sparrows; everywhere: in the fields, on the roofs, in the houses. Let the earth be covered with them, the sky black with them. One would live, eat and sing with sparrows. He felt suffocated, wanted to take his gun and clear the air of them.

One by one, almost noiselessly, the sparrows fell. . . . His cheeks creased in a slow smile . . . the Graews were lying beneath the green turf of a neat cemetery and the birds of the air sang in the trees. Peace at last . . . one was done with the Graews . . . peace. He was already at the iron grill of the cemetery (painted every year at his expense because he wanted the dead to be surrounded by the elegance of a beautiful garden) and though busy entombing the Graews (with his forehead against the window) Carolle's breathing was in his ears along with the sound of his own footsteps on the sandy path of the cemetery. Why was her breathing so quick? Too quick! He bent his head slightly, his ears searching for the cause of it, but the rest of him was with the Graews. The sparrow story had not ended; one does not dispose of God with a gun, and Jonathan Graew was alive—a successful sparrow, sturdy and tough. He listened carefully and went on with the diagnosis, following Carolle's strangely uneven breathing with difficulty. Tomorrow he would really examine her, and he began

to imagine how she would object; he almost laughed
outright as he remembered her rebelliousness to that
sort of thing, and as he searched for the words he would
use to calm her, the vision of Jonathan Graew drunk
at the roadside became clear. His mind followed one of
those insidious and confusing paths that present themselves and interfere with logical thought. He now saw
Jonathan Graew one Whitsunday morning, standing
motionless by the hawthorn hedge in his English shoes,
his broad proprietary back gently caressed by the spring
wind. His smile was luminous and the hedge was white,
each flower seeming all the whiter for his smile. "But a
tough customer, just the same. . . ." Guillaume Alérac's
forehead and right hand were against the windowpane.
The wind sang in the splindle trees and the laurel leaf
was still shining, but less brightly. The wind must
have blown down the stable lantern. He was thinking
of Graew, the hawthorn hedge, and what it was that
could have brought a Graew there to stand absent-
mindedly.

Enough of that! He must light his lantern now and
put on his shoes. His hands got cold at the prospect.
How could he drag Graew into the kitchen? With
Gottlieb's help? No, not that way. Make Carolle and
Mlle Huguenin help him?

Outside there were huge torn clouds traversing a

restless sky. Guillaume Alérac breathed as though he were drawing the odour of wet grass into his lungs—as though he were holding a handful of it under his nose. Heavens! How rutted and full of mud the roads would be—and the dogs dripping wet! And your rheumatism—your heart, Alérac! And what about your left foot? "He is seventy years old." Suddenly he saw his mother as distinctly as one sees a landscape just before a thunderstorm. She was holding a pen and there was an oval spot on her right ring-finger. The smile which had always moved him so deeply was upon her face; it was a smile full of dismay and frustration. His memory of it was so terribly poignant that he almost called out to her: "Mother, Mother, what can we do to keep death away?" But Mme Amédée Alérac was also in the cemetery with her bit of turf, her Biblical verse, and her flat stone.

Then, while he was looking at this landscape of memory, as through a telescope, a tiny round spot of red detached itself. It was bright, not quite poppy-red; more lacquer-red, perhaps, with a little yellow in it. The sight of it filled him with joy and he tried to explain its source. Then suddenly he knew the reason for his childish pleasure: the red spot was the wing of a cock inside the first cup he had ever drunk from. What a long way it had come with him! There it was now, signalling to him. Was the time for departure at hand? Did it mean that one was near death when things reappeared like that? The red wing of a cock inside a cup, shining like a new toy. Or was it merely a glimpse through the curtain of memory, signifying nothing?

CHAPTER FIVE

*T*HE silence spread slowly and smoothly like a patch of oil on water; it reached Carolle, who drew in her legs, Gottlieb, and then Mlle Huguenin. The latter, with a faint motion suggesting a swimmer, plunged into her knitting and began to count the stitches with the little whispering sound that a spring makes when there is almost no water in it. The silence seemed to be looking at her: "Is she making that noise? One wouldn't have thought it of such a pitiful creature. What about the other one?" The other one was curled up like a dog in her "seal" pretending to read *Robinson Crusoe*. Her eyes furtively and anxiously sought the figure leaning against the window. How still he was! "If only one had more customers like him," thought Silence, "business could carry on." But Gottlieb was the best of all; he was looking over Carolle's shoulder at the pictures in *Robinson Crusoe* and each time one appeared he traced its outlines with a knitting needle. On any other evening Carolle would have leapt from her chair in horror—scratch *Robinson Crusoe* with a knitting needle! The book she prized as much as her Bible! She declared they were alike, both stories of adventure, and that they both dealt with celestial matters. Mlle Huguenin would tell her she must be mad to speak of Christ like that, and her face would be pale with anger at Carolle for confusing the sacred with the profane. She took Robinson with her everywhere; she showed him the Pyrenees: "It's cold, Robinson; cover up your parrots. Let Friday see." Friday was Gottlieb's favourite, his idol. For him, Heaven was an island covered with Fridays, oranges, and birds, and with Carolle there too, sitting under a blue parasol.

But that evening was like no other evening; *Robinson Crusoe* could be scratched, tattooed, cut to pieces. . . . She was with her grandfather standing at the window, following him step by step—where was he going? Was it the path of surrender? "Ladies and gentlemen: this dangerous and difficult journey for the small sum of ten centimes. . . . " Idiot! That was what she had once heard at the Circus; her grandfather had taken her to see the tight-rope dancers. "Stretch the ropes . . . stretch the ropes." And then that figure in pink tights standing in the air high above her.

Silence was now spreading through the countryside; it had visited the Orphanage, had seen lights in the

Graew stable, for Colinette was going to foal. Jonathan Graew and Mme Vauthier were there; something was steaming in a bucket and the stable boy kept his hands over his ears. Silence thought he would have done better to put them over his eyes. The church beyond the hill was lonely among its graves. Mlle de la Tour was sleeping in the Parsonage and her brother was probably tiptoeing about to find a book, for there was a light in his room. He had not been called out; Silence would have known it if there had been anyone dying in the parish. Abel and Maman Rose slept also—how they were sleeping, those two!—he thin and hunchbacked, she fat and round. In the dark together they made one mound of happiness, dreaming peacefully. "I am ready, my Redeemer," Abel said. And Maman Rose: "Think for a moment, Catherine; you'll have printed silk dresses, and in church you'll sit just behind the Aléracs." Catherine was not dreaming; she lay as still as death with her eyes wide open.

The church bell was Silence's worst enemy; the cocks were its enemies too, and sometimes dogs. Men could be counted on to sleep eventually. The bell tolled: "How many? All right. I've plenty of time." Silence was alone now, but it preferred a night with stars; there would be none tonight—one would have to do without them. Ah,

well, they would shine with the first frost. Silence hesitated at the edge of the village . . . those houses and
streets! But it liked empty buildings well enough—the
night watchmen always slept soundly at their posts.

"It's true that chairs look like seals," thought Carolle;
"in the dark one can imagine them breathing." Guillaume Alérac moved towards her; in the book he saw a
picture of an island with palms on it. He glanced at
Mlle Huguenin's back, then looked down at Carolle,
and in the magic calm spread by the candle light his
face bore an expression of mild cynicism.

"I am going to speak to him." His voice was too loud
for the time and place. Mlle Huguenin stretched out
her pull-over as though to dry it and she watched Guillaume Alérac with eyes full of repentance. Her chignon
seemed to be in danger of collapsing again, and Carolle's
voice rose: "Don't spoil my chances, Grandfather; let
me do it." Then it fell again.

Gottlieb turned a page impatiently. It was the picture
of Robinson with a beard; he had a parrot perched on
his finger. "He looks like Jonathan Graew!" Gottlieb's
laugh shook the walls of the kitchen.

2

"Your chances? . . ."

"Oh, I didn't mean anything." She threw herself at her grandfather and clasped him in her arms. Her beige dress made her look like a tawny forest animal; she held him, tightened her arms about him: "All I want is you." And she clasped him the more tightly.

"Little lunatic!" It was he who held her now, dried her eyes with his yellow silk handkerchief—the one with the green squares on it which they had christened "Isle of Tears" because he always used it to comfort her when he had scolded her a little too severely.

"Your grandfather is a dreadful old man, isn't he?" He pushed away Carolle's protesting hand. "It's time now to learn how to love people for what they really are." O Heavenly Father, couldn't she stop thinking of him as a Saint Francis or as one who said: "Suffer little children to come unto Me?" He was Guillaume Alérac and that was enough; and Guillaume Alérac's pleasure, did she but know it, had been to oppress others —he had taken an evil delight in doing that. "I paid and paid—I who love you—until you were as poor as a mutton bone. And why do you think I paid? To save my honour? Because I was fond of my farmers? No! It was simply because I wanted them." A cruel expression

94

which was almost pathetic spread over his face. Bending towards the fireplace, he grasped the poker and very slowly split an ember in two; a little puff of smoke rose up out of the green and pink fragments. How closely he resembled the ancestor in the hall now! The one with the ring on his finger. "There is a cruel sweetness about him," someone had said, on first seeing the portrait.

"They're often disagreeable, Carolle, the strong ones of this world, the ones who oppress." How she hated the way he laughed now. It was a throaty laugh, at once challenging and sad. "What do you think those farms mattered to me? It was the farmers, and the farmers were responsible to the Graews, and the Graews were going to be responsible to *me!* That was my battle. They were Alérac farmers and they were going to stay Alérac. It required money to keep them Alérac. I would get the money. I enjoyed that battle waged with bank notes and guarantees. It made me feel that I was living; that was the important thing. Oh, the money those Graews lent!"

He straightened himself to an unbelievable height. To his companions, that tall spareness and his eager, wind-blown features, with unblemished teeth shining maliciously in the candlelight, made him irresistible. If not even a single sparrow could fall to the earth unnoticed, how did God take care of hawks and eagles?

95

". . . Well, I would teach them how to lend money: 'Do you want a horse, you fool? Well, here are two and don't forget it.' 'Your cow is dead? What good is one cow? Here are four—get along with you.' 'What? They are going to take your house? Tell them they'll have to deal with me.' How do you suppose the Graews were thought of in heaven? They came here with scythes, two goats, and a cage of birds. 'Turn round, friends; the road is free. We'll settle the account. . . .' "

Guillaume Alérac was gazing into the embers; he stood with his foot resting lightly upon one of the fire-dogs and in the insufficient light his expression was continually changing; a momentary suggestion of proud gaiety seemed astonished to find itself hovering round his mouth; one wondered at the delicacy and the strength of the mouth's modelling. Is it one's soul at work, altering here, adding something there, taking away something there? One is this; one is that: quickly changing to the eyes of a careful observer, and how slowly for some other who is in misery and feels himself to be a hundred different beings that no one can possibly know about. Mlle Huguenin asked herself: "Why, oh, why is life so disjointed—never the same for more than a moment at a time?" Her face was flushed and pale by turns and her lips moved continually. She was no longer being wafted about in holy places, but found herself now firmly on the earth. She had been taught that God's ways were inscrutable; that evening she found them merely arrogant. She thought of Jonathan Graew's figure disappearing round the turn in the road, and the joy of that memory burned her, suffocated her; the shame of it bewildered her.

". . . I should have been more careful of your money, Carolle—bought phosphate and tin shares for you, and followed the market day by day." She shrugged her shoulders. "It was too late; the farmers were coming to me now. But nothing could change the figures in the Graew ledgers. It was a terrible business—I paid, I discounted, I gave security. Every piece of land and every farm that was turned over, I kept. . . ." He clenched his hands so tightly that one could hear the bones crack like dry branches. ". . . I mortgaged fields, crops, the very tiles of your roof. I wanted to crush the Graews like lice with my fingernail, beat them down with my thrashing-machines. It was the last play, the most spectacular of all: check for the Graews or . . . checkmate for the Aléracs. Well, it was . . ." His voice trailed off into silence with the hollow sound of a frozen bell. He stood there astonished, listening, silent. He no longer saw Carolle or Mlle Huguenin, or the fireplace, or Gottlieb crouching at his feet and gazing up at him

97

with half-closed eyes as though searching the topmost branches of a tree for something he had seen moving there.

3

When he recovered himself, Mlle Huguenin again thought he looked like a Rembrandt. The light fell upon the right side of his face; his profile was magnificent and there was something indescribable in the way he was smiling. It frightened her because she could not account for it; her heartbeats began to pump fear through her body. Then suddenly, like a flash of lightning: "If I did not love Jonathan Graew, nothing would happen to him. It's my fault." She saw him lying, forever still, his feet in new patent leather shoes. She felt she would die of misery and her love for Jonathan Graew seemed like a useless rosebush watching her with all its roses.

The Rembrandt now put his hands on Carolle's shoulders; they pressed heavily upon her and her eyes sought his face. The unequal glow fell upon both their bodies, making patches of light and darkness, like a game in yellow and black—pale yellow and deep black; their faces both remained in the same unchanging pool of yellow. . . . He felt the slow yielding of her shoulders—he wanted her to understand him. At difficult

REDWOOD LIBRARY
NEWPORT, R. I.

moments—and there would be many—those hands would be on her shoulders. He gazed into her eyes as no man would ever gaze into them in this world. His love for her would never be equalled by that of any other man. He could do nothing for her, but in his eyes there was the knowledge of life that his seventy years had brought him. Bending towards her, he seemed to pour out everything, as one vase fills another: his strength, his violence, his youth, the good things he had never had, the days he would have liked to live, desires that still had all their sting and bitterness (they would pierce her too one day, make her bleed as he had bled), his suffering, his patience, sorrows that had clouded his life like the dust from an emptied coal-scuttle. There was no sieve holding anything back; all was given, everything—even a very secret love, so secret that he no longer thought about it but recognized its perfume.

Carolle felt all this piling up in confusion within her, then finding its place somehow. Later, she would have time to get straightened out, examine things, and distribute them properly. One could be a Cartesian in her family, but for the moment she was engrossed by her efforts not to weep, to keep her eyes open and full of courage. What was it all about? Lost properties, the Alérac house, Jonathan Graew . . . the important thing was to keep up one's courage, to be an Alérac.

He took both her hands, kissed the palms: "It's checkmate, my dear." Then he closed them quickly and kept them in his own. But his voice was still unsteady; the body's weakness saves the soul from many ordeals. Carolle had not yet tried her strength and she could answer carelessly, almost saucily: "Not quite, Grandfather, not yet. Suppose I don't want them this side of our white fences?" And because everything was lost, she added quickly, almost laughingly: "It's settled then; they stay the other side." She held out her hand to seal the bargain.

"Oh, Carolle, if only you were a boy!"

"But she's a very beautiful girl!" Gottlieb looked so furious that all three of them began to laugh. He was holding Carolle by the hand as though she were little and he about to take her off to school—and woe betide all who dared lay a hand on his goddess! He gazed at Guillaume Alérac with anger blazing in his eyes.

"I will give you *my* house, I will give you *my* house," said Mlle Huguenin breathlessly.

"Yes," thought Carolle, "after he has stolen this one from me." And her mouth began to tremble again.

CHAPTER SIX

*D*ARKNESS concealed the figures of those who
sat by the fireplace that evening almost
completely, but a hand or two could be seen gleaming
obscurely like phosphorous wood. Possibly those who
do not live near a forest are not familiar with phosphorous wood, and perhaps it is fortunate for them,
because its colour is that of a dead body lit up somehow
from within. The colour of the Aléracs was a little like
that. Carolle was at her grandfather's feet with her chin
resting on her knees; her hair had a mineral radiance
upon it. One of Mlle Huguenin's hands fluttered in the
gloom, and there was a spot of light on the left side of
Guillaume Alérac's right heel. Nothing else. The night
had imposed itself upon the house and nothing could
be heard but the faint creakings within its walls and
the breathing of the Aléracs. This breathing seemed to
have no connection with their bodies; it was more like
the Breath of Life that was given to Man on the Sixth
Day. The Garden of Eden was not yet created, but there
was grass and Man lay upon it, drying under the new
sun. Then the Breath entered his torpid nostrils and

he sat up for the first time to look at the world. Since
that day the Breath has entered billions of bodies and
has been rejected by them, but it is always rising, falling, and rising again; all else is merely accidental:
whisps of straw, motes hovering in sunlight. The
Aléracs were made of phosphorous wood—worms were
eating the chairs; darkness swallowed up the world and
the Everlasting Breath caused breasts to rise and fall
in saecula saeculorum.

The Aléracs sat thus, each in silent self-communion.
Each mind was filled with its possessor's private
thoughts and ideas. A finger laid lightly upon one of
their faces could have followed the changes and the
rhythms of the thoughts behind it, could have felt the
most secret anxieties dwelling there. Figures had massed
behind Carolle's brow: debts that fell due on All Saints'
Day. Figures came running, collecting there and adding
themselves up: butcher 543; dentist 600 (engraved upon
a card and presented three times already: Dr. Jacques
Macquart); 1200 for the annuity; the grocer, the
plumber, this and that . . . She was examining and
considering each one. Could this one wait? Surely it
would be dreadful not to pay that one this time . . .
invisible fingers pulled at the skin of her cheeks; she

did not move, but the figures kept on mounting with each breath; she felt as though the tumult of her debts were rising up within her and would one day suffocate her.

Behind Guillaume Alérac's temples a tiny insistent hammer was striking, always on the same spot: *quod, quod . . . Athenienses damnaverunt Socrates quod . . .* that *quod* seemed such an important word that one had almost the sensation of having struck the keyboard of a typewriter causing a letter to leap up. It must be bedtime, else why had *quod* with the subjunctive chosen to rise up that way in his mind along with an inexplicable vision of a necklace of blue beads? . . . *quod, quod,* and the phrase ended with a little bustle of syllables: *juventutem corrumperet.*

It was hard to tell about Mlle Huguenin, she looked so calm; but it was the calm of a person enraptured: "He would speak to Jonathan Graew. He would speak to Jonathan Graew." Her heartbeats were strangely uneven for those of a happy woman. She was first cold and then too hot. "What would he answer? What would he answer?" She thought of King David and of the prophet Nathan. "Thou art the man." No, it wouldn't be like that; there would be no sackcloth and ashes, no bed of state. Guillaume Alérac would be wearing his tweed cloak and his yellow scarf, and he would put his malacca stick in a corner, throw his gloves into a chair: "My boy . . ." And merely from his manner of saying "my boy" the other would understand everything.

THIS CHURCH IS BURDENED WITH HEAVY DEBTS

It was printed on a placard at the door of a Catholic church. Carolle could still see the church, the street, those red letters on a grey background. She had given something. Did it matter that she was not a Catholic? She knew what "burdened" meant when there was a question of money. She too was burdened.

The dentist could be paid with the money from the beets—no, the annuity—no, the new roof. The beet money began to be divided, subdivided, torn to pieces. Nothing would be paid; she would hardly have the comfort of a thin bandage upon those wounds which one is told are not fatal.

Guillaume Alérac took out his watch—a huge antediluvian turnip of a watch—and shook it. It said ten minutes to twelve, and it must have been about that. The Aléracs did not like to listen to time passing (clocks had been stopped or let run down) and they were so used to the everlasting midnight of the hall, the nine o'clock of the dining room, and those brief glimpses of eleven minutes past two in the study, that, if the clocks had been set going again, they would have been rather unpleasantly shocked, as by an intimate friend's sudden change of coiffure. Also, time caught in that way at different stages in its passage had a certain dignity and mystery. Perhaps at those moments, in other worlds, important things had taken place whose secret occurrence was now recorded forever.

Tomorrow she would settle the money problem; she would go to the Morédans. No, she wouldn't go. Yes, she would. She'd have to take herself by the scruff of the neck and drag herself to the Morédans. How awful it was to borrow money! She saw herself in her black dress; but no, it didn't matter what dress she wore—nothing mattered.

Athenienses damnaverunt . . . undoubtedly he had been studying his Latin grammar one evening at bedtime when very sleepy, but that necklace threw him off the track—he was sure he had never worn a necklace of blue beads. The Latin sentence had a cold, wintry connotation, but he could not evoke the book that contained it, or the long narrow schoolroom with its north windows looking into the high-walled street and beyond at the three fir trees touched by the thin eight-o'clock sunlight. Nor did his teacher seem to have any connection with the Latin words—a very real and strict teacher he was too, one whom they had never made fun of and who could stamp to and fro in front of them in a terrible conquering silence. No, the phrase hovered in some other silence; it made him shiver as he shivered when he took off his clothes and stood naked for a moment before getting into bed.

He sighed at the memory of those young days when one went to bed thinking of a Latin phrase; then he began to wonder, but only with that casual curiosity which was all he could focus upon things that concerned himself, whether he would hear *Athenienses damnaverunt* at the moment of closing his eyes forever and whether that *quod* with the subjunctive was going to watch over his final sleep.

Suddenly there was a sound of footsteps in the passage—hadn't Masha gone to bed? They looked at each other and at the door. Even Gottlieb. But no, they must have been mistaken.

Would she know how to ask for that money? Would she know . . . Of course she mustn't be arrogant about it—when one is timid one has little control over one's manner. And when one is ashamed . . .

Now that the general question of settlement had come, she would settle with Michel. The Michel business had lasted too long. A few words spoken gently . . . there must be some way of saying things like that without hurting a person's feelings. Oh, what did people mean anyhow with all that about love? "I love you —you love me." It was as senseless as the slamming of a door. "I open. I shut." No more of it for her! "And if I love someone else?" Come let's turn the page:

"It's a long way to Tipperary."

Mlle Huguenin was thinking of the next day's waist-coats; she would have to sort out her silks. Then she wondered whether Jonathan Graew would marry Catherine. She knew that Catherine was not the woman for him; she was hard, self-centred, and vain. No, perhaps she wasn't all those things; perhaps that was unjust. Her judgment could not be trusted, because they both loved the same man. Still . . . yes, Catherine *was* self-centred. She remembered one day when Carolle and Catherine were sitting on the cemetery wall with their noses in the same book. She had seen them from the road and had come up behind them until she could read the title of the book: *Ivanhoe*. The little girls sat very still; she could hear them breathing and turning the pages. She stood near Nathalie's grave (Nathalie who had loved little white lambs); everything was peaceful and she listened to the cowbells tinkling. Suddenly, without raising her eyes, Catherine remarked indifferently: "They've got into the clover." Whereupon Carolle jumped down from the wall, took Catherine's whip, and ran off. Mlle Huguenin had heard her voice in the clover field; she knew that Carolle was afraid of cows, horribly afraid of them, and felt sure that she was shaking with fear at that moment. Catherine read on imperturbably, her curls sweeping the pages of the book. She wasn't merely pretty; there was something more in her face than that, something almost regal—a look of proud independence. Carolle came back and sat beside her, but she kept on reading without raising her eyes. Carolle did not have to mind the cows; it was Catherine's work and she was paid a little for it.

At that moment Jonathan Graew had appeared at the opposite gate of the cemetery; he had seen the children and if one saw them one usually saw Mlle Huguenin too. He held out two marshmallow sticks; Catherine twisted the green one round her wrist and Carolle, to whom he gave the pink one, said it preferred the sunlight and laid it out on Nathalie's gravestone. Then she ran off quickly and Mlle Huguenin saw that she had a hole in her sock. What a way to thank Jonathan for his kindness! Mlle Huguenin was mortified. Later, she said to Carolle: "But I thought you liked marshmallow sticks."

"I do, but not when they come from Jonathan Graew."

Mlle Huguenin had been tempted to get another one from the shop, but no, it was impossible; she was too fond of Jonathan. Instead, she bought her some licorice drops, but Jonathan Graew was cross with her just the same, thinking she did not know how to bring up children. The next day at school Catherine boasted that she had eaten both sticks.

No, Catherine was not the wife for him. It was not for her to say, but she couldn't help feeling it. It was true; heavens, anyone could see that she was not a suitable wife for him. She sat looking straight in front of her, as though questioning God whom she regarded as the only person one could be friends with, the only friend who would not deceive her. Her mind told her this, but her heart was beating for someone else.

Carolle too was thinking about Catherine—not whether Jonathan Graew would marry her, but whether

she would accept him. One could never tell about
Catherine. If she did marry him, they would certainly
live in the Alérac house. Catherine would sit here—
by the fire—in the "seal." Catherine would be the one
to see the jonquils come up. Amazing how their rôles
had changed since the early days when her toneless voice
had said: "They've got into the clover." That August
evening was very clear in Carolle's memory; she could
almost feel the greasy handle of the whip with its worn
hair binding. A strange little girl Catherine was, on her
first morning at school, so pretty and so silent. When
asked where she had come from, she made her usual
gesture of raising her hand, and said nothing, as if the
answer was of no importance. At school she was thought
stupid because she almost never spoke, but the look
in her eye made one suspect that she knew everything.
She had come out of an orphanage. "What's an orphanage like?" "Cold! And you have to be careful of your
uniforms." That was all.

Did she love Jonathan Graew? No one would ever
know. "Do you love Jonathan Graew?" She would raise
her hand slowly, without spreading her fingers, and
smile gently. . . . People said he was mad for her, that
he wanted desperately to marry her, that he would walk
to and fro beneath those ancestral portraits of his, asking them to forgive him because she was poor and he

loved her. He spoke aloud, poured out his words (a servant had said), and after that he would sit there holding his head in his hands.

How long would Carolle be mistress in the Alérac house? Where and how would they live afterwards? Her grandfather was so old! Her ear was touching his knee and it seemed to her that she could hear him thinking the same sad thoughts. On the white flagstones two bright points of light were shining; they came from the toes of Mlle Huguenin's patent leather slippers. The two-spot! Who would win the game? Who had the double six?

Carolle looked up. Gottlieb must have been watching her for a long time. She saw him gazing at her now with radiantly trustful eyes. But his faith did not enable her to postpone until tomorrow the evils of today; nor did it tell her that her grandfather would not die, that her house would not pass into strange hands, that Mlle Huguenin would never have cancer—nothing of that kind. Nor was it the sort of faith that makes hosts of people put "I know that my Redeemer liveth" in gilded letters upon granite slabs.

Perhaps Carolle did not need to hear the answers to those tormenting questions. It was the humbler gift of peace and consolation that she required: "It is I; be not afraid."

With a finger on his mouth, Gottlieb watched her in anxious expectancy, his eyes brimming with delight. "You understand? Tell me you've guessed. Of course you have! I went to get her. You see. . . ." Suddenly it was overwhelmingly clear to Carolle. The orange, the green candle—it was she. It was Mother. She nearly cried out, but managed somehow not to; they never spoke of her mother. Perhaps she had worn a green dress, or if not, then a yellow dress, like the one in the portrait in her grandfather's study. And it was because one did not speak of her that he wanted her to be there that evening, radiant and gentle, in the house that would soon be taken from them. "See, it's Carolle. She's a big girl now, your daughter, almost as beautiful as you are. She's talking—you can hear her. But there's no need for you to talk; you are so sweet and you shine so brightly."

She looked at Gottlieb and, their eyes being thus joined, something of his enchanting smile appeared upon her features. As she understood more and more, his gaze became less and less intent and was absorbed into the darkness of his mind. Soon, in those marvellous eyes, there remained no more than a glimmer of what had been—as faint as the gleam on a knitting needle—and he started to polish his nails on the edge of his trousers.

She shut her eyes again, and would have liked to hold out her arms, but she knew no one was there, that the chief anxiety of the dead was *noli me tangere*—still, she would have liked to hold out her arms. She sought her grandfather's hand with her cheek and one could hear its almost imperceptible scratching against the rough cloth upon his knee. He slid his hand under her hot face. Every crease, every line of that hand was familiar to her as well as its odour of new leather. His wide ring pushed against her temple which she thought of as the flap of an envelope taking the impress of his seal. She wanted to feel the very bones of his hand, to be joined to them, never again to be threatened with the separation of death, to have done with all that and to seek refuge with him in an eternal *noli me tangere*.

She was trembling with emotion now, and her grandfather laid his free hand upon her warm hair without speaking. He merely placed it there. They remained thus, motionless, silent, with Gottlieb lying at their feet like a good dog who is happy with the scent of man in his nostrils.

Mlle Huguenin rolled up her ball of wool.

PART TWO

Jonathan Graew

CHAPTER ONE

*I*T WAS annoying to meet them like that, very annoying. He should have taken the road past the cemetery instead of always stupidly coming home the same way. Still, it was his usual way and he liked it. They were going to take it from him, were they? He couldn't come home the way he liked, couldn't he? He'd be asking Mlle Alérac's permission next. She objected to meeting him on the road, eh? Of course she objected, and he'd show her how much he would put himself out for an Alérac. . . . He had drunk so much that the rain looked yellow to him. He leaned against the hedge muttering: "Yellow rain fell on the fields." He moved forward again. "Yellow rain fell on the fields—that's three steps—yellow rain fell on the fields—that's six. The rule of three works like this: if a man's step measures 20 inches, how many times does yellow rain fall on the fields. If a man's step . . . a drunken man's step . . . no, not drunk; Jonathan Graew isn't drunk, Jonathan Graew walks straight, Jonathan Graew often plays the harmonium in church . . . if a man's step measures 20 inches, how many times

. . . no, darling; no, no, my little gazelle, don't look
at me that way. Come, shut your eyes; there, that's right
—you make me drunk when you look at me like that.
Shut those lovely eyes of yours—there! Now you look
like Mother—don't open them! None of that! Mother is
. . . where she is, and she's all right."

The bitter scent of the hawthorn sobered him a little.

"It's queer, but when I'm drunk the other one's eyes
look at me from everywhere; when I see them, I know
I'm drunk." He laughed loudly. "When Jonathan
Graew sees Mlle Huguenin's eyes reflected in the ruts,
it means he's drunk.

". . . oh, you look like her again—all right, away
with you. 'Let the dead bury their dead.' That's in the
Bible." At that moment the eyes were staring at him
from over the hedge. Mother's eyes were angrier than
ever: "Come on, grumble, scold me, say something!"
But there was a look in those eyes now that gave him a
flash of complete soberness. He straightened his hat.
What floods of rain! The water in his shoes went cloc,
cloc, and the earth was full of it too. What a huge cloth
it would take to dry off the earth!

> *Car tout n'est que men—son—ge*
> *L'amour même est un son—on—ge*
> *Fer—me tes jo—lis yeux.*

His voice echoed in the soaking thickets, trembled for an instant in the maples and lost itself behind him in a swirl of wet leaves. That bitter scent followed him like a lost dog. "Hawthorn's a word that doesn't go with this rotten weather. It's white, warm and sweet. It's lovely. You want to stroke it like a bird—now it's black and it smells bitter." He had reached the difficult stage where his drunkenness was beginning to subside and his heart to expand. Every man was his brother and Saint Martin had not done his duty; he should have given his whole cloak.

The ruts were treacherous because of the tree-cutting. How much wood had gone over that road today? It was soft and swimming in mud from the heavy teams. Here and there the bottom of a hole was stamped with the criss-cross marking of a horse-shoe. How the whip must have cracked over the heads of the leaders with their netted blinkers, their straining breast-pieces and their lean hocks, shaped like butt-ends of guns. Four, six, eight horses; two octaves of bells and long ends of timbers scraping the mud; chains rattling, axle-trees creaking, harness steaming and the strong, sharp smell of the bark—all pink underneath. Good Lord, it must be like that when you die. If you are born here you're made of things like that: a piece of a tree, a horse pulling, bark torn away; or you're like a bit of the sky above the tops of the pines. And the wind hurries you all the time; no spring at all—suddenly the flowers are all in bloom: meadows of buttercups; whole fields of forget-me-nots, up to your knees, up to your waist; and when the sage blooms it's time to cut the hay. Then winter comes quickly. How he loved this rough country, these forests, these hedges of hawthorn, elder and hazel. Lord, how wonderfully clear the air was sometimes!

But tonight, with the darkness covering the earth and the wind blowing, you didn't quite know where you were or whether it was the night coming down upon you or the earth rising up to suffocate you with all its leaves. You heard the voice of the wind blowing in the trees, and it was a monotonous sound like surf on a beach of pebbles and shells.

From behind, Jonathan Graew looked like a sailor because of his swinging, dance-like gait. His voice could be heard now and then, but it was muffled by a fabric woven of watery threads hanging about him. Of course they would find him propped against a tree with glistening beard—uselessly crucified. The end of Jonathan Graew—his farmers would be delighted, but . . . "No, no, friends, not so fast!" He was not to be downed so easily. The thought of this joy of which he would deprive them as long as possible tickled his palate like a tasty morsel of food. What a comfort it was to be alive and warm in this deluge of rain, to hear his heart beating steadily under his waistcoat! They would still pay rent and that was a warm and comforting thought too.

He flicked off an exasperating little leaf that clung to his cheek and the touch of his hot hand smelling of his wet pocket was also pleasant. He realized perfectly that there was no one he could rely on, and a warm hand on his face was something. It was one thing to lend money, to do business with people—that was his rôle in life; to be loved was quite another. No, Jonathan Graew was not loved by anyone. He began to laugh, but with less gaiety than he imagined. About ten paces ahead of him a white animal gleamed in the darkness; that was the Aléracs' fault, for they were tenants of these fields. And with what? You might well ask that! Poorer than church mice and full of pride. People came to the Graews for money, but they did nothing without the Aléracs' approval. The latter paid neither bills nor wages, but they were served just the same, and spoken of as lords and masters. When the day came for him, Jonathan Graew, to take possession of their house (it would come soon) could you blame him for wondering whether or not the the village would let him enter it? And what was left of that moribund race? Nothing but debts, an old man, and his illegitimate granddaughter.

The groaning of two heavy branches caused him to look up; he was walking between two hawthorn hedges which, stretching away to the turn in the road, became higher and thicker; they were cut in tiers and they bloomed pink and white in the spring. Then the road forked off across flat country; great tall trees, impressive in whatever light you saw them, lined these roads and were joined by long white beams, thus providing recognizable boundaries to the Alérac land. Everyone admired these white fences and wouldn't have had them changed. Jonathan Graew liked them too, for he had good taste, but he had the power to change them, because nearly all the land was his now. It delighted him to walk on Alérac land. The air seemed laden with the perfume of strawberries; he might have been moving among beds full of them—no, it was even sweeter, and his heart leapt within him. It was the perfume of the earth itself, of this earth which was at last his own, which he would keep until death supervened—yes, that was the legal phrase: "until death supervenes." He smiled again his strange inexplicable smile. What lay behind it? Sadness, shame, or a sneer?

There was always a contradiction between his smile and the look in his eyes, something that divided him against himself and made him seem both brutal and gentle at the same time. You would have known that he was sunburned, tall, a fine figure of a man, even in the obscurity that surrounded him now. What was it that made the Graews look at you that way? It had been the same with his parents and his brothers . . . but the four Graews were in the cemetery now with the Aléracs, the Biblical verses, the lizards in the wall and the white poppies. There wasn't much left of all that now—just this one Graew on the road, rubbing his beard with the back of his hand to get the water out of it. Oh, why did it have to rain like this? He might just as well get along home. . . . Who was left now: Carolle Alérac, 20 years; Guillaume Alérac, 70 years, finished, ready for his grave; Jonathan Graew, 32 years (description above); Mlle Huguenin; Catherine, too young (Death is always frightened of Youth); the others didn't count. . . . A little cemetery with low walls, clipped box hedges, not too crowded—so nice for lovers. . . .

2

A funny sort of man, this Jonathan Graew; he would laugh with you whole-heartedly, his large, weak mouth open, his teeth shining, his eyes almost closed with his laughing, and his beard pointed like a demon's—then

suddenly he would stare at you so seriously that it made
you feel queer; and you thought of God, the Bible and
Immortality. It was a look that shrivelled you up—cold,
inexplicable; you didn't dare to say: "Stop trying to
be Saint Paul! Stop it, will you?" and anyhow your
mouth was sewn tight when you owed money. Carolle
Alérac was the only one not afraid of him—a young girl
as pale as the moon, with gleaming hair and magnificent
eyes. Still . . . poor little thing!

It was said . . . yes, it was said that her mother and
a Spaniard . . . well, in those days the Aléracs were
always dealing with rich Spaniards in the Islands:
cotton, watches, sugar-cane. Then a day came—what
was Guillaume Alérac doing? He was making the
rounds of his estates, visiting his farmers, wasn't he?
And while he was away she played the harp and sang
a little—not long, for singing tired her—and the Spaniard turned the pages. They did not talk of love; she
merely sang some old songs. In the evening, Guillaume
Alérac looked at the stars through his telescope. He
knew their names and would say: "That's Betelgeuse
and that's Orion. Look!" And those two would look at
the stars. Think of such a thing—a Catholic and a
Protestant! She was *his* daughter, mind you, *his;* he had
no other. He was so certain, so absolutely Guillaume
Alérac. Who would have dared to soil her whiteness?

The whiteness of snow. And so beautiful, and smiling so gently; the name of Alérac and a long avenue of elms protected her—all the land she could see was Alérac, right up to the sky. Even the church was hers, and hers the privilege of entering it first. Once she wore a yellow dress to church and the sunlight seemed to be singing beside her in the pew. She was said to be engaged to the Pastor who spelt his name with a "de" like hers (there was a "de" with the Alérac name in those days; coronets too, and Counts; you can tell by the gravestones) and then the Spaniard came along . . . What was there left of her whiteness? She was just a girl like any other in a hayloft. No, no, not in a hayloft; no one knew where it happened, only that it happened. And it turned out badly, because she died. They say that Guillaume Alérac was in the next room while her daughter was being born, but that he wouldn't go in to her. She died while he sat there in that other room as still as one of the stones in his court-yard.

Good God, what rain! And this wind that flung the water from all the cisterns of the sky at you and blinded you with whirling, soaking leaves. Usually he loved to feel the sky pressing down on his shoulders till it spread itself upon the heavy, oozing earth all round

him. But now the cold raindrops beat sharply upon his
face and never had the bitter scent of the elder leaves
made him feel so squeamish. What was the matter with
him? The rain, probably, and the last of the whisky
fumes. Hidden memories rose up and cried out within
him; he thought of the women he had loved and imagined he could see them among the thrashing branches
over his head and that he could hear them asking why
he had not loved them better. As if he knew! Lord,
how the wind shook everything, came rushing along the
ground, leapt up through the branches, then down
again.

Was there nothing this man shared with anyone?
This man alone on the dark earth, walled away from
everything by the pelting rain and the mist, walking the
road alone in his English shoes.

He was twelve years old when he first saw the little
Huguenin girl, looked at her with eyes that really saw
her. She wore a white dress and was carrying a big
bunch of dandelion tufts. She blew out the candles with
all the lung-power she could command and the tufts
swirled about her like white mosquitoes. She had
raised the bunch of dandelion tufts high above her
head; he had seen under her arm and had wanted to
fling himself at her and bite her there, in the place he
afterwards found was called the armpit. She turned

and called out to him: "Jonathan, Jonathan, I'm eighteen today!" And he rushed away into the fields like someone crazed. Lying flat upon his stomach, he bit into the earth until his mouth was full of blood, but it was not the blood and earth in his mouth that made him cry.

What idiots people were! Of course he had been taken with her (man, like the earth, had his seasons and she had been his spring, that was all); in fact . . . he found himself wishing that something could have happened; a few moments in church, a few bells rung and then . . . peace. Heavens, how he wanted that kind of peace! It would be like a warm sheet enfolding him, soothing him until he could shut his eyes and let everything go. He could evoke the sensation—a warmth and softness upon his body and all his troubles departing on tip-toe. . . . For a moment he experienced this imagined bliss; he closed his eyes and walked in an unearthly silence wherein he heard the faint sound of dripping leaves. He heard his own footsteps and they seemed somehow heavier than his weight should have made them . . . he threw off the warm sheet . . . no, his life wasn't worth any more than that puff-ball which he had just crushed with his foot, or a piece of rat dung.

Peace . . . was it renting out farms, clearing land, winter sowing, roads, fences—was that peace? Continual fussing about leases; the people at Grand-Combe wanting a new roof. Would the Brandons pay or wouldn't they? Would he have to take their household goods? He didn't like dispossessions: a woman hovering over her furniture; a cow that wouldn't leave its shed; a farmer who had been filled with drink to prevent him from noticing his goods being taken from him; the Pastor on Sunday who never forgot to speak of the cruel rich man; and he himself, Jonathan Graew, leaving his seat to play the organ for the hymns—all that annoyed him exceedingly and he would have liked to be done with all of it: dispossessions, women, cows, the whole tiresome business. "The poor ye have with you always." An odd idea, that. And now the little Huguenin girl, an old maid today (it wasn't true, but he enjoyed thinking it was), sewing waistcoats at her window! There were geraniums on her window-sills: pink for the drawing-room, red for the rest of the ground floor, and white upstairs. Eighteen windows and a shiny door with number and knocker. School children came to see that door every year; they were brought there because the house was an old one of historical interest, and while they were looking at her door she would flee to her kitchen, turn the tap full on and make an infernal clatter; she couldn't bear to hear her family talked about. She believed that people were all alike and did not amount to very much; therefore it wasn't worth while to put on airs and have school children looking at one's door. The only important thing in life was to draw near to God. . . . The rowan tree across the road watched the geraniums day after day until its fruit turned yellow; then the time came to take the geraniums into the house because the ground was freezing up and there would soon be snow. Mlle Huguenin was thirty-eight now; the years went quickly, one had so few to live—thirty-eight, forty-eight, fifty-eight in no time at all. Guillaume Alérac, done for; the Huguenin girl, done for; Carolle didn't matter; that left Catherine—Catherine and himself. The thought of Catherine almost brought him to a halt; it drained the strength out of him. A love like that takes all of a man's energy—sometimes he could hardly breathe. He had loved other women, had laughed and sung with them, but now he didn't feel like singing. This was altogether different. He dug his clenched fists into his damp pockets and shut his eyes—oh, Catherine! His tongue was a withered leaf and he had scarcely enough saliva to swallow the lump that rose up in his throat. What a fool! Was he going to weep?

Was that why he went in? Was that why he pushed open the door and found Jean-Louis Favre looking like a codfish and Sam Tissot like a polecat in jelly?

What if one of them *was* looking at his glass with his head in his hands and the other lying like a dead man with a cigarette hanging from his mouth? They were all brothers, so what did it matter? First he had smelt gingerbread and then the delicious perfume of that little glass of absinthe . . . he had heard music, bells tolling . . . he really liked mournful records best, with negroes singing about a muddy river rising up and flooding the world: the *Hassayanipa*. He was floating there with his little Catherine, both of them dead, she with her head on the arm he had put out to receive it—resting just where he had wanted to bite the little Huguenin girl—floating on their backs with their faces turned to the sky while the negroes sang.

He had only lately taken to drink.

So few years to live—no time at all . . . now he was thinking again about Mlle Huguenin. Very annoying to meet them on the road like that. What did he care about that silly Alérac girl? He could have snapped his fingers in her face . . . walking in the paths that belonged to him! The signs said: "Private Property. Penalty for trespassing: twenty francs." He wanted to humiliate her but did nothing, and she smiled at him as if to ask: "Penalty twenty francs?" What she said was: "I'm afraid I trod on this dandelion. Sorry, Jonathan Graew," and put the crushed flower in his hands.

How like her that was! So different from Mlle Huguenin, who knew he was drunk (saw it at once), would
keep on trying to get used to it and suffer fresh torments.

He had passed the avenue of elms; the rain continued
to fill up his English shoes. His hat was tilted forward
like a crooked chimney, but hats were not important
compared with shoes. He cared about shoes, insisted on
having brown ones, English, hand-sewn, elaborate stitching on top and soles as thick as beefsteaks. . . . That
was the dog at Grand-Combe barking, and the other was
Albert Calame's pug. . . . Catherine was nineteen; the
difference between nineteen and thirty-two was thirteen,
a bad number . . . "for better or for worse" . . . you
said that when you were married. It would probably be
worse.

What about your fields, your farm-houses and your
dead mother gazing at you fixedly, critically? Are you
going to stop here, Jonathan Graew, and let the wind
and the rain finish you off? Don't you hear the owl
calling? Don't you understand the warnings? Stop thinking about the time when you can have Catherine in
your arms for as long as you want, or it will be the end
of you. That will be your fate.

The trees rose up before him in the enveloping darkness and the trailing mists were the mute accompani-

ments of his thoughts. There was a long low wall still to pass, with iron lattice-work upon it; behind the wall was the thick gloom of a neglected arbor vitae walk leading to the-house-where-no-one-lived: a very beautiful empty house where they said a woman in white stood at the door on All Souls' Day night holding a candle in her hand. But that wasn't true; it was like the story of the green knight who rose from the pool on the second night of the May moon with three stars on his breast because he had repented and a broken cross upon his head because you may not take your own life . . . that was where Carolle Alérac would live when she was left alone. She'd live there with the rats, the white peacocks and the tigers—he hoped there would be a great many tigers. And the cat's yew-tree! He and the little Huguenin girl could remember all that. "There's your yew—there's your cat." She was too religious to allow him to put up a cross, but he painted a little yellow one on the wall behind the grave. They'd see what God would think about a cat's cross. It was going to rain. All right, He would leave them some of it; probably cats had no right to more than half a cross. . . . How long ago all that was! White-bearded memories. What had happened to Mlle Huguenin's cat in the earth; and what of the yew-tree now that there was no one to clip it? Maybe it had become a chimpanzee, too tall, very sad, and sick with the sickness that comes to a chimpanzee when it cannot leave its tree.

Sometimes the heart changes in a different way: things out of the past suddenly become as new—a cat's death blooms in your mind like a clump of white phlox. Dear shy little Huguenin who never raised her eyes—she makes brown waistcoats now, or grey ones, and what does she think about? Geraniums, perhaps, because they're so lovely and so still . . . his memories of her were not very numerous and could be examined one by one, like a handful of Mirabelle plums—no worms, not a single one. He had not forgotten that love of his youth; it seemed to be invading his heart now with timid fingers.

His own gate looked whiter than usual in the rain: a rich man's gate, made of finished wood from the mill, and painted; a poor man's would be made of rough beams with the bark still on them, the knots showing, and the ends often bristling with twigs. Even in the uncertain light you could tell that the trees were tall and splendid and the avenue between them seemed long because the house with its dimly-lit windows was almost hidden in the mist.

CHAPTER TWO

*H*E NOTICED with satisfaction that the dead leaves had been raked from the paths and that the vines had been tied up. He reached out and felt the knots of raffia on the tall stakes and knew that the work had been well done. His two dogs appeared and stretched themselves heavily and silently at his feet; he leaned over and stroked them. Their big grey bodies were scarcely distinguishable, but their fierce yellow eyes glowed with adoration. Just another reason for hating this Jonathan Graew: why couldn't he have dogs like other people's? Dogs that were friendly, that pulled at their chains, welcoming you with slobbering mouths, hysterically twisting bodies and swishing tails—creatures you could at least be certain were not wild beasts.

The dead leaves had been raked into piles at every fifth tree; the misty avenue seemed to be filled with the odour of rotting leaves and wet dogs. Mme Vauthier, busy in the kitchen, heard his steps as he walked past the vegetable garden into the yard. He enjoyed coming upon his people like that, letting his cold gaze pry snake-like into their work. He inspected the dairy, looked over the lanterns, scolded a farm-hand for not having waxed a set of harness and because a fork was lying on the stable floor. He was one of those masters who thought praise was bad for his servants. When he had a thing to do he did it, and it seemed to him a simple matter to follow his example.

There was still that trouble over the length of the tether-ropes: "I've told you a hundred times they're too long!" At last he felt the pervading peace of the stables, though, in a way, it came down around him like one more burden. For a moment he stood still; the lantern hung from a beam. All was dim and peaceful, like Christmas. No doubt the Holy Child had not lain in such beautiful straw. The half-filled mangers dreamed of miracles—it was not their fault if nothing happened —and this lovely clean hay was surely worthy to receive a woman with child! There was room for the angels, and what did it matter that there was one ox too many? It was almost always asleep. The ass was the other side of the partition, but the farm-hand was always ready to go and get it.

The light fell upon Jonathan Graew's soaking shoulders and the hind quarters of three cows, as heavy as great skin-covered ships. The rest was not only invisible but enveloped in darkness so thick that you

could almost take hold of it. Jonathan Graew walked
over to the window. The animals seemed to be having
a lesson in breathing to which they gave all their attention. Everything was so motionless and warm that it
was difficult to tell whether a world was being born
or whether you had drifted quietly into the life that
follows death, in which it would be rash to make any
movement. Even the sound of a fly darting here and
there would have been a shock. Jonathan Graew bent
over till his forehead touched the windowpane; then
he lowered his eyes with something like determination.
If you could see nothing, if the night did not wish you
to see, if it had come down upon the earth and if the
wind was blowing too, what, then, did you want to see?
He turned from the window and his eyes blinked,
though it was only the light from the stable lantern
covered with cobwebs that shone upon his face. In his
arms he caught a calf that was always trying to get to
its mother, lifted its chin and scratched its forehead; he
could feel the place where its horns would sprout. It
was warm and a little damp, and its uncertain blue eyes
with lashes like worn paint brushes were full of malice.
"Well, Biki, what do you want now?" He looked at the
calf as though it were a naughty child. In the dim
light his face wore a sad expression, suggestive of youth
and tired inexperience. Several times he put his hands

136

up to his face and then seemed to be looking for something in his hands. A cow suddenly dragged at its chain,
making a fearful noise, and, though there was no reason
to, Jonathan Graew jumped and looked quickly behind
him. The noise vibrated through him, right out to his
finger tips. Blinking, he could feel his lashes cold on
his cheeks. God, he had no absinthe! His beard seemed
to pull at the flesh of his cheeks. How stupid it all was!
The shame of what had happened at the *Petit Monaco*
that afternoon so overwhelmed him that he threw his
arms about the calf's neck again as though it were a life-
buoy. . . . How ghastly life was! His soul was in confusion and, consequently, everything else. Hundreds of
little annoying things began to rumble inside him, rose
up to exasperate him.

He had firmly resolved not to go to the *Petit Monaco*
and at the door his resolve had risen before his eyes
with all the clarity of something written in chalk on a
blackboard. But he had gone in and dropped some
coins into the music-box. How he hated those pink dolls
who danced like little girls in pink spotted dresses. It
filled him with horror to see them putting out their
pointed toes over the *Blue Danube,* yes, it was their
pointed toes he hated; and *O Sole Mio* made him want
to weep with sadness; he saw himself in the classroom
with a man's face—a little boy with a beard. The ab-

sinthe was blue and sugary . . . oh, those dancers' feet on the spangled metal cylinder, those little dolls putting their eager pointed feet on his stomach! . . . and when she came over to him with her kiss-curl stuck flat between her eyes, there was only one way to make an end of it. . . .

But that was nothing—to feel the warm, trembling flesh of a woman beneath his own was merely lying with a woman, nothing more. Her big globe-like breasts under her dirty chemise made him sick when he looked at them later, but that, too, was nothing. The terrible thing was that short sleep that always followed and brought the same dreadful dream with it. In the dream he had the three of them in bed with him: Catherine, the one from the *Petit Monaco,* and Mlle Huguenin who was the least frightened. Ah, no, not all three together! No, no! The one from the *Petit Monaco* saying "Why not?"; Catherine smiling wanly, and Mlle Huguenin—oh, not Mlle Huguenin! He could have fallen on his knees to beg her to forgive him for dreaming of her like that . . . and that dog dragging at its chain when it heard its master's footsteps; they had tied it there purposely so that they would not be caught. The shame of that almost suffocated him.

What a despicable man he was, never to be able to think of one woman at a time; now it was three—what a cad he had become! And all because of her. God, how he hated her! He felt like crushing her against his breast till he hurt her, but she was his Catherine, his little girl. It drove him mad never to be able to find out what she was really like—never to get anything out of her. He felt like grasping her little white neck and bumping her head against the wall: "There now, does *that* make you feel something?" His nostrils were trembling and the lines of his grey face had a death-like austerity.

The calf came towards him, drew back, came to him again, rubbing itself against his hips, full of coquettish tricks; and its warmth communicated itself to Jonathan Graew—the joyous, leaping warmth of a young calf. He felt it rising from his knees to his stomach. Then the calf began to lick his hands rhythmically with its hot tongue. If anyone had ever told him he would console himself with a calf . . . well, never mind. How stupid it was to kill animals; how stupid to take Biki to the butcher. "Well, Biki, what do you think should be done with you? What would you like to be, Biki, a bull in a rich pasture or a 'veal cutlet *au citron*'? Choose!" The calf capered round him. No, it would never have parsley in its nose; that was definite. Still . . . could a bull without a pedigree be kept in the Graew stables?

The Great Danes were waiting at the stable door, ears

erect. They walked with him, one on either side, and in the dim light from the barn lantern Jonathan Graew looked like some fantastic beast—a centaur with three heads moving through the mist on dogs' feet.

2

The kitchen door slammed and he walked quickly over to the fire. Mme Vauthier looked at him severely, her hands in a pile of flour. She was a tall spare woman of fifty-eight. A wedding ring shone through the coating of flour on her hand and her strong white arms were bare almost to the shoulders where she had pinned her sleeves. Her closely fitting grey bodice surmounted a full skirt of the same material which was imprisoned beneath an apron of chalky whiteness.

"I met that silly Alérac girl," he snapped out sneeringly. His pointed beard, high cheek-bones and the frustrated violence of his gestures gave him a sullen look. Sharpening a match, he began to clean his fingernails. Mme Vauthier leaned over the white deal table, long and rounded at each end; she shaped her flour like a crown and poured about one cup of milk into it. Then she slowly pushed the flour towards the middle, and, already kneading with her left hand and still hold-

140

ing the milk jug in her right, she said simply: "I have just cleaned my kitchen, Jonathan Graew."

He glanced quickly at his shoes; a yellow, widening patch of muddy water surrounded them. The patch looked like America, but Labrador was missing; he formed it with one of his toes and went from the room without another word.

"Your things are on the bed," said Mme Vauthier in a low voice, without interrupting her kneading (that would have been criminal), "the socks on the chair, and your bath is ready." Slowly and patiently she worked the dough with her fingers and palms, pressing it as a boy does a snowball; then she rolled it out in the flour that remained on the table, covered it with a cloth and left it.

Several times the kettle lifted its lid and spat out water. Mme Vauthier bent over the stove. You could see her image reflected in the variously shaped pots and ladles: she was thin and spare, plump and round; yellow and red in copper, and bright blue in nickel. But there was nothing capricious about her utensils; those lids would always be lids covering saucepans on her stove. Between Mme Vauthier's hands and her utensils there was a sort of pact never to be broken. Though she was very matter of fact about all that she did with them, the existence of her pots and pans was a succes-

sion of exquisite odours and her oven knew many hours
of similar delight. The perfection, the exact blending of
her dishes, seemed like the result of dreamy speculation.

Now she took salt from the jar and while she sprinkled it (as though saying to herself, "Two grains for
each turnip; three for each carrot") she was thinking of
Carolle and Jonathan Graew: no, he had no right to
speak like that. Her expression did not change and her
hands were unhurried. She put on some water to boil
for the black coffee, turned the ham, and, having a
moment's leisure, she wiped her hands and said aloud:
"No, it's really not right to speak like that." Then she
bent over and closed the draughts—dinner was ready.

He had shocked her and this thought warmed him
even more than the body brush with which he was
frantically rubbing himself. She was a kind, thoughtful
woman and he could count on her. What a pleasure it
was to put his feet into those warm, dry socks she had
knitted for him—a special pattern that never chafed
his tendons. No one could run his house better than
she did; she thought of everything, had even put out
another pair of braces to replace his wet ones. His collar
buttons were in their box, scented with bergamot, and
she had laid three cravats on the coverlet for him to

choose from. No, he could not possibly complain of her. And with all her efficiency she had great dignity. At Christmas, when he had offered to raise her wages, she had said: "I know what my services are worth, Jonathan Graew; you can use that extra money for something else." He supposed that was how women behaved who belonged to those sects—Baptist, Anabaptist; or was she a Darbist?—they were all sombre and serious, like the cover on a Bible; and his potatoes were more carefully taken care of than the children of God!

His shoes were warm; they had been kept at the right distance from the fire so as to avoid their drying too quickly and cracking like cardboard. Yes, she was the perfect servant. He wondered how she would get on with Catherine and what she would have to say about his marriage, for she would say what she pleased and in that case . . . Well, it was easier to stop a windmill in a hurricane than Mme Vauthier if she wanted to talk.

He slipped into his comfortable velvet jacket with its leather buttons like chestnuts and held his heavy gold watch in his hands for a moment—his father's, his grandfather's? . . . one didn't know, for it was heavy and contained lots of gold. Its weight and its roundness pleased him greatly, also its flat face and Roman numerals. How many Graews had held it in their big, careful hands? Yes, he had a real affection for that watch. Carolle Alérac thought him a boorish man, but he had a sensitive feeling for watches. For the general run of people it must be admitted that he had far less, and he was beastly to servants. They hated to work for him and would never stay a day longer than their contracts called for, except Mme Vauthier who read the Bible and knew that this earth was a vale of tears.

3

The moment of sitting down to dinner in a country kitchen can be perfect; here were forks and knives of solid silver, a bunch of marigolds on the white cloth, neat curtains at the windows, the haymakers' bench against the wall and all the kitchen things of copper and nickel hanging above: utensils, containers, all worn and polished until a breath would have stained them; easily put out of sorts, these utensils, shining like sunlight on sea-water and then fading inexplicably. You may say there is nothing drearier than a tarnished saucepan, but oddly enough the spirits of those at table are just as vulnerable.

Mme Vauthier's large feet carried her silently over to the stove; she took the lid off the soup pot and you almost felt like bathing in it, the odour was so enticing.

And when she cut the ham into rich hot slices you wanted to get them into your mouth at once, no matter how. When you were out in the cold wind and rain, and felt somehow responsible for the desolation of the world, it was amazing, almost shameful, how the thought of white steaming potatoes and cabbage with bacon could comfort you.

Mme Vauthier's reply to his remark about Carolle Alérac accompanied a marvellous piece of pastry, hot and golden, crackled like an old painting—and such a colour! She, like her utensils, had her moods and reserved them for unexpected moments. She put the pastry before Jonathan Graew and stood beside him, pale and severe in her grey dress. He was clearly on the point of complimenting her, being in that state of grace which follows the eating of good food, when the body is warm and has no concern with the soul and its torments—rare moments that should be preserved from any intrusion. She stood there with the plate and the pie-knife in her hands and spoke in the even tones of a servant, as if saying: "Would you care for some sugar?" or "Shall I bring in the coffee?"

"Carolle Alérac is not what you say she is, Jonathan Graew, and I'll thank you not to talk that way again in my presence." He wrinkled his eyebrows and the knife in his hand was poised in the air for an instant:

"She's a devilishly unpleasant young woman, your Carolle Alérac." Then he resumed his eating.

"Then that makes everything all right, Jonathan Graew, because . . ."

"Because what?"

"Well, she doesn't think you're very pleasant, either."

"Oh, well, Madame Vauthier, the opinion of the daughter of a . . . well, the daughter of someone who wasn't much! It doesn't matter what she thinks."

"Carolle Alérac the daughter of . . . Be quiet, Jonathan Graew," she drew herself up, "or I'll leave your service! I knew Alexandrine Alérac better than you did and I will stand up for her till I die! Such a lovely girl; and our Carolle is like her, only Mlle Alexandrine was gentler and paler. There's more pity in a rat or a rabbit than in some men I know—much more!"

As she poured out the coffee she looked suddenly old and feeble; he realized that they were going over dangerous ground, but how could you stop an angry woman?

"And God forbid that I should judge anyone, but was it wise for Guillaume Alérac to let a lovely young girl . . ."

"Oh, now you've started in on Guillaume Alérac." He put down his cup crossly. Couldn't he have his dinner in peace without all this wrangling about the Aléracs?

"You've generally got something to say against him," continued Mme Vauthier in a low, thick voice. "You'd be lucky if you knew many people who have borne misfortune as bravely as he has, very lucky indeed. First of all, the death of Mme Ishbell . . ."

"They say he wasn't very fond of her, Madame Vauthier."

"Death is always death, Jonathan Graew—a heavy burden, and perhaps heavier when people aren't very fond of one another; and Monsieur Jérome's money all going into pills and hospitals and goodness knows what other pious and expensive things." She spread out her dough on a cake platter. "Really, he might just as well have cleared the estate of its burdens, for I don't suppose the prayers they say for him in his hospitals do him much good where he is, in God's just heaven—at least I hope not. And the other misfortune . . . well, Jonathan Graew, it's better not to talk about that." She stopped suddenly, but her face spoke for her.

"You mean the arrival of the Graews in these parts, Madame Vauthier?" A loud laugh showed his teeth; he was comfortably at home in that kitchen of his and would be, always.

"Yes, that's what I mean, Jonathan Graew, the arrival of the Graews." This time she looked him straight in the eye.

He shrugged his shoulders. Had it been anyone else he would have given her her week's wages and let her go, but you couldn't treat Mme Vauthier like that; she was too valuable to him and he didn't really mind her frankness. She had not stopped working; anger was in her words, but not in her hands. At this moment she was putting some big blue plums in the yellow dough; the dull blue plums and the yellow dough formed triangles between her fingers like a backgammon board. After a silence, during which Jonathan Graew lit his pipe, she spoke to him in a very different voice. She might now have been addressing a friend who could understand her; there was a glow of gentleness in her cheeks which he remembered when speaking of her later, and his listeners could not believe it for they always thought of her face as earthy—"yes, the colour of potatoes," some said.

"You see, Jonathan Graew," she smiled and there was something almost exultant in her expression, "with them you didn't feel that you were a servant; you shared things with them and there was never any grudging or calculating; everyone went to the same school and they paid the schoolmaster. I'm not complaining of you, Jonathan Graew; I'm perfectly satisfied

here, but with them it was different. . . . Do you remember the nights little Alexandrine used to spend at
her father's farmhouses? After dinner with her parents
she would go to one of the farms for the afternoon and
fall asleep over her bread and milk in the evening. I
don't suppose her mother really liked it, but they
usually kept her there till the next morning; it was a
sort of custom with them."

"Well, I don't like it, Madame Vauthier." He puffed
at his pipe . . . it was flattery, but at the same time
the farmers were made to believe you were God's repre-
sentative on earth and should be treated with reverence.
No, it was not his way—they wouldn't find him playing
up to them like that. He had his position—such as it
was—but there wasn't any of that kind of arrogance in
him; he didn't put himself up as someone to be
venerated, and if Mme Vauthier or the farmers expected
it they would be disappointed.

He leaned over to tighten his shoe-laces which were
loose over the tongue strips and he tied them again
carefully.

"Don't expect me to praise Carolle's mother, Alérac
or not, Madame Vauthier. She had a child out of wed-
lock, didn't she? We are not supposed to admire that
sort of thing very much."

"I believe in forgiveness, Jonathan Graew," Mme

Vauthier's hands were idle for the first time, "and she was so ignorant." Her voice was almost inaudible now; he had to raise his head to hear what she was saying. "So ignorant and so young, and Masha talking to her all day long about 'a great love, darling, a great love' and weeping as she read her palms. He was a handsome fellow, I can't deny it; he seemed to have plenty of money and ships, and he was always talking of his mother, the priest, his house, his sister Pepita, and I don't know what else. No, no, I swear to you that she wasn't what you say. You can believe me, Jonathan Graew; I don't often lie. And we shouldn't speak lightly of the dead; no, we shouldn't."

Silence fell again, but this time a pleasant silence in which one could smell the bitter plums Mme Vauthier had sprinkled with sugar and placed in the dough.

As long as there were people in this world like Mme Vauthier the conflict between the Graews and the Aléracs would be more than one of mere farmhouses, fields and fences. Jonathan Graew knew it to be a struggle for power and he knew that power did not always come from the money you had, but rather from the respect in which you were held by the people around you. All that annoyed him intensely. And now Colinette was going to foal: "Hot water, Madame Vauthier, lots of it; the lanterns; something to drink; it'll be a hard time—her first." He drummed with his fingers against the window. "And there is a risk, of course." He felt terribly alone, overwhelmed afresh by an infinite sadness that always came to him when one of his animals was going to produce young. The curse of the world was on him too. . . . He put on his hat, threw a cloak over his shoulders and went out to the stables.

4

The lanterns were being put in place. "She tries to lie down, and she groans all the time." The stable-boy stood watching as Jonathan Graew approached. It would be six or eight hours more, but they would stay with her now, poor thing. The links of her halter-chain rattled against the manger. "All right, Colinette, all right." He stroked her smooth forehead and when she looked at him with her big frightened eyes his inability to help her became almost unbearable.

The stable-boy lay near her on some bundles of straw; beside him were bread, cheese, two apples and something to drink in a brown jug. Lying close to the apples was a thin worn volume: *Le lépreux de la Cité d'Aoste.* "Are you reading that?" and for the first time Jonathan Graew looked into his stable-boy's face. But when he said: "Come and get me in two hours—sooner, if she's not all right," his voice was harsh and gruff. Nevertheless, he fixed one of the lanterns so that the boy could see to read.

On the window ledge were brush, curry-comb and a comb for the mane; and everywhere the smell of new leather and horse-hair. Colinette was stamping and rattling her halter-chain as anyone would who was restless and in pain.

CHAPTER THREE

WITH a wave of his hand he sent the dogs
to their kennels and began to walk to
and fro in the yard separating the kitchen from the
stables, so as to keep the farm hands in suspense and
Mme Vauthier too, who, it must be admitted, was full
of curiosity; they were all furious with him. The yard
was a spacious rectangle, planted with maples, and it
gave to the house the solemn appearance of a dwelling
that could not escape its destiny—one felt that something had happened there which those trees would keep
to themselves. What drama of love, jealousy, vengeance
or hatred was still to be enacted within its walls?
Except for a faint rustle of falling leaves the dark
silence was complete. Jonathan Graew paced back and
forth with that seamanlike, swinging gait of his, and
when he passed Colinette's window his figure cast an
almost imperceptible shadow on the pages of *Le lépreux
de la Cité d'Aoste;* then for a moment Mme Vauthier
could see him through her window. When he passed out
of her vision she thought he had gone into the stable,
but no, there he was again and he could probably see

her polishing a copper pot. The farm hands at the end of the yard would say to themselves: "Good. There he goes at last," and sigh with relief . . . but the dim shadow would fall again upon *Le lépreux de la Cité d'Aoste.* The little stable-boy lying in the straw nervously drew his knees up under his chin: "He's not a rat, he's a polecat; no, he's not a polecat, he's a camel; no, not a camel, a crab." He put his hands up to his face and frowned with annoyance; then he got up and walked all round Colinette, carrying the lantern. She was huge and bloated. "Stupid, what did you do it for?" Then he began to talk to her as though to his brother who was walking with him, a long way from home: "Come along, we'll soon be there." Colinette's nostrils looked like two wet, pink poppies, and there was a white stripe running right up to just between her beautiful brown ears (they were so long and silly). In some ways they made you think of those leather bottles in *Ali-Baba and the Forty Thieves.* "Ali-Baba is a good name for a colt, but the master wants to call it Jupiter; and Babine, eh, Colinette? That's a pretty name for your daughter, what about it?"

The boy patted her between the ears. . . . Lord, how she groaned!

The "crab" kept on pacing back and forth . . . soon there wasn't even the faint rustle of a leaf or the rattle of a halter chain in the stables. Mme Vauthier thought he had gone to have a look at Colinette, and she breathed hard upon a soup-ladle that needed no polishing. Poor Mme Vauthier, so worried; and worries, she had always noticed, aggravated those varicose veins in her left leg. Yes, she must go to the doctor one of these days. But the pain probably wouldn't last, so why go to the doctor? And it wouldn't be long before they took her to the cemetery anyhow . . . oh, she wouldn't mind going. After all, death was the best part of all; no one could disturb you there.

Her sadness was mixed with self-pity; she considered death regretfully and tenderly, and began to think about wreaths and hearses. Tears came to her eyes. Oh, yes, "faithful servant, deeply lamented." Such words would be well deserved—she looked at the table covered with shiny utensils of all sorts and at one end the sacred battalion of forks, knives and spoons—all ready to be put in leather cases. But God knew the human heart and wouldn't pay much attention to all that on the Day of Judgment. No, she did not like her master. There! she had said it. . . . His presence pleased her about as much as the flood did Noah, and she reproached herself because it was God who had appointed

him and he was her master, even if she didn't like him
very much. She breathed hard on the ladle she was
polishing and it shone brilliantly in her hands.

"In my Father's house are many mansions. . . ."
That was a fine thing and God be praised—He was always ready to correct your rash judgments. But one
thing she knew and she would say it: her fellow parishioners would be much happier not to live in the same
house with Jonathan Graew. She sighed, holding a
colander poised for a moment in her hand. She knew
she should not think such thoughts, that there would
be a time when she would not think them (at least so
you were told), though it was strange how anything
good could come out of your dust when you died . . .
she was certainly a long way from her Heavenly abode
at that moment; her varicose veins warned her that cold
weather was coming—there would soon be snow.

She saw nothing more to do in the kitchen and hung
up the ladles and pans on the wall. The red-bordered
dish-cloth on her arm accompanied her like an attentive,
obedient child, rather apathetic but not wanting to miss
anything. . . . No, she didn't like him, but she ate his
food and accepted his money; and he knew nothing of
her perfidy—yes, perfidy; the word wasn't too strong for
it. Carolle Alérac had been able to keep the Anges
field, but where had she gotten the money to do it?

How many times had he asked her, pacing the kitchen floor, "Yes, Madame Vauthier, but with what money?" . . . "With yours, Jonathan Graew; with what I have earned in your service." Well, she had never told him that, but she kept his kitchen spotless. Was there a single tarnished pot or kettle anywhere? Look at the ladles? Was there a speck of dust on the shelves? No, in Jonathan Graew's house everything was in its place and spotlessly clean. The kitchen maids in the district were sick of hearing about the perfection of Mme Vauthier. It would have been better if their mistresses had kept quiet about her; the girls were honest at least.

The poor soul was trying to redeem herself; the taps bore witness to it, and if the door-knobs could have talked they would have told you that they were exhausted with her polishing. The last grain of dust was put to rout, brooms were worn right down to nothing, and when Jonathan Graew hardly dared to set foot upon his shining floors he did not know that the odour of wax filling the house indicated the presence of a soul buying repose for itself.

Mme Vauthier got out the knives and began to clean them. It wasn't the day for knives, but there were moments when she had to rub them: carefully, one after the other, with a champagne cork and emery powder. She did it gently so as not to scratch them, knowing that when she was done she would feel better. Now and then a tear fell on the knife in her hands; if it dropped on the handle she paid no attention, but if on the blade, yes: with her cork she would spread the tear out, combine it with the powder and rub the mixture.

With Mme Vauthier, to mingle religion with her regular occupations was much more than a habit; it was a need that she felt not only at night before getting into bed, kneeling on the cold floor to say her prayers, but all the day long. God was near her when she washed the dishes, cooked, worked in the garden or cut wood, and he was a severe God. What would she have done if he had not been severe? She thought about Heaven too —Heaven, where you entered by a narrow door. But of her last day on this earth she could not allow herself to think. "Industrious and deceitful servant! What hast thou done with thy life?" Why, she had worn herself out polishing pots and pans, making preserves, guarding secrets that made her heart beat like the heart of a hunted rabbit. And the worst of her troubles was not the dead baby she had borne, but it was bad enough, for when they said, "All's well, Félicie Vauthier," she did not cry out, and then . . . he was dead.

She appeared to be talking to the bone-holder. Some-

one must have dropped lemon juice on it; she rubbed
gently, with a lightness that one would hardly have
expected of those hands, and the bone-holder began to
shine. . . . When her husband was so ill—even when
his sickness had wasted him so that he weighed no more
than a child . . . oh, she supposed it had been terrible
to see a person you loved in a coffin—embroidered pillow and all. But there was something which meant
more to her than anything in this world, or could in the
next—something that she would never give up. It had
been with her through everything: the birth of her
dead child and the death of her husband; and it was
something which, in tears and shame, she would have
to answer for, and she would never deny it.

"You were on the road?"

"I was on the road."

"And you looked at him?"

"And he looked at me."

"Then?"

"Then everything was shining; the horse's coat
glowed like a polished floor."

"Then?"

"Then he leaned over and held out the flower to me;
yes, the one he had been wearing. He gave me his
mignonette. . . ."

"And though you loved your husband you had this

159

thought in your mind: 'Now that he is dead, if Guillaume Alérac wants me . . . will that be a sinful thing?' "

Of course she had had such a thought, and when the great day came she would be called: "Stand forth, Félicie Vauthier." Then she would have to kneel in the dust, but would there be any dust in Heaven? In the stars? No, it would burn up. In the clouds? No, there'd be no horsemen in the sky on that day. And when she bowed down before her Lord and Master, she knew she would still be holding the mignonette in her hands.

She had put the spoons in piles of twelve; the knives were laid out on a chamois skin. . . . And now Jonathan Graew would be taking their house from them. . . . Mme. Vauthier's fingers were busy with the forks and the silver polish. Then she took her buckskin and in trying to rub away the misfortunes of the Aléracs she merely caused Jonathan Graew's teapot to shine with greater brilliance than ever. . . . Ten o'clock and no hot water for Colinette—all those memories and a sprig of mignonette had distracted her, but God knows, she couldn't forget—no, she couldn't forget.

Everything was tidy and beautiful. The opened lid of

a leather case showed the carving set, bright with polishing; it looked like some barbaric ornament.

If she had a daughter who came to her with tales like that—God forbid that such a thing could happen—she would say: "How can you get into such states over a man? Is there any sense in it?"

She closed up the last case and the kitchen suddenly seemed enormous to her; she felt as lonely as a tree in the desert. After sheltering the lamp from the draught she put on her wrap. What could those men do for Colinette now? What did men know about such things? Nothing, of course. She would have to go at once to the stables.

2

The lantern almost dropped from her hand as Jonathan Graew came suddenly out of the kitchen garden through the mist, his cloak fluttering: "Why do you have to come at me like a ghost? I thought a tree had begun to walk and my heart nearly jumped out of my body." The yard was wide and she was carrying a lantern, but he had walked straight towards her, his eyes and thoughts upon other things.

"There are no more ghosts, Madame Vauthier." His laugh was dry and forced. Devil take the woman! A flock of magpies could keep his secret better than a servant in his house.

"You know more than I do, Jonathan Graew, but if there aren't any more ghosts the people who've taken their places are much stupider." In the light of the stable lantern she saw his face, drew back, and then went on speaking in a lower voice: "I suppose I should congratulate you, Jonathan Graew; the time has come, hasn't it?"

At the door he stopped and turned to her crossly: "What do you know about it, Madame Vauthier?"

"What do I know? Well, it's not hard to see. When a man looks like a disciple coming back from Emmaus it doesn't always mean that he has seen the Lord. So I'm congratulating you—that's what I know about it."

"Very well, Madame Vauthier, you're right. It's been decided. But as to your congratulating me, I don't know. . . ." Instinctively, they moved away from the door and spoke quietly.

"It was high time you stopped making a fool of yourself, Jonathan Graew. You won't find anyone prettier—she's like a white tulip—and she's got a heart about the size of a pin-head, but yours isn't much bigger. She's lucky," Mme Vauthier took a deep breath, "luckier than a flighty girl like that deserves. God keep me from ever having such a responsibility, but if I had to choose for you, she would never be mistress here. Steady practical girls aren't the only ones of course, but there is another kind."

"Are you thinking of Abraham Huguenin's daughter, Madame Vauthier?"

"No, Jonathan Graew, I'm not. I would never pick her for you. She's an angel from Heaven, but, if I may say so, an angel is not what a farmer wants. She could join the Heavenly choir—you have only to watch her singing—but I don't think she would be very good at bearing children. Good Christians don't produce them like rabbits and there must be plenty of children on a farm."

"Then who was it you wanted for me, Madame Vauthier?"

"No, no, Jonathan Graew, don't ask me." He felt that she was smiling amiably at him through the darkness. "When the wine is poured we must drink it. We are in the hands of God."

"Then you'll stay at the Vale?"

"I will stay if it suits your wife," she spoke without bitterness, "and if you need me."

They pushed open the stable door and found other occupations awaiting them.

CHAPTER FOUR

*W*HILE Mme Vauthier was thinking he had gone into the stables and the farm-hands were wishing the devil would take him, Jonathan Graew had merely walked down the avenue away from the house. He was not concerned with tulip or hyacinth bulbs, winter wheat, catalogues or market prices; and thoughts of his fire, his leather chair, the old couch that smelt of pipe smoke and the maps of his land were far from his mind. His high bookshelves were crowded with old volumes, some of which had certainly not been opened for a hundred years: several huge Dutch Bibles, an Erasmus and many others whose worn yellow leather bindings were all he knew of them; the chest-like cupboard beneath the bookshelves with his pens, pipes, bill-files, his tray of seeds in little compartments—these things might have been called the "mothers of his soul," but tonight he wanted none of them. The very thought of finding himself face to face with those Graews, of being appraised by each one of them in turn (portraits always had plenty of time for that sort of thing) made him shudder. Good God, if the dead possessed you more than the living! What could you do?

With his cloak flapping against his chest and his hands in his pockets, he moved past tree after tree like a youthful ghost who didn't quite know how to deport itself. There was an odour of dead roses near the orchard wall—a *Gloire de Dijon* or a *Belle Jeanne* had been blighted by the damp and the cold. The mist curtained off whole apple trees; poplars wore night-dresses. Every noise was muffled; your footsteps pressed upon strange soft things that regained their shape with little juicy sounds after you had passed. The super-natural, hypnotic calm of a smugglers' night hung over the tree-lined avenue . . . all Jonathan Graew wanted was a certain young woman.

2

The other house was an old, tumbledown one with a steep roof; its front windows looked into an orchard and the forest rose up behind it. The wild grape vine trickled its clammy wetness down the window-frames and on to the strawberry plants. Jonathan Graew walked awkwardly in the soft garden mould, a poor footing for anything but a tree. He stood there, however, in the misty dark, looking about as cheerful as a bean-pole. If the house seemed to be squint-eyed it was because its two lighted windows shone unequally; there was a lamp in one of them, but from the other which appeared to interest Jonathan Gracw so much came only the intermittent glow of a dying fire.

There wasn't much there: two shadows against the opposite wall; and there was no great wealth indicated by the plates and bowls you could see. Flickering gleams slid over the plates, played a game on a teapot and did a dance on the lid of a saucepan and, cat-like, left everything just where it was; but at the edge of the hearth he could see two hands shelling beans. "My mother-in-law," thought Jonathan Graew; he almost laughed aloud. Was he, the owner of many acres and cattle, merely standing there to discover that rain could wet a landed proprietor just as quickly as a pile of dead leaves? He thought his feet were going to sprout like potatoes in a cellar, but he stood there without moving, terrified of sneezing at the windowpane.

When the fire brightened, which it did slowly and with much spluttering, he could see a man's feet, large and muddy, and a hand poking the fire with a stick. There was no talking in that room; when the body is weary with years of labour, communication is silent: the elbow asks something and the knee replies. The beans continued to fall into a bowl—how calm and peaceful it was! . . . He watched, his chin on the window ledge, determined to understand the peace in which these poor people lived—he kept on looking, but it was still incredible to him: a little fire, a hand, three feet, beans dropping into a bowl. . . . A puff of wind made a faint rustle among the leaves and he slid along to the other window like the flap of a night bird's wing.

His heart began to flutter at his closeness to her. A hammer tapped dryly in his head like a woodpecker's bill on the bark of a tree. The sight of her in there almost made him weep. His throat hurt him, and if he had spoken, his voice would have sounded as though his throat were full of gravel. There she was in her room, just the other side of the thin glass pane, sitting in the light from the lamp and a steadily burning fire. The shadows did not fling themselves crazily here and there, but seemed rather to be moving cautiously about a young girl lost in thought. Her face looked strangely beautiful and her lovely, graceful hands, lying crossed on the table before her, seemed to be even more securely enmeshed in her dreams than her features. The joy of something inexplicable and immediate had caught her hands and fixed them in a pose of absolute beauty.

A sort of madness possessed the man who stood there in the darkness with the wild grape leaves putting little cold kisses on his cheeks. The girl in there, breathing contentedly almost under his nose, busy with her dreams, had nothing but scorn for him; she would send him off with a box on the ears so that she could be alone with her happiness. . . . His heart was beating at such a rate that his temples seemed packed with ticking watches. He wanted to burst into the room and tear everything to pieces—especially the skeins of silk and all that silly paraphernalia—and see her sitting in the midst of the débris. He tried to laugh but tears rolled down his cheeks—let them roll—could he stop them? Could he do anything? What did he mean by skulking under people's windows like a thief?

If she hadn't been so preoccupied she would have seen a body rising up like the branch of a tree in the wind. Let her look at him. He didn't care. He could see everything now: the woollen frock, the pointed shoes, her lovely pale face, her soft mouth. . . . What was she after all? A girl from an orphanage. Nothing. Catherine who? Catherine what? All the show of elegance annoyed him. But for the Aléracs she would have been a servant—the Pastor's maid-of-all-work. A frilled cap, prayers at every meal—that's what you'd have had, my girl. But no, they had educated her. Mademoiselle did embroidery: shepherds and shepherdesses, trumpets worked on satin. Embroidery, dreams, driving out to

pay calls in a carriage . . . and those two shadows and
the bowl of beans: her family—what of them, Jonathan
Graew? His impulse was to wrench those silken shepherdesses from her and throw them on the dung pile
like chickens' heads. . . . Her lips moved a little. To
whom had she spoken? He dug his nails into his palms
and felt them going into his flesh; it didn't hurt him.
His suffering was of a different sort.

You may ask what men can know about hell. His
hell was himself, his wet feet, the rain on his back, the
girl in there, his thumping heart, his congested throat
and his fists striking out automatically, beating down the
hedges. . . . The grey frock rose and fell gently as she
breathed; nothing could disturb her; thousands of
angels guarded her dream-like seclusion. His chin was
again resting on the window sill, and every time he
winked the panes seemed to push him farther away. Big
cold drops fell upon him from the grape vine, and when
a puff of wind shook it he was drenched with drops and
showered with grape leaves till he looked like a sham
tree.

If she had turned towards the window she would have
seen a white face against the pane and two lustreless eyes
fastened upon her, but she was far away. Well, he would
change his tactics; he would put her out into the road
now. At once. All her trunks and bundles. The law was

the law after all. When rent isn't paid, well, what happened then? It was all right to wait three months, but six was foolish. To give a year's grace was idiotic. Well, they would find out what an idiot could do. This time they'd know. "It's the girl or the money." That's what he would say. He'd had enough of Jesus Christ, the poor, and the parish since he'd begun to run after her like a goat that smells saltpetre. "Tell me what there is in this house that doesn't belong to the Graews. Tell me or I'll choke you."

She opened her eyes as though she had heard him, looked casually about her at the things of this world and was gone again. "Catherine!" His throat was so dry that his cry could scarcely be heard. His skin tingled as though he had lain in a bed of nettles. His farmhouses, his fields, and the big flitches of bacon hanging in his chimneys, everything, the whole village—all was there behind him roaring with laughter. Play your old game, Jonathan Graew; you knew how to take farmhouses, land and hedges, but a simple country girl you cannot take; you can do nothing if she doesn't want you.

The weather vane on the roof creaked as it had always creaked, turning round and round like a crazy, blind magpie, and water dripped from the gutter with the same hollow, dreary sound . . . those half-wits never went into her room—no one talked to her—it was like a church where you had to enter on tiptoe and speak in a low voice. She was too petted, too sacred; her hands had to be kept smooth so that they wouldn't fray her silks, and she always had to have the best lamp in her room. "Oh, the little one is all right for us; we don't even need that one for what we're doing—just imagine— shelling beans . . . no, people like us don't do Catherine any good; we don't know the right way to talk."

Oh, they had spoiled her—the little girl who had come to their house one June evening. And they had prayed so hard, so hard! . . . Fools! Idiots! Bible-sellers!

3

Your anger blinds you, Jonathan Graew; Abel Grosjean didn't sell his Bibles, he gave them away. He was a pedlar who sold blacking, nails, shoe-laces—tubular ones like thin licorice sticks with little metal ends, almanacs, and letter-paper. First he was a truck-driver and a cask fell on his back, but he was not killed—God must have wanted to keep him on the winding roads of this country. Tall, beautiful men with straight backs had their work cut out for them: "Increase and multiply"; but for those who were alive after casks had rolled over them God had other plans. First of all, they were no longer tall and beautiful; misfortune had curved their backs and their arms hung down like shovels. Some of these unfortunates tramp the roads with pedlars' baskets and the Word of God. That's what happened to Abel.

The whole countryside knew that bent figure; his basket contained shoe-laces like bouquets of mouse tails, pearl buttons, matches, needles, pins, threads, silks, and little pieces of canvas for children to embroider with a duck and "happy birthday to Papa," medicines for horses, cures for erysipelas, facial soaps . . . and his dog running ahead but coming back every ten steps to wait for him. What a dog! God had to keep an eye on him, for he had his troubles too: deformed hindquarters, short-haired except for his ears which were covered with curls inherited from goodness knows what spaniel (the sins of parents are so hard on children), but Abel always looked on the bright side of things and thought his dog beautiful. After a steep bit of road, exhausting them both equally, Carton would sit on his haunches awaiting his master and seeming to smile at his slowness. Then Abel would put down his basket and look at his dog: "Carton, He didn't have a dog when He went to the Garden of Olives," and Abel no longer dared to wipe the sweat from his brow. A cat would have answered: "He didn't have a wife, either," but dogs are slow thinkers and they don't know how to express themselves very well.

At the farmhouse they saw him coming: "Mummy, there's Abel," and they went out to meet him—the child sat down on one side of the basket, Carton on the other; leaning over them were Abel and the black-skirted farmer's wife with her sleeves rolled up to the elbows and her brows wrinkled in thought: "Give me some thread today, Abel, and a large stick of licorice. I've got pins, but I'll have to have some needles . . . What's that, a necklace? Oh, no, Abel, you spoil her too much. Look at her strutting round with it. She's only four, but she never passes the pond without looking at herself in it. I must admit I was like that too . . . Oh, I almost forgot; have you any more yeast? and I'll take two sticks of cinnamon and three of vanilla."

Abel took out the vanilla: "It won't be long now, Madame Girod; perhaps tomorrow, perhaps sooner." As he handed her the vanilla, the cinnamon, the yellow matches and the other things, he spoke of the end of the world: "The day is drawing near, Madame Girod."

"Look at this, Madame Robert. Look well." He took from his pocket a tract illustrated with a picture of the sun and moon drenched in a rain of stars, rushing through space towards a world submerged by unmanageable floods in which trees were tossed about like cabbage stumps.

"The King of Heaven is coming, Madame Perrenoud; perhaps tomorrow, perhaps this very day." And when he saw that she was afraid: "When God wills it—maybe not until the day after tomorrow."

It's hard for people like that to find wives, but Abel had one when he was a truck-driver and she had stayed by him. Maman Rose was short and fat, but so gentle and so good! When she sat by her garden wall and began to sing . . . of course her gooseberries were never stolen; the village school was almost next door and her bushes were loaded, so there must have been a spell on them that kept the children away . . . her voice was more like a little feeble bell than a voice and she generally sang *The Good Shepherd*, but sometimes it was the song beginning:

> *Encore un jour et le monde va passer.*
> *O pèlerin, marche sans te lasser.*

Her faint, tinkling voice was so strange and so sweet that, instead of laughing at her, the school children began to sing themselves; and it was very moving to hear their fresh little voices hurrying the pilgrim on his way:

Encore un jour et le monde va passer.
O pèlerin, marche sans te lasser.

But they paid no attention, or very little, to what they sang.

Maman Rose's great sorrow, and Abel's too, was that they had no children. He, poor man, thought the fault was hers and she of course blamed him. When he asked her to read to him in the evening out of The Book, it always opened at the same places—in the Bible too there were people in anguish because they had no children; it opened at Abraham being visited by angels, then at Elisabeth, the wife of Zachariah . . . When she had finished reading he took her hand; perhaps he thought babies were made that way, or perhaps he didn't and was merely ashamed. Then the darkness would mingle with their prayers and God saw that children were needed in that house, but what could he do?

The days passed.

"He hearkened to Abraham, and to Sarah; what about us?"

"Abraham was not a cripple, dear."

"He hearkened to Elisabeth."

"She wasn't fat like me."

And late one afternoon when Abel and Carton were passing by the Parish Orphanage they were shown a little girl who needed special care: "Could Maman Rose take her for a few months?"

4

She it was at whom Jonathan Graew was now looking; for her he was trampling down the heliotrope; on her account his hands were bleeding and his voice mumbling and swearing among the bean-poles. He refrained from putting a fist through the window because his feet happened to be more restless than his hands. Entering the house through the kitchen, he shouted "Graew" at the two shadows who almost fainted with terror; the beans were upset into the fireplace. He slammed the kitchen door and walked over to Catherine; she half turned towards him and waited with graceful indifference for him to speak.

"Is it to be yes or no this time, Catherine?" He did not greet her and he came across the room so quickly that she thought he would go on through the opposite wall, like a phantom eager to get back into the darkness.

"You look very wet, Jonathan Graew; won't you sit down?" Her voice was soft and delicate, seeming to fall upon his consciousness like dust sifting down upon furniture.

"I'm asking you whether you will marry me, that's all. My clothes can be dried later and I don't need a chair; I can hear you without sitting down." He leaned towards her, fixing her intently with his gaze. Her hands were in her lap; they were long and beautiful and trembled slightly. For a long time she looked at them silently; then she lifted her head, rested it on the back of the chair and slowly examined Jonathan Graew from head to foot.

"Catherine."

She was conscious of the rapid beating of his heart as he took a folded yellow document from his pocket, put it down on the table, and moved his hand towards her.

"Is it yes or no, Catherine?"

Her lips were ever so slightly opened and there was a cold look in her eyes that frightened him.

"Catherine!"

She thought she felt his will weakening and hers grew stronger; she kept her eyes fixed upon him as though he were an animal to be dominated: not a word, no change in the expression of her lovely mouth, not the slightest movement of her vivid young body. She had been through this sort of crisis with him before: he would weep, ask her forgiveness, tell her that he loved her and that he would keep on waiting . . . but now he stood there with a pale frozen look on his face, a huge lead soldier bearing down upon her with, it seemed, the whole room behind him; even the trees outside and the low, menacing sky and the darkness of the night had come to his aid. She waited in silence and terror.

His hands now pressed heavily upon her shoulders and he spoke again to her in a low, hoarse voice that was going to sound in his own ears for the rest of his life:

"You can have the Alérac house if you will marry me."

He felt her warm shoulders relax. What a coward he was! A dreadful feeling of nausea attacked him. He was sure he could taste and smell this shame that over-whelmed him—it was like iron rust. He wept, but the flooding anguish within him prevented his knowing it.

She lowered her eyes a little and her smile faded—then it vanished entirely. The delicate vein at her temple was like the green spray of a fern leaf, and though she was as still as death one could sense the force of her mental conflict. How small and weak she was, and yet how violently she struggled with herself! She was cling-ing desperately to something she could not bring herself to surrender. Would she surrender it? No. . . . Again she fought hard and the fern leaf stood out vividly upon her temple; then it faded, her nostrils trembled and a smile reappeared about her mouth. There was no resignation in it and her grey eyes now looked insolently at Jonathan Graew—a shadow of distress there, perhaps, but it quickly vanished as other thoughts began to declare themselves behind her sensitive features. Then she shut her eyes again . . . her head was bent a little forward now and there was something about her so withdrawn, so shut away, that one thought of a wax-sealed flask of perfume, shaped like a sleeping woman . . . her eyes opened again and she asked him smilingly, as though discussing an order for a piece of embroidery:

"What day would you want it?"

He could not answer her; his lips refused to form words. The only thing he wanted now was to get away, throw himself down on the straw beside Colinette and forget.

"Are we going to live in the Alérac house?"

He nodded.

"You're sure they will not be able to pay?"

He waved the folded yellow document at her and it fell half open upon her knees. Without changing her expression she glanced furtively at it and read: "Payable to the order of Georges-Jules Perret." The sum was a large one and the name was unknown to her, but she

saw Guillaume Alérac's signature below it. She raised
her eyebrows and asked quietly: "Georges-Jules Perret?"
Despite his misery, he smiled maliciously; then drumming his fingers on the table he pointed to his breast
as much as to say: "He is here, Georges-Jules Perret";
and a look of triumph spread over his face.

She understood at once that the name had been made
up, that it stood for some lawyer or bank and that the
mortgage on the Alérac property fluttered there on her
knees in the draught from the chimney which was
spreading ashes all over the room. The document
opened and shut, showing first Alérac, then Perret, then
the figures and zeros. Catherine's face was now perfectly calm.

"Will everything be sold?"

"Yes."

"Are you sure?"

He nodded.

"Even the things in that closed room?"

He knew she meant Alexandrine Alérac's bedroom
which the antique dealer had declared was full of
treasures and, remembering the Aléracs' kindness to
Catherine, he said nothing. However, he waved a hand
expansively and she realized that everything would be
hers.

5

She was again sitting with closed eyes, but her hands now seemed to be examining things with passionate care and attention; her face had lost its terrible impassivity and clearly indicated the thoughts that were rushing through her mind. . . . It was too much, too much even for Catherine—she would see the Aléracs' jonquils coming up in those urns! She would be able to sit in the "seal"! No new chair (of course she would be able to buy twenty if she liked) could ever be so desirable as Carolle's old "seal"—the one that had been hers, but would now come to Catherine along with the other things. Her whole body tingled with pleasure and her thoughts were in a confusion of delight. There was nothing vulgar in Catherine—no greediness. The joy she now experienced came from a deeper source: the suffering which had poisoned her youth was ended.

The day would soon come when she could stand on the threshold of the Alérac house like a wingless arch-angel and say to Carolle with an avenging gesture of her arm: "Stand back! You cannot enter my house." Oh, how she had suffered! Her shoulders were trembling at the memory of it. "No more of your frocks for me! Did I ever ask for them? Did I ever ask you for anything?" Even that first morning at school it had

been: "Where did you come from?" She hadn't answered and had seen Carolle looking at her frock, the
only one she had. She didn't want another, but in the
afternoon one had arrived and what a fuss had to be
made over it! I was pale and dirty and when you said:
"Now we'll be just like two sisters," I wanted to tear
it to shreds and throw it at you. But I had to thank
you for it, try it on while you watched, turn round and
round with Maman Rose and Mlle Huguenin saying:
"Thank her nicely, Catherine." At school too the
teacher said: "Have you thanked her for it, Catherine?
Why, you are just like two sisters now." You were so
pleased and put your arm round my shoulders, and I
felt like biting you. But I smiled—I always had to smile.
Then your shoes, hats, handkerchiefs and stockings—and
always: "Say 'thank you,' Catherine." If someone saw
me reading a book, it was: "Did Carolle give you that?"
And the ring that no one could find anywhere—you had
given it to me and I was so happy watching you on all
fours hunting for it under the furniture when I had
thrown it down the water-closet. When the blue bead
necklace disappeared you couldn't understand it:
"There must be a curse on those necklaces I give you."
I was the curse myself. You said: "I'll give you a prettier
one," and then, mistaking the cause of my embarrassment, you told me it was all right because you enjoyed

giving me presents. I could have scratched your eyes out. And when you had diphtheria I prayed that you might die. I don't want your clothes, do you hear? I don't want your blouses; I don't want your hats. I want a father and mother like other girls. I've had enough of strangers. I don't want Maman Rose to be always saying, "Thank her nicely, Catherine." That time when we were reading *Ivanhoe* together, I knew you were afraid of cows and I said they'd got into the clover and sent you to look after them. Maybe I did turn the pages while you were gone, but I wasn't reading; my heart was dancing with joy because the Alérac girl had taken my whip and was driving the cows from the clover. I had to wear your clothes, but I could tell you to go and chase the cows and you didn't dare to refuse me—me, the little girl who had been given a clean pinafore and sent off to play at the Aléracs' . . . you were always there, inside the iron fence; and everything behind you was yours—I never had anything to give away.

Wait till I get your house! You'll be coming to beg for *my* frocks then. "Thank her nicely, Carolle." You'll have nothing left. He's just told me. I'll be the one to see the jonquils coming up. Do you think I will ever forget how you said: "Catherine, I've seen the jonquils coming up"?

She was weeping now, miserably and triumphantly. There was something in the past that filled her mind— a memory that had both heaven and hell in it. She was thinking of that bedroom door which you had to pass so quietly. It was the room where Carolle's mother had died; no one ever went into it. Once the door had been open just a crack, and Catherine had looked in. And as she looked something had happened to her: all the strained, hard feeling inside her and that soreness in her throat which must have come from always having to laugh when she wanted to cry—all this left her as she stood at the door of the forbidden room, and a wonderful new joy came to her. It was like finding she had a father and mother after all, and that no one had ever made her wear other girls' clothes. She loved Carolle in that moment, loved her more than anyone in the whole world and imagined them both in the Heaven you learned about at school on Sundays. . . . Then Carolle came and told her to walk quietly past and not to look into the room, and all her joy vanished completely.

Well, she was going to live in that room! She would have it for her own now, and that joy would come back to her—it would deliver her from her misery.

But there was a pitifully disillusioned look on her face as she turned to him, and when she said: "It will be in the spring," he was so moved by her frail beauty that he took her in his arms gently, as he would a little child. He did not dare to kiss her, but the warmth of her young body rose up in him as the sap rises in a tree, and he was pervaded by a strange happiness and a fitful sense of repose.

CHAPTER FIVE

HE TWO old people in the other room had lit the small lamp; naturally they wanted to listen and Maman Rose moved close enough to the door to hear quite distinctly. Abel got up too; his hump made him look like a big loaf of bread moving across the room on soft feet. Though he walked with the utmost care, one of his feet knocked against the poker and (the devil must have had a hand in this) it fell on an empty preserving kettle which rang out in the stillness like a cow-bell. Talking stopped at once in the other room. As a matter of fact there was never much that you could get your teeth into when Catherine and Jonathan were together; they talked less than fish in Lent. And what faces! Hers like a statue and his like the sole of a shoe. You could easily understand the poor fellow's being discouraged. But Maman Rose had done her duty; she had talked to Catherine: "Think it over, dear . . . all those fields, farmhouses, pigs to be killed —new shoes, printed silk dresses. And you would be able to sit just behind the Aléracs in church." She had even tried to draw Abel into it, but he could only think

about the end of the world. He was too busy with his
vision of a gaping chasm for all sinners, tottering cliffs,
stars raining down upon a grey earth that was splitting
into pieces like a cake of chocolate; red fields under the
pale midday sun; cries, gnashing of teeth; and the pro-
phetic animals at the four corners of the firmament; the
Angel sounding his trumpet above the rushing waters;
the mountains, the houses, the shop in the rue Neuve
all floating about like empty jugs; and the company of
the chosen on a piece of dry land changing their shoes
and preparing white robes for the wedding feast of the
Lamb. . . . He couldn't take a flower in his hand
without saying: "Tomorrow, poor little thing, perhaps
sooner. Thy will be done, my Saviour." All he had said
was that the Kingdom was not of this world—just what
Maman Rose thought he should not have said, but men
were like that, and of course the Abels were never
wicked; otherwise Abel would have killed Cain.

When Jonathan Graew pushed open the door and
said: "The wedding is to be in the spring," Maman
Rose's head swam.

"Oh, Jonathan Graew!" All those fields and farmhouses rose up before her. "Oh, Jonathan Graew. Say
'thank you' nicely, Catherine." If only she could keep

Abel from talking about the end of the world! He said
nothing, but gazed at the man who seemed tall and
handsome in the dim light from the little lamp.

"He is straight like Abraham—like Zachariah!" Something was torturing him, something far worse than a cask
crushing his back. "Oh, Abel, it doesn't make any difference. What if he's as straight as a telephone pole.
Haven't I told you that Sarah wasn't like me? You never
saw her." She squeezed his hand to make him look at
her, and then, in a low voice so that no one else should
hear, she tried to comfort him: "Abel dear, you know
it's not a man's fault when there aren't any children,
don't you?" Nevertheless, she felt his disgrace deeply.

Then from the shelf in their bedroom Abel got his
Bible and his verse-box full of little slips of coloured
paper, each bearing the indication of a verse. Jonathan
Graew chose one, Catherine another; and Abel read
out the verses they had drawn so that they could know
what God's message to them was. Catherine's came
from *Revelation:* "I have somewhat against thee, because thou hast left thy first love," and no one understood it. Jonathan's was from Job: "Skin for skin; yea,
all that a man hath will he give for his life," and that
pleased no one. Then Abel read his own from one of
the Gospels: "I come not to bring peace, but a sword,"

and when Maman Rose's turn came she read: "I am with you alway, even unto the end of the world."

The four of them sat for a while near the fire. It was a tiny one for such a grand occasion, but with scarcely any wood in the house how could you have much of a blaze? It was a little poor man's fire, continually being piled up on itself, quite content to burn as it had always burned. It wasn't going to waste its strength in flames and petulant crackling: a gentle, amiable little fire, perhaps a bit embarrassed because it could not dry out Jonathan Graew's wonderful shoes properly. In that house you got used to wet leather and worn soles; you were never called upon to give such quick service.

It was an odd-looking semicircle of feet—like a lot of leather fishes. You could almost see their eyes, mouths and gills. Abel's big ones—so much cleverer than his head—knew the surrounding country by heart and if feet could talk his would be able to tell everything there was to know about the ground he walked on: every little stone on the narrowest road. They knew the difference between the feel of the grass in the morning and at seven o'clock in the evening; they knew that ruts could best be crossed diagonally; they knew that the country never looked nice when you had a corn and they were perfectly familiar with everything from the outside world that got into your socks. Sometimes you were nearly blind with weariness and wanted to sink down at the side of the road; at such moments, when the landscape seemed to be rent asunder, you could count on them to guide you, even though they were in a torment of pain themselves . . . and when the earth was all music and sunlight and daisies bloomed in the meadows, those big feet of Abel's knew the joy of it. Amazing—almost laughable; but it was true.

Catherine's feet were the sort that hardly touched the ground; she seemed afraid it would burn them. Maman Rose's would have been just right for a table and, if you worked over them a little, splendid for a piano. Jonathan Graew's took possession of the world every morning at five o'clock. The earth was theirs, but the love of a young girl was not.

Ten o'clock! Engaged or not, it was time to go to the stables; each one knew that Colinette's hour was drawing near. They were country people and had learned to submit almost reverently to the exigencies of the weather and the stables, so they got up from their chairs.

The pedlar's basket in the corner of the room was full

of treasures: mother-of-pearl buttons shone like real pearls and the gilt edge of a Bible gleamed like the Star of Bethlehem. On a box of shoe-blacking you could see half a lion's mane, a quarter of a lion and a red tongue. Wedding presents would soon have to be bought.

"You're going to call it Jupiter, aren't you?"

"Yes, Maman Rose."

"And if it's a filly?"

"Choose a name, Catherine."

She thought of the green Niobe in the piece of *petit point* she had just finished mending and said absent-mindedly:

"Would Niobe do?"

"The one who lost her children? Certainly not; I don't want all my colts dying."

"Well," bending her pretty head, she gazed into the fire for inspiration, "Singapore?"

"Singapore?" He looked suspiciously at her and a little anxiously, but his vanity soon came to the rescue. "Singapore would sound well on the race track: Jonathan Graew's Singapore will run next Tuesday at Planèse in the *Croix de Berny*. All right—Singapore, if it's a filly."

He got up and Maman Rose, who knew what good manners were, said: "Catherine, you may go with Jonathan Graew." But it was raining too hard.

PART THREE

Difficult Situations

CHAPTER ONE

*S*HE HEARD someone set down a jug of hot
water outside her door. Carolle Alérac's
whole body knew it was quarter past seven, though there
were remnants of the night still clinging everywhere,
remnants of a late autumn night—cold, damp and un-
yielding. The inside night extended from the bed to
the window, where it joined the night of the lawn—a
great pallid mass, solid above but pierced below by
shafts of light from the ground floor windows, warped
and twisted by the trees and the wet iron fence. After
that came the night of the village which belonged to
everyone.

The night of the bedroom was of a peculiar warmth
and closeness; it was a sort of house in itself, a Noah's
Ark full of sleep, odds and ends of dreams that rose up
slowly into the mind from goodness knew what depths,
and faded again . . . and in the midst of it, sufficiently
awake to hear Masha and Gottlieb in the kitchen, lay
Carolle, her mind still in the borderland. Through the
thin filigree of her dreams she saw the whole day ahead
of her, taking her in its grasp, and she retreated again

into the night, lay as one dead . . . just a moment
more of the darkness, the blind bed clothes, the little
place in the pillow that sang like the sea in a conch-
shell . . . then, alas, the moment was upon her.

Days began with a tub and a jug of hot water—a
whole day of activity: feet in the tub, back shivering,
a sponge rubbing a languid breast . . . it's you, Carolle
Alérac. Don't you recognize your own arms? And naturally you're late . . . brushes, comb, skirt, pull-over,
belt fastened on the way down stairs, and a kiss for your
grandfather smelling of tooth paste and pumice stone.
What about the Troglodytes, the Esquimaux—diet of
seal blubber and clothes of wolves' fur—the great deeds
of the world aren't done with soap! Did the Saints wash?
Were there any bathtubs in the Garden of Olives? Idiot,
are you Jesus? Or Pico della Mirandola? Well then, get
washed!

Carolle sighed and put her right foot into the water.
The day had begun.

2

"There you are, my dove, light of my life! The peace
of angels be with you—it's breakfast you're wanting
now, isn't it?" If all the arms Masha needed for carrying, cradling and caressing, and all the legs for going up
and down stairs, rushing about to get this and that, had

been visible, what an odd-looking animal she would have been! All arms and legs, and a wonderfully soft bosom to rest on. "Oh, my beautiful, for me it was always babies—and snow, snow on the cupolas—and babies everywhere. First lift up the little legs, hold them like a bouquet, cotton everywhere, gently, then roll them in linen, so carefully; carry them about for a bit, then lay them in the cradle . . . then unroll them and lift the little bouquet of feet again. How angry they can get! So much passion in a tiny body; little feet thrashing like whips and their foreheads all wrinkled over their eyes: God sees you—eat, my sweet lamb; you're hungry. . . . Mme Ishbell's first three are dead now and that cousin of yours—oh, he was so tall and strong! Killed by a hunting spear! And little Nathalie in my arms, yes, I tell you, in my arms! Thy will be done . . . and now . . . all of them . . . gone!

One day she was looking at her icon a little unsteadily, as though she had just regained consciousness: ". . . those beautiful hands . . . this little ring," and she gave Carolle a girl's gold ring with a blue stone in it.

"Is it Mother's ring, Masha?"

". . . beautiful hands—oh, how lovely they were! And those little straw shoes, oh . . ."

"Made of straw, Masha?"

"Yes, straw shoes, and tiny—oh, so tiny. . . ." Then everything was confused: "The Tsar's daughters . . . blue ribbons. . . ."

How many little Aléracs had kissed, slapped, sucked, pinched and slobbered over that spacious bosom now leaning towards the samovar in the dim morning light? Its full, generous curves made one think of almost anything but a woman's breast. Tea was being got ready now: "Steaming hot, my love—for you and your grandfather. And here's the lemon."

An old house with a wing, a lean-to, and out-buildings is generally full of old people whose occupations are vague, and often their names too. An old shepherd might knock at the stable door—some hairy old Esau who had lost his sheep:

"What does he want?"

"Some dinner."

"Let him have it."

"Pickled pork?"

"Yes, give him that."

He would be apt to say that he had known the neighbourhood well in the days of M. Jérome, and that would satisfy them.

Or it might be a ragged old crone sorting lentils at the fire. Amazing, the number of derelicts a fireplace will attract from nowhere, especially in a country kitchen in winter. This one would probably say she had done washing for M. Jérome's second wife—then for Mme Ishbell. Then marriage, children and grandchildren . . . and the old mother, instead of letting herself be carried down the tide of her offspring, had stemmed it, and here she was back again with the Aléracs!

"What does she want?"

"Dinner."

"Give her some. We don't turn people away hungry."

"Of course not."

The fate of the Aléracs seemed hopeless to Carolle and Masha in the mornings. It was a dreary round for them; Carolle's face was grim and Masha lumbered along like a seal in her flounced dressing-gown. An arm would go into the seed bin right up to the elbow; sausages had to be angled for, and a piece of fish. "Think of the Lord's two fishes, my child. Two, I tell you. He

touched them with his hands and there were thousands.
You must believe it."

In the cellar they walked from the carrots to the potatoes; then to the leeks. They decided on turnips . . .
rows of empty bowls and jugs on the shelves spoke elo-
quently of a faded glory. "Grandeur and decadence of
the house of Alérac," thought Carolle as she ran her
eye over them. Faint streaks of daylight came in at the
narrow windows near the ceiling. Accompanied by
Masha's short, hurried breathing, they climbed the
stairs, "God's will be done, my child." . . . Gottlieb
was close to the lamp peeling vegetables and Carolle
sat near the stove, elbows on her knees and chin in her
hands, looking at an account book with a hunted expression on her face.

"God knows better than you do that you have need
of these things, but you won't believe—you won't believe!" Masha's face was full of pity and despair. "She
believes," Gottlieb concluded. . . . For a moment
nothing could be heard but the sound of Carolle's pen-
cil and her whispered figures. Somehow there were always two courses, and Masha was never without her
stew with bacon and lentils.

"And when there is nothing left, I tell you that God
will lay his hands on the roof of your house, and you'll
see. . . ." Masha would stand before her icon and her

short, plump hands erected cross after cross upon the flounces and frills that covered her wide bosom.

3

Every evening Masha read to Gottlieb from the Gospels, first touching his forehead with the Holy Book. She really believed that one day the evil spirit that possessed Gottlieb's mind would emerge like a black dove flying this way and that, and that God would cause it to fall into the lake and perish. She believed this and she believed that the Holy Book contained everything. When Good Friday came she would declare: "They have murdered Him, I tell you, murdered Him!" And the tears would run down her cheeks.

Even at the Graew's she had put up her icon for a while: "Your house needs it." And they let her have her way. . . . To the angry father of an erring daughter she had said: "Don't you know anything about the patience of God?"

She adored Abel and would always let him have some soup or a bowl of curds when he came to the door, but she did not think his idea of Heaven was sufficiently imposing. "What about the Saints? Do you think God has forgotten them? . . . What, you don't pray to the Virgin? Then may the Queen of Heaven pray for you!"

When food ran short (the supply of chickens and ducks sometimes came to an end and butchers had an unreasonable fondness for their dead cows) she would take down a gun and give it to Gottlieb, making the sign of the cross on his brow, both hands, and the breach of the gun: "Go, my child!" Carolle's face would grow pale and she would grit her teeth. Who would have to be taken home on a stretcher—one of the customs men or the game-keeper? "God's will be done." But he would come back with a grouse or a couple of rabbits, still warm.

She was indispensable; one could no more imagine the Alérac house without Masha than the end of the world without a cataract of stars and a rushing tumult of waters.

For lunch that day there were peas with bacon, and dinner would be followed by a chocolate soufflé. Not so bad for poor people? "God understands your need of these things. He understands."

CHAPTER TWO

*I*T WAS about nine o'clock when Guillaume Alérac passed in front of Mlle Huguenin's windows. The morning was raw and shivery—just the sort one would expect after such a night. As Guillaume Alérac greeted her, his soft hat raised and his gold-topped stick clasped under his arm, a shapeless, pale sun, paler than straw, shone for a moment above the sparse hedges. At the turning of the road the sixteen windows of Belle Maison gleamed briefly—just a timid little flare reminiscent of youth. Then all was grey again and snow began to fall slowly and softly from the wide sky. Guillaume Alérac turned up the collar of his coat, tightened the scarf about his neck and walked down the road with his long stride that seemed only at rare moments to be that of an old man.

The snow began to cover up the fields; to Guillaume Alérac, it seemed magnificent; he knew this would be his last winter: house, pictures, silver, furniture, all sold, and he free of debt. In six months, not a day more; he had it all worked out. Why wait here to die? There were enough Alérac ghosts watching over lands that no longer belonged to them. It didn't matter to him where he was buried. . . . Carolle thought they might go to Paris—why not? A big city was better than some shabby provincial boarding house. She had leanings towards painting and would be able to work at that. Anonymity would be the best thing. The past could be more easily forgotten: when a thing is finished, it is finished. Poor little Carolle!

The white slanting snow fell in absolute silence; not even the twittering of a bird. Once, then again, Guillaume Alérac had to stop because his heart was giving him discreet warnings—good old machine wearing out so gracefully: "Yes, you still need me, and I need you too, because I enjoy living. I do all I can, so please help me out. Why are you in such a hurry?" "All right," replied Guillaume Alérac, "compose yourself. Can't you see I've slowed down?" He held himself very erect and stopped to draw some deep breaths and enjoy the feel of the cold air in his lungs revivifying his sluggish veins. His keen gaze swept the grey landscape.

He had known how to enjoy life, and the things he gazed at now were so beautiful: the pines rising out of the bare fields that sloped up to the pale, low-hanging sky; the circling crows; a maple-lined vista that did not lead to a deserted château, but to some more secret place—a glade enclosed by poplars or white birches.

Nothing, no one, not even a dog. Just the crows circling silently over the bare fields.

No one could love his land as he did. His old heart beat steadily and his feet possessed themselves of the road with a kind of anger. He would think of all this; wherever he was he would see it; he knew that visions of it would come to him so abruptly that if Carolle were with him (in a Paris street, for instance) she would turn to him and say: "They're cutting the rye now." And he wouldn't answer, but the fields, the poplars, the elms and the long grey house would be there before them, barring their way; and they would both stop as though Carolle had dropped a glove. . . . It didn't matter—Graew was admirably fitted to administer the estate (he would tell him so); astonishing how he always made everything pay! In his time there had never been winter ploughing like that. And how splendidly it was done—careful, methodical work; and what furrows! No, the man knew what ploughing meant. Carolle was obviously unfair to him. He looked at the wet, brown fields where the barley and oats had been. Graew certainly had his points; he had qualities which Guillaume Alérac admired extremely; he was a real landed proprietor, and in certain mysterious ways he was like Carolle and himself (how furious Carolle would be if she knew he thought this); it was true, but of course he was very different in others. He, Guillaume Alérac, had never urged his people to get more out of their land.

He stood still for a moment, not from exhaustion, but because there was no other place in the world that pleased him as much. What a peaceful spot it was! The cold air blowing on his cheeks smelt of new snow and he was intensely, violently conscious of his need to live.

What he loved about those little old farms of his was their poverty, the wind blowing softly over their rye fields, their still sunsets and their melancholy solitude. When he was far away a sudden longing would come to him for the sight of the still, mirror-like water in the peat bogs, a longing to return and find everything just as he had left it: the same fields, the same birds in the air or on the yellow gentians, the same rain wetting the leaves.

"Produce" was the watchword now; it appealed to the young of course, though, oddly enough, it had been Uncle Jérome's too. Guillaume Alérac's idea was to let things alone, not to touch anything—the world was very beautiful as it was. He had his own way of being a landed proprietor and realized well enough that he was out of date. He belonged to a world that was no more.

He turned homeward and on the left, beyond the little town, his eye caught the new pink roof of the

Jérome Alérac Cancer Hospital. If that was all one could "produce"! He smiled and turned his back on the cancer patients. The snow fell more thickly as he descended the steep road.

2

As he came near the grey schoolhouse the song of the swallow floated out to him across the garden:

> *C'était sur la tourel-le*
> *D'un vieux clocher bru-ni . . .*

and he was so pervaded by memories of his childhood that he pushed open the door, shook the snow from his shoes and entered (he was, incidentally, inspector of schools). The song ended abruptly, but with a wave of his hand he started it going again, and from thirty throats emerged thirty swallows amid a hubbub of pupils reseating themselves.

> *Coura-ge dit sa mè-re*
> *Ouvre ton ai-le au vent.*

The little ones, the middle-sized and even the big children sang. There was a pleasant atmosphere in the room; the sun was shining faintly again and one wanted to go out to meet it, to offer it encouragement. Against the garden wall the hollyhocks were already coated with snow and bore gracefully the weight of their new white flowers. Against the sky above the hedges, the flakes whirled about, falling and rising. It was hard to tell whether the hedges were being blown up into the sky or whether the sky had been torn into millions of little grey shreds: soft, grey, beige; and when they came close to one they were white. A felt carpet was laid over everything; the trees were greyish green, but the hedges stayed black underneath, with their fingers bearing tiny loads of white.

In the silence, accentuated by the breathing of thirty pairs of lungs and the schoolmaster, blushing and anxious, walking after him with his yellow wand, Guillaume Alérac glided from one pupil to another. Occasionally there was a seemingly unattached foot which had forgotten that the Inspector was examining the class, and the noise of its rapid removal from the aisle was unexpectedly loud. Then the embarrassed master would hunt for the erring foot, and its owner would suffer inhumanly—he would be ashamed of having feet at all.

Questions were asked; history, geography:

"What do you like? You don't know? Hand me your note-book."

"And you, what do you want to be when you grow up?"

"Mechanic."

"And you?"

"Schoolmaster."

"And you?"

"I want to make dresses."

"And you?"

"I don't know, sir."

"You don't know. Well, who's going to if you don't? Go to the blackboard." Once upon the platform the wretched boy seemed to have nothing but hands and feet, and his short fustian blouse looked like a bird's tail. One could see that he was intelligent, but terrified. He was soon covered with chalk and his hands made marks on the blackboard too, where a square root dropped its ornamental ladder rung by rung, the last figure fitting into the corner next to the yellow wooden frame.

The Inspector asked the strangest questions which had nothing to do with the curriculum—no grammar, no participles; and his dry voice gave you no idea whether you were right or wrong. He stood there by the platform, towering over you and staring into your face with his cold eyes. Why did he never ask you the kind of question you expected, but always pop tricky ones at you: "What time did the sun rise this morning? What do you think they are doing in London at this moment? Does electricity interest you? Where does it come from? Have you read *Quatre-vingt-treize?*" Or else he held a picture under your eyes for two seconds and then made you tell what you had seen, and when it was over and your chalk had melted in your hand, he would put one of his narrow, glistening feet on the platform, lean forward, arch his eyebrows and ask politely:

"What book do you like best?"

"*Les Trois Mousquetaires.*"

Inexplicably, the whole class, including the master, burst out laughing. Guillaume Alérac laid a hand on the fustian musketeer's shoulder and gazed into his troubled little face:

"Is it Porthos, Athos or Aramis, then?" He might just as well have asked, "To whom have I the honour of speaking?" and his smile—no words could describe its beauty.

"Aramis."

"I liked Aramis too. And it's a memory you'll always have with you. You'll see . . . Why not come to my house this afternoon? You can take my Dumas," he turned to the class, "and the rest of you! A little walk and a few moments by my fire! What do you say?"

3

They got up from the bench where, as a boy, he had sat for seven years: "Here, next to Africa (when I put out my arm I could touch it just as you can now); stretch out your hand. What's that under your finger, your index finger?"

"Zanzibar."

He seemed to be cutting a huge piece of bread out of the sea with the wand; it was Africa. "Who wants Dakar, the Cape, Alexandria?" He showed them how America began with seals and polar bears; then turned into a land of wheat, cotton and cities; then slipped down through the narrow strip which led to tigers, coffee and palm trees. Brazil, the Pampas, the Andes—and then the land contracted . . . seals again, icebergs and cormorants. He cut out big pieces for them; they could touch icebergs; ice-floes swept into the class-room between the peat stove and the arithmetic frame with its red balls strung on wires. Harpoons shot into water holes to kill seals, and a white cold stillness spread over the class —not a foot stirred. Ink, hands and tongues were frozen. Seamanship: haul in the braces, take in a reef . . . the smell of tar; sailors shouting as they sailed a course between a row of potted geraniums and a school bench. They were off . . . Guillaume Alérac's voice rang out harshly, sounding above the waves, up through the rigging to the very masthead, and the face of little Aramis shone like an archangel's. . . . With Columbus, Pizarro—to Tumbez, Santa Clara, the Ile des Morts . . . then the equator and the mangroves . . . thirty heads humming with visions of seals and icebergs; shabby yellow desks gave place to groves full of ibises and cockatoos, rubber and cinchona trees—perhaps it was like the beginning of the world.

The pupils were breathless: the little Gindraz girl held out her hands, and later on Lili Braun said, with that odd way she had of elaborating some syllables and skipping over others, "Oh, it was lovely. I thought I was on my honeymoon." And the clumsy Landry boy, who was destined to cart earth and dung all his life, whose hands showed that he would never drive anything but some jaded nag, he too was riding his Pegasus to the summit of Heaven—one could hear his breath "missing" like the engine of a motor car.

When Guillaume Alérac had put the earth and the oceans together again for them, when it was all there upon a slightly tilted globe that could be turned with a touch of the finger, he told them that eyes were to see with, ears to hear with and that the earth was theirs. And when he took the little Gindraz girl over to the window to look at her throat (she had been listening with her mouth open and breathed badly) she half closed her eyes and, since nothing seemed impossible and it was snowing, she thought white parrots were falling from the sky.

Then Guillaume Alérac wrapped his silk scarf about his neck and put his gloves on. Five pairs of hands held out his stick to him. He turned up his coat collar and went out.

CHAPTER THREE

*D*ID YOU meet my grandfather?"

"No, Mademoiselle, I did not have that honour," replied her visitor.

"Splendid!" thought Carolle; the bitter morning seemed at once more endurable. Of the two monsters who were ravaging their kingdom, the more odorous (though many people would have assured you he had no odour) had just come up the elm avenue. He was tall and dark, with a slight stoop; his hands were genuine, but he had the head of an imitation Christ—he was a dealer in antiques. Jonathan Graew was concerned with the living; one might have called him the slug in the Alérac garden. But the antiquary had a vulture's taste; he was interested only in the dead.

When the faint odour of decay, emanating from a piece of furniture one is obliged to part with, gives it a richness and a gaminess that are irresistible, and one suddenly develops a passion for one's chest of drawers, chair, or Venetian mirror, then along comes the antiquary to carry it off. Who has sent him? One doesn't know. But there he is, wiping the sweat from his forehead. The faint odour of corpses must be perceptible a long way off. But what of the closed windows, the thick hangings and those walls, well able to withstand an invader? Obviously someone must have gossiped in the village.

"I was just passing by, Mademoiselle Alérac. . . ." He looked at the house, read the date aloud, laid a hand on the wall: "It's going to last longer than we will, Mademoiselle."

"It's worth more than we are, too."

"Fancy your saying that—what could be worth more than you, Mademoiselle Alérac? It's our business to know about works of art." He looked at her more closely. Was he going to put a price on her, appraise her as he would a bench or an armchair? "Well, you are easily worth the house," he rubbed his hands together, "and I'm not the only one who thinks so. Plenty of others would ask nothing better than to . . ." He looked away. "There's someone who's set on getting you; he's really serious."

Mlle Alérac said nothing; she ran her fingers along the fringe of one of the curtains, while the room went round her like a skipping rope. The imitation Christ became more and more amicable, seemed almost to be wearing himself out with kindness.

"In the event of a—a dispossession," the word was

merely breathed—rather suggested than spoken, "the house would go for very little; it's too big and it's not modern"; his voice rose, "the roof is in bad shape. Who would want it? Graew—Jonathan Graew might. I can't think of anyone else." He gave a little mirthless chuckle that left his lips caught above his teeth.

"Well, Mademoiselle Alérac, what answer is it to be?"

"That I wouldn't hear of it."

The same mirthless chuckle—then: "Think it over, Mademoiselle Alérac, and don't take too long, because . . ."

"You make large commissions on such arrangements?" Her youthful gaze was direct and searching, but there was behind it a misery and despair that wrung one's heart. The watery sunlight that shone upon the schoolhouse windows where Guillaume Alérac had made his tour of the world now fell upon the hands of the imitation Christ and made them look very long, green and unreal, as though under water.

"What a beautiful chest you've got there! You mustn't let things like that go under the hammer." His voice sounded thick, "You know, Mademoiselle Alérac, you've got an offer of marriage now." He looked down as though he had seen something shining on the floor, "marriage."

"Are you in the habit of offering less?"

He straightened up and looked at her oddly, as much
as to say, "Oh, come now, you needn't be so proper;
your mother didn't bother about things like that." She
felt as though someone were sticking needles into her
heart, but as she watched him walk slowly down the
elm avenue one could have guessed nothing of her feelings. He wandered from tree to tree as if in the depths
of his shop or stopped as if to inspect some object that
was to be the property of someone else. He muttered:
"Nice place, that—with the snow on the trees it looks
a little like a Breughel. It's rather tottery; just a little
patience and it will tumble into someone's lap, girl
and all. They've sold their Sèvres already. Wonder
where the rugs are. Don't know who's got them. Maybe
that old hag (Mlle Huguenin); probably. Only one of
the lot is worth anything, but that's a Bokhara, a
beauty." His nostrils dilated—he might have been tast-
ing a delicious piece of Bokhara. "I could sell it to
Chanriond . . . must watch that chest. God, how long
ago did I promise it to the Bernards? But, hell, the
longer they wait the more they'll want it, and there
won't be any haggling over the price. All this calls for
a cigarette." He took out his Marylands and tapped one
on the back of his hand. "Damn the girl, they say she
sold her beets to someone else right under my fine
Jonathan's nose. . . . Wouldn't be surprised if he's

dabbled in Alérac mortgages. . . . She can take care of herself. Must have a temper too—and what legs!" Carolle Alérac's legs gave him a slight pain in his side. He stopped. What had he eaten yesterday? Lord, if he could no longer eat what he liked! Was it his liver?

By the roadside he saw a yellow gentian almost covered with snow. His cigarette was out. What was it about yellow gentians? He threw away his match and thought for a moment. What did they remind him of? How he got from yellow gentians to Carolle Alérac's mother he couldn't imagine. Unpleasant story, that . . . what a smile the girl had . . . "What the devil?" He started back, "Do you often jump out at people that way?"

"If you hadn't been so absorbed in that telegraph pole I wouldn't have seemed to jump at you. Has it a patine on it?" Jonathan Graew came and stood beside him. At the bottom of the hill lay the town under the sifting snow.

"It's pretty, isn't it?"

"Yes, it's pretty." The antiquary's cigarette was burning rapidly in the wind. "What do you think about the sale at the Aléracs', Jonathan Graew?"

"Oh, I've heard of it for some time now."

"A nice property, anyway."

"Would you want it?" asked Graew.

"I didn't say I wanted it; just that I thought it was a nice property."

"From which I take it that you're interested, Monsieur Berthoud?"

"How you go on, Jonathan Graew! It will bring a big price and several people are waiting for it to come into the market; the bidding will be high. A good sale, I tell you. Unless . . ."

"All right, old fox," thought Graew, "I'm better off than you'll ever know, but if you think I'd pay a fancy price for that place you're mistaken." Then he asked casually: "Unless what?"

"Oh, adjustments are possible where there's a pretty girl concerned. A marriage can patch up lots of things."

"But from what I hear, the place is loaded down with debts." Jonathan Graew leaned towards the yellow gentian.

"The debts would go with the girl—that's understood."

"But, Monsieur Berthoud, what chance would there be of a solution like that in this place? He would never let her marry a farmer, would he?" He straightened up and blinked several times in the pale sunlight. "I don't know who there would be in this neighbourhood."

"What about you? Why shouldn't you be the lucky man?"

"I'm accustomed to investing my money carefully, Monsieur Berthoud. Other people's debts . . . Sorry, I'll have to go now; haven't had my shoes off since yesterday evening. Colinette's colt is all right—splendid—but she herself wasn't getting on very well this morning. I've got to get back . . . Yes, yes, you're right: highly bred animals are like women. You can't be away from them for long."

The lonely house was behind them. What an odd name it had: *The Seven Hearts!*

2

When would they take it—when would they take her house? Never! . . . Something cried out within her, so loudly that her mouth opened automatically and the word sank into the oak beam by the fireplace across the room, just below a knot with dark circles around it. She gazed at the mark it had made; the word looked back at her, fascinated her; and as she gazed, her lips moved: "Never, never!" . . . Could she balance the scales? The thought of all those heavy beams and that massive wainscoting drained the last trace of colour from her pale face. What a weight against her! How could she hope to do anything. Her hands clenched till the finger joints cracked. She was hot and cold by turns. The antiquary's words hummed in her ears: "The house . . . for very little . . . too big . . . not modern." Her features were grey now. Never had they worn an expression of such blank despair. She seemed to be addressing an invisible person: "But not until, not until Grandfather . . ." Her whispered words startled her. But her grandfather was alive, alive; that was the important thing: life! Nothing else! Her body cried out against this marriage; her house cried out against the intrusion of strangers, but the word "death" sounded in the depths of her mind. Throughout the house Death could be heard crying its name. An expression of grim determination spread over Carolle Alérac's face: "Nothing shall be touched here until he dies."

With a new strength and sureness she walked over to the fireplace, letting her hands rest on the chairbacks, reassuring the chandeliers, giving the globe map a turn with her finger: "Not one of you shall go, I tell you, until he . . ." She stood erect in the great room, her little head thrown back courageously: "It is written in the book of Job: 'Skin for skin; yea, all that a man hath will he give for his life.' All right, 'skin for skin.' We'll see."

On the chest there was a tall Bruges candlestick with a red candle in it; then a recessed doorway beneath a pointed arch—the door was not high but it had a beautiful lock. A frayed wicker chair with a cat lying in it filled the corner, and then came a high, narrow window with green fringed muslin curtains. In front of the window lay a thick, badly shorn rug—not candy-pink, but deeper, almost apricot; dark blue shadows bordered the patches of light that fell upon it. The table stood on this rug, spread, at that hour, with a stiff white cloth.

Carolle Alérac sat down in the "seal," crossed her legs, emptied her purse into her lap and counted its contents. Then she took a stitch in one of her gloves, slipped into her fur jacket and went out.

3

Her grandfather had taken the right hand road, but she followed the one to the left which, though it seemed to lose itself in the still sky, turned sharply and led down into the town. She walked quickly and the stone walls, lightly covered with snow, were like long white animals accompanying her. She crooked her fingers in her woollen gloves in order to warm them on her palms, but her feet were comfortable in snow-boots. As each season came round she was provided with a new pair of feet: summer feet; eager, vigorous spring feet; she had her winter feet today which delighted in snow, skis and the squeak of new rubber on rough roads. She too looked at the solitary yellow gentian by the roadside, but did not stop. She saw the narrow prints of the antiquary's feet and the wider ones beside them—the marks in the snow had an extraordinary air of expectancy about them and the gentian was like a long pointing finger. High outcroppings of yellow limestone bordered the hilly road as Carolle made her way rapidly towards The Quarries. Behind the tall yellow rocks jagged pine trees waved in the wind.

Yes, she would be able to meet disaster. The cold air did her good, strengthened her. She needed money. If only they would trust her and let her alone! She knew what loans and securities were by this time. Securities? She stood still and ran a finger along the secret pocket in her hand-bag; then she walked on again thoughtfully.

She could just see Jonathan Graew's house, The Vale, at the end of its long avenue and concluded that the washing had been hung up between the trees, for white walls seemed to have sprung up round it. The fields lay peacefully under the snow; not a human being could be seen, no sound could be heard. Her motionless figure rose up among the falling flakes like a little tree of fur. Before her were the Alérac fields, the roads, her house, the low sky and the crows flying . . . if she married him she could keep everything. Why did he want her? What was there about her that appealed to him? And what was there about him that did not appeal to her? He was neither old, nor ugly, nor bald; in fact not un-attractive at all, and his smile was rather charming. What was lacking? What essential quality was it that he did not have?

A squirrel looked at her from the branch of a tree; she would have liked to toss it an almond, but there was nothing in her pocket but a sou. The squirrel made a face at her and the sound of her laughing filled the still white spaces; one could almost follow it about among the snow-covered branches. The ground was covered with dainty little weasel tracks.

Her grandfather was at Jonathan Graew's at that very moment, and the thought of this made her hold her breath. How he had changed! Much more frightening to her than if he were ill. Those visits he made; his quick proposals, as if there were just so many days left in which to settle everything. And the way he talked to her about God and life! That was his mortal illness—that was his cancer.

People with grandfathers who became self-centred,

greedy and peevish had a bad time of it, Heaven knew, but her own grandfather, with his cool resignation to fate, filled her with terror. Oh, if only he would go into one of those towering rages which could send every one off cowering before its violence! This was usually a hateful experience, but she would have preferred the most savage anger to his pious acceptance of the future: "I shall go and talk to him, Carolle." And he had said it with an expression that made her long to say: "Oh, but, Grandfather . . ." and to have him reply: "Carolle, you must be mad!"

Everyone seemed to be robbing her, stealing everything she had; and the most cherished of all her possessions was this grandfather of hers, full of pride, anger and wilfulness. They had taken him and given her this extraordinary stranger in his place.

She had made good time and the Morédan house, high above The Quarries, was already in sight—an oddly shaped dwelling which looked more like an owl than a house, because of its wide roof pressing down over its narrow sides.

4

From her perch, Mlle Noémi Morédan had seen Carolle approaching. She walked over to Mlle Constance, who was sitting at the other window working at a piece of embroidery.

"Carolle Alérac is coming to pay us a visit."

"Are you sure, Noémi?"

"Quite sure, Constance; she's coming along the quarry road; she's wearing her fur jacket."

Carolle was so absorbed in her thoughts that she almost collided with Gottlieb when he came through the hedge. Here, at least, was someone who never changed! He stood there, open-mouthed, gazing at her as he would have gazed at a celestial vision. His gun rested on his shoulder, his clothes were covered with cobwebs and pine needles, and there was something soft inside his jacket that made it bulge out. The steep sides of the limestone quarries rose up around them—huge, yellow, chaotic. Things managed to grow somehow in the pitiable disorder of rock and sand: stonecrop, thistles, brambles, moss, ragged grass and even woodbine with its pink berries. Solitude . . . desolation.

"What have you brought us, Gottlieb?" She touched his bulging jacket. "A bird or a rabbit?"

He looked at her with half-closed eyes now, and shook his head ever so slightly.

"What is it then?"

A crow sailed over them on motionless wings, cawing harshly. They both jumped.

"A crow." Gottlieb spoke and silence fell again; they could hear their hearts beating. Then, with his eyes still upon Carolle, he stretched out his left arm and the soft object which had made his jacket bulge out fell to the ground. At first she didn't understand; then she went up close to him and asked weakly:

"Gottlieb, tell me where you got it."

He laughed, taking the dead hen by the legs and twirling it round and round. Its white feathers looked yellow against the snow.

"Gottlieb, tell me," she besought him, her hands now resting on his shoulders and her big grey eyes searching his which were gleaming with pleasure. "Tell me, Gottlieb, tell me."

How terrible it would be if he should take to killing chickens! She could imagine the fury of the farmers at anyone molesting their live-stock. They would go straight to Graew (he was mayor that year): "What, he's killing your hens? It'll be goats, pigs, children next, if the fancy takes him. He'll have to be locked up." Heavens! What if they were to put him in the asylum? What if . . . "Tell me, Gottlieb, where did you get it?"

She could imagine him in a grey uniform pacing back and forth behind the walls like a wild beast, hunting for Carolle, crying out in anguish. She knelt in the snow, taking the spread wings in her hands and beseeching him: "Tell me, Gottlieb!"

He came closer and spoke again, his eyes almost shut: "The finest, the fattest of them all, Carolle . . ." His joyful fingers opened and closed like the feet of a swimming duck and a malicious smile fluttered across his face like a feather belonging to some nameless bird. Carolle sat with the dead hen in her lap, trying to think what was best for her to do. Not a sound could be heard save the rustling of the grass and thistles among the yellow rocks. She stood up slowly, holding the hen by its feet. What should she do with it? To whom must it be returned? Should she keep it? Gottlieb was laughing now—an intermittent laughter that started and stopped with a strange regularity. Once—twice it escaped him . . . then: "The best of the Pastor's hens, Carolle," and the laughter trailed off into silence.

"The Pastor's!"

But Gottlieb was gazing up into the whirling snow. Nothing could be done with him now. Carolle, the hen, everything had gone from his mind. He spread his arms out under the broad white sky and the snowflakes fell upon his upturned palms.

Carolle took a piece of paper from her bag and scribbled a note: "Masha, don't ask him any questions; I'm going to the Pastor's now." She put the hen in his game-bag. "No, not under your jacket, Gottlieb; she'll like it better here." Then she fastened the game-bag and, instead of turning in at the Morédans', hurried down the road to the Parsonage.

5

Constance Morédan raised her narrow face from her needlework—she was working on a jaguar's claw. "Carolle Alérac is taking a long time," she thought, "Noémi must have been wrong; she's near-sighted."

Noémi, guessing what was in her sister's mind, asked: "Isn't Carolle taking a long time about it, Constance?"

"You were wrong, Noé; it was someone else."

"But I recognized her fur jacket. Do you want me to go and look from the north room?"

"Yes, go to the north room and then tell me."

Noémi Morédan's fat, pink body moved down the hall that smelt of beeswax and stopped before a door; she pushed it open quietly and stood for a moment looking at the flowered green curtains in the room. She could have gazed at them for hours without moving. All the things that were kept in there: laces, lavender sachets, family relics, books full of pressed flowers—all of them had an odour that took you back among the dead, among people you had never seen. The mahogany wardrobes were full of bibelots; an album of dried sea-

weed lay upon the oval table and a blue and gold butterfly from Brazil spread its wings under a glass globe.
Noémi Morédan walked over to the window, laying a
hand on the mauve silk sofa. It would never have occurred to her to sit in it. Was the mauve silk sofa for
her to sit in, that is, was it for the Noémi Morédan that
you saw every day, the broad-bosomed, wide-hipped
Noémi Morédan who was too big everywhere and had
so much hair that her chignon dragged at the back of
her head? No, the sofa was for another Noémi, for the
one who came to life every evening after the clock had
struck ten and sleep had laid its hand upon the house.
Then, in a peaceful mahogany bedstead, under eyelids
scented with lavender, a tall, slender, exquisite, un-
believably beautiful Noémi Morédan came into being.
She was nineteen, maybe twenty, and she wore a yellow
dress; her head was covered with curls that could not
be arranged in a chignon and her lovely mouth curved
over her little gleaming teeth. She rode horseback and
the farmers raised their hats to her as she passed. When
she walked, her father went with her—a very elegant
father dressed in grey and carrying a gold-topped
Malacca stick. Her wedding was near, her trousseau
bought, the chapel ready and there was a new ring in
the house . . . and then one day . . . the real Noémi
had sat down on the edge of the bed . . . the shadowy

room made no difference; it wasn't the room she had seen, it was something outside, through the window where she was standing now. The willow-herbs had smelt so sweet that she hadn't even seen the brambles or the nettles; the larks were singing, the whole earth was fragrant and the quarry was full of sunlight and the humming of bees . . . oh, that day . . . Noémi Morédan's hands sank into the soft coverlet and her breath had come quickly, pantingly. On that day she had seen the "yellow dress" in the quarry and the Spaniard walking beside the "yellow dress," almost dancing in the bright sunlight—they walked that way in his country. She had seen the Spaniard take the girl in his arms—from the window he seemed to be clasping a long yellow plume to his breast; he was speaking eagerly, anxiously; she listened to him without moving and a hawk sailed over them on motionless wings. She saw it all every night. When she closed her eyes she was a girl in a yellow dress under a hawk's spread wings.

"Well, Noémi, where is Carolle Alérac?"

"I've looked everywhere, Constance, but I can't see anyone."

"There she is. Don't you see her? She's just turned off to the left. You ought to have your eyes attended to."

CHAPTER FOUR

MAZING the amount of clothes a landed proprietor could possess! It seemed to Guillaume Alérac that for at least a quarter of an hour he had been walking past shirts and drawers. What Carolle had seen from her lonely field was indeed the washing at The Vale, but though her eyes were as sharp as those of a poacher or a Sioux Indian she had not been able to distinguish the figure of the man who was walking past the maple trees. Lines had been stretched between the trees on both sides of the lane in true peasant fashion. The long arms of the shirts waved crazily, swelled large and white in the wind, and the drawers followed suit, both legs of one garment sometimes kicking out in the same absurd movement. Behind the shirts and drawers hung the sheets like a herd of thin white cattle; then came tablecloths and dish-towels, and finally a dark grey collection of socks which were beginning to stiffen in the frosty air.

As a laundry landscape it was successful enough, with its rows of sham corpses under a low sky, but the hands that were going to gather in those flat, crackling bodies and coil up the lines on which they had hung would make their owner cry out in pain.

Guillaume Alérac was now walking past pillow-cases —absurd the way they bellied out like frilled bladders. Ridiculous that a maple tree should suddenly bristle with shirt sleeves and that a row of gooseberry bushes should look like a horse trapped out for the Crusades! The bath towels waved stiffly, like big pieces of white cardboard.

2

Jonathan Graew stood at his office window, wondering who could be coming up the lane; a sheet would blot out the whole figure or a towel leave only the legs visible. Finally a grey hat appeared above the dish-towels; then he got a glimpse of shoes and recognized Alérac. The colour rose to his cheeks: what a day for him to choose! No one had ever had to walk up to the Alérac house through rows of shirts and drawers; Alérac lived in style . . . his face soon regained its brownish pallor. Why Mme Vauthier always had to hang the washing so close to the front door, she alone knew. How explain the stupidity of some women—one needed a special kind of intelligence to do that. Couldn't it have been hung in the orchard? . . . And now Alérac with his stick and gloves! What had he

come for anyhow? Donations to the poor? Paid.
Widows? Paid. The Orphanage? Paid. The Church
Council? Arrangements all made. What was it? His
engagement to Catherine? What business was that of
his? Did he even know about it? Suddenly he remembered the yellow document—no, that was impossible!
His lawyer was under too many obligations to him. No,
the person had still to be born who could get him into
trouble of that kind. He didn't have to worry.

Consequently it was with perfect assurance that he
went out with his dogs to meet Guillaume Alérac at the
front door.

"Well, Monsieur d'Alérac," he restored the "de"
which his host no longer cared to use, "I hope you will
excuse all that washing hanging out there. I've told
Madame Vauthier twenty times not to do such a stupid
thing, and now you've had to walk through my dish-
towels and socks."

"They used to hang there in Uncle Jérome's time,"
replied Guillaume Alérac imperturbably. "I remember
that very well, because . . ." He laid his gloves and
stick on a chair.

"Because?"

"Oh, we used to play tricks on him, nasty ones—with
his shirts, of course . . . what a temper he had!"

"I've heard he wasn't easy to get on with."

234

"Quite impossible."

They laughed mirthlessly in that bleak room which had rarely known Uncle Jérome's laughter. From their frames the immovable Graews gazed down at Guillaume Alérac with arrogance and severity. Inconceivable that this Alérac should feel so much at home in *their* leather chair; inconceivable how calmly he crossed his legs in front of *their* fireplace!

They discussed flowers, seeds, leases, tenants and such matters. On the shelf beneath the bookcase were samples of wheat, rye and oats in little trays; jonquil and narcissus bulbs were laid in rows of twelve upon newspapers, and between the legs of a card table piled with farm records and ledgers stood a yellow bowl full of chestnuts.

"I like your new hedges, Jonathan Graew; the height is just right and they mark off the Pargot land splendidly. Expensive, I suppose?"

"They're always expensive when they have to be paid for; all good things have their price. Now those Roman tiles—I've worried a lot about them, but I'm not going to spoil my roofs with cheap modern substitutes. You, Monsieur d'Alérac, would never expect me to do that."

Guillaume Alérac was full of understanding for this man who loved his property so deeply, who had such an enduring passion for the earth. Perhaps he would one day get back the money he had put into it. . . . While they spoke of farm management, crops, swedes and his worries about Colinette, Jonathan Graew leaned against his Louis-Philippe desk, wondering what it was that Guillaume Alérac wanted of him. The old man's presence in the house that had once belonged to the Aléracs was always embarrassing—of course the old busybody was looking at everything with a critical eye, and though he realized that he himself knew more about farming than any Alérac he understood that the house must have looked very different in the days of Uncle Jérome. And now, with that document in the desk, it was intolerable to have Guillaume Alérac in the room. . . . He walked over to the desk and turned the key with a defiant glance at his guest.

"What a beautiful piece of wood!" Guillaume Alérac slid one of his hands over the polished surface.

"Do you think so? I don't see how you could like anything here very much. It must have been so different in Uncle Jérome's time."

"It's the same old house, Jonathan Graew," he looked up at the beams supporting the ceiling; then, "the same black oak floor, and—wait—there was a leather couch just like yours and in the same place. And books, here —books that were never opened."

"Then, in one respect, they were like mine." He looked at his crowded shelves. Let the rats have them —but perhaps the bindings were worth something? . . . He found his cigar case under a pile of papers and offered it to his guest.

"I only meant that no one ever read them," continued Guillaume Alérac, cutting the end off his cigar. "When I emptied the shelves I found every book stuffed with dried flowers—just imagine it—a herbarium, not a library at all. Flowers, you know, were his hobby. No, it was more than that—they were his passion. . . . Uncle Jérome's world was made up of his bank account, his hospitals and his flowers. At Easter it was marvellous here," he waved a hand towards the clotheslines, "armfuls of crocuses, tulips, hyacinths! And he was the one who said that every expense was a mistake —well, the garden was full of mistakes. None of his three wives ever received as much attention as one of those white tulips. It was real love, I tell you."

"Oh—love." Jonathan Graew's voice was so low that Guillaume Alérac asked:

"Has something gone wrong, Jonathan Graew?"

"Is there ever anything that doesn't?"

"Yes, often; and I notice plenty of things here that are doing very well indeed—almost too well."

"Too well?" What did he mean? Did things ever go

too well? He supposed it was just another one of those Alérac-isms.

"Didn't you say six thousand bundles from the Vale land?"

"Seven thousand," he corrected savagely, "five of rye —wheat and swedes did well too." He leaned over to put a log on the fire (how long was it since there had been good cedar logs like at the Aléracs'?). The two Great Danes sat on either side of the chimneypiece— huge, alert and majestic. "I suppose one might say the land had me in its clutches." He got up and stood near the desk again. "My mother wanted me to be a minister, but that wasn't any good. I tried—I passed examinations. We had to read Plato and all I could think of was the east wind and whether the hay was in or not. I tried to learn ecclesiastical law, but I was always wondering whether the frost was going to kill the rye—it wasn't any use."

Guillaume Alérac puffed at his cigar, wondering at the weariness of his host's voice: "What's wrong, Jonathan Graew?"

"I'm engaged to be married."

"And what's wrong with that?"

"Oh, it's a queer business," he dug his hands into his pockets and paced back and forth in front of the portraits, his eyes on the floor. The boards cracked under his feet and the Great Danes got up uneasily to await his bidding. Guillaume Alérac knocked the ash from his cigar—a long, pinkish-grey ash that smoked quietly for a moment in the ash tray.

"Madame Vauthier doesn't think much of it, nor do they," he glanced at the portraits, "and I agree with them—no, it mustn't be!"

"So then? . . ."

Jonathan Graew laughed and there was a fleeting look of adolescence on his face as he said: "I can't help it." He stood before his mother's portrait: "She wouldn't approve; no one here would—not even the house. I know better than anyone that I mustn't—but I've got to have her, that's all!"

Embarrassed at having said so much, he grasped the decanter, poured out two glasses of brandy and drank his own at a gulp.

Guillaume Alérac could not help thinking of Mlle Huguenin and then of his own life. He was full of pity for the man standing at the window with his head in his arm, struggling for composure. Until the end of the world things like this would happen.

"Twice I fell in love," he spoke quietly, "and both times I knew it could never come to anything. The difficulties I saw ahead were too great." He crossed his legs and laid his long hands upon the arms of the chair.

By the slight tightening of his eyelids one could gauge the depth of his emotion. "The third time all went smoothly, but the result was disastrous. You never know how those things are going to turn out, never! You don't know why you're in love or why your love is not returned. All you do know is that there is nothing you want except the hell you've made for yourself."

Why was he talking of these things? Strange that he should speak like this here, in the very room where he had brought his young wife to receive Uncle Jérome's blessing. He had not had an hour of happiness with her. Money, family approval, everything; and how lovely she had been! . . . Then that other love —the most poignant of them all—no, he would never say who it was! Nobody could understand it, unless perhaps someone who had been through a similar emotion. But he did not want to match his experience with anyone's; he knew enough about love. Life could teach him nothing more.

It was peaceful in the room now; the fire had burned down and the dogs were back in their places. Jonathan Graew's hands were still plunged in his pockets, but not so deeply now, and his arms looked like the two handles of a vase.

"Things are better with you than with me," he said, "there's no doubt about that. Your troubles are behind you. Mine are still ahead of me and I've got to keep going. I can't help it." Again the boyish smile; Guillaume Alérac was touched by it, wondered what was in store for Jonathan Graew, and again the thought of Mlle Huguenin rose up in his mind.

Every time the old man's eyes rested on the shiny wood of the desk Jonathan Graew looked down to hide his anger. What right had Guillaume Alérac to lecture him about life? He wanted to put his fist through the thin polished wood and show him what one might find in a Louis-Philippe desk at eleven o'clock on a snowy Thursday morning in the country! . . . But he went to the decanter and poured himself another glass of brandy.

Through the window Mme Vauthier's aprons could be seen fluttering like warning signals, but who knows how to read warning signals? . . . Replying to his host's observation that he seemed tired, Guillaume Alérac said: "Oh, I've come a long way this morning. I'm just back from a journey to Brazil. I took the whole school with me. It was marvellous! . . . What could I have been thinking of a moment ago when I told you that love was all that mattered in life? I'm an old fool. There's so much more, Jonathan Graew: my granddaughter, all those children, books to read. That's a lot when you come to think of it. . . . By the way, there's

an interesting youngster there named Randal. Do you
know him?"

"Which Randal? There are at least twenty Randals
in the parish."

"I mean the stone-mason's boy; his mother does
washing. He ought to be pushed, and it wouldn't cost
very much. Monin could take him first. It would be a
pity not to let him have a chance."

Jonathan Graew came over to his chair and examined
him carefully, as though preparing to read the inscrip-
tion on a monument or a tomb.

"I don't much like undertaking that kind of thing;
you always get in deeper than you want to. You help
the boy, and before you know it his parents are on your
hands." (The Aléracs had had bad luck with their
charities and he wasn't fool enough to follow in their
tracks. Let someone else be Santa Claus this time.) His
upper lip twitched with annoyance. "Good works are
usually repaid with ingratitude. Tell me, hasn't that
been your experience?"

Guillaume Alérac got up from his chair and crossed
the room to rest an arm on the Louis-Philippe desk.

"You're right, Jonathan Graew; more often than not
it's a waste of money . . . although, in cases like
that . . ." He tapped the flap of the desk with his fingers.

"Just above that yellow document," thought Graew, watching the drumming fingers with increasing uneasiness and a certain feeling of exultation. Later, however, he was forced to admit to himself that the moment had been one of the worst in his life.

An inscrutable expression hovered in Guillaume Alérac's eyes and was gone. "We can do only a part of what should be done for our fellow beings. We are permitted to hope that there is Another who will do more than we can, and this is very comforting. Don't you think so, Jonathan Graew?"

"I was not thinking merely of the money; please understand me. . . ." His eyes had met those of his guest and he fell silent.

"I came here this morning to talk to you about something else," Guillaume Alérac started to put on his gloves, "but another time will be better. Nevertheless, I'd like to say this now: in every marriage there's always one who gives more than the other and I think the one who gives the most has the best time of it." He looked at the tall, handsome man before him with the eyes of one who has learned by experience what it is that women expect and what it is they need: "Well, there's a good deal more to be said."

They left the house in silence and walked down the

maple-lined avenue—one swinging along sailor-fashion and the other stiffly erect.

"That *Petit Monaco* sort of thing is all over, isn't it? Promise me that, my boy, won't you? You can't undertake matrimony and keep on with it . . . well, goodbye, Jonathan Graew . . . it looks as though winter had come."

CHAPTER FIVE

$\mathcal{C}$AROLLE ALÉRAC stopped in front of a grey house with a beautiful doorway; she pushed open the gate, ran up the steps and went in without ringing. In the hall she took off her snow-boots and hurried up the familiar wooden staircase which always smelt of quince jam. She was anxious not to have to talk to—what was she, a cousin or a cousin once removed? She could never keep her relatives straight. At all events, Mlle Cécile de la Tour, the Pastor's sister, asked too many questions and was always going on about how Christian Science had saved her. No, she couldn't face that. She climbed two flights and knocked three times on the third door down the passage. A voice replied and she entered: a leather couch, some lovely old chairs, an austere-looking portrait on the wall and a man's head bent over a grey blotting-pad. The man pushed back his chair and came forward, and the floor cracked loudly as it always did. Carolle seemed paler than usual and tired, he thought . . . snow still on her fur jacket . . . was it coming down as hard as that?

It was a severe interior, but sympathetic: white curtains in the windows and tobacco-coloured ones at the sides, the smell of leather and old books, and two tall silver candlesticks. A fire, ready to be lighted, lay upon a pile of white ashes. He led her to the couch.

"What's the matter, Carolle?" Evidently something was very wrong.

"I came . . ." She began to speak and then, as though surprised by a storm or a sudden gust of wind, she found herself weeping. He leaned over her—tall, black, a little ridiculous, trying to protect her from some danger that threatened.

"But what is it, Carolle?"

She was asking herself despairingly the same question: "What is it, what is it? What's the matter with me?"

It was all going to be so easy: she full of assurance and everything so simple: one thing to say to the Moré-dans, another to the Pastor. It had been just like two strong columns which she was to walk between, and then go on about her business—and now she was weeping! He wouldn't go away; he stood there looking at her, frightened, clasping and unclasping his hands . . . what could he say to this girl who sat stiffly on his couch, crying noiselessly, with tight lips and a stubborn look on her face? Her tears fell slowly, regularly, endlessly.

She didn't apologize, she didn't wipe her nose as most

people do when they weep, and she didn't press her handkerchief into a little wad, but she couldn't stop her tears from falling.

He took one of her hands and it was easy to see that he was not used to touching women's hands. He held it as though it were a bowl from which one was surprised not to see a wisp of steam rising. She withdrew the hand and it lay upon her lap—long, narrow and white. It was like an extra hand that she carried about with her.

He stood beside her hesitatingly, ineffectually. Could it be her grandfather, the house, Gottlieb, Jonathan Graew? . . . She had taken off her toque; her head rested on the back of the couch and her knees were pressed tightly together. So young, so pathetic! . . . A deep uneasiness began to take possession of him; he went to the window, put his forehead against the metal knob, and gazed with unseeing eyes upon the quiet snow-covered landscape. There could have been cactus plants, elephants, fireworks, someone playing a mandolin, and he would have noticed nothing.

2

The cold white light, into which he had been staring, darkened the room for him as he turned away from the window. A book lay open on his table: Théodore de Bèze. . . . What splendid heads those Reformers had! What cold piercing eyes! "I, God the Father. . . ." Interesting, the difference between the heads of Catholics and of Protestants: female structure and male structure—as different as the heads of zebras and horses . . . what, in a moment like this, could have made him think of such things?

"Is something the matter with Masha? Tell me, Carolle. That's it, isn't it?" Was she merely tired out, or something more? Carolle shook her head. She knew at last what it was that had come to her so suddenly. It was this, then! No wonder her strength had left her; it was all perfectly clear now . . . the world had fallen to pieces: her house, her grandfather, Gottlieb, the debts . . . she was gasping for breath . . . the white hen, almost yellow now, with a little spot on its neck, was flapping its wings above the confusion of her life.

"Carolle, you must explain what is troubling you . . ." How could he find out anything when his words died like bubbles on water?

What was she to explain? How could one explain anything when the world had come down about one's shoulders? . . . Her head was still resting on the back of the couch and he stood watching the pulsating artery in her neck.

Carolle was like a ghost in his room. His eyelids fluttered, the corners of his mouth went down and he was
conscious of the peculiar trembling sensation in his
cheek that he always felt at difficult moments in his
life. His face bore the signs of conflicting emotions:
misery, tenderness and anger; it was like a puzzle, but
one could easily see how to put it together again and
recapture the peaceful countenance one knew.

He wondered whether man was fated to relive certain experiences of his life. Another woman had sat
weeping on that couch, neither to the left nor to the
right, but on the self-same spot—he was sure of it—just
under the Rembrandt copy. She had worn a yellow
dress; it was too thin for the time of year, but she had
not felt cold. She had sat just as Carolle was sitting, her
head resting on the back of the couch, and he had seen
the pulsations of the artery in her neck. She too had
refused to speak to him, and she had wept.

During all these years, he had never passed the couch
without seeing Alexandrine Alérac get up, put out a
hand and then withdraw it as though someone were
pulling back her arm. Then she had gone. . . . Poor
little girl!

He ran one of his hands through his coarse grey hair,
and the anxious expression which had contracted his
rugged angular features vanished completely: "Since

when? How long, I wonder?" He searched for the answer and from somewhere deep within him he heard: "You wouldn't *allow* yourself to believe it," and he realized that it was true. He was still perplexed and uncertain, but he was glad to be able to say to himself: "I knew it, of course I knew it." His lips began to tremble. . . . How desperate had been his struggle for peace! Twenty years! For twenty years he had lived with the Psalms, his books, the poor, the dying; with his beloved sister who played Couperin and was always happy, who would walk through a cemetery as though it were a drawing-room full of friends, believing that death was an illusion and that, if one but knew it, the people there were more alive than the living. Twenty years! It had been a heart-breaking task to build up a life after everything had crumbled, broken into pieces. One had to gather it all up and hold it carefully. In the beginning, how hard it had been to construct even one day out of those little odds and ends of courage, out of the desert of his misery.

And now? He was approaching old age—a lover of silence, books. Was it all going to begin again? Was he to be caught up in the whirlwind—beaten and bruised? No, it could not be! But the thumping of his heart made him realize the uselessness of that resolution. . . . He was mad to be thinking of her in a parsonage, surrounded by books—a girl no more than twenty! It all seemed sordid, horrible! She was young enough to be his daughter. Fool!

He was filled with rage at his own blindness and cowardice. Couldn't he have foreseen that this sort of thing would come to him? It was the usual fate of a man near the end of his life to be so tempted—the final flaming up of passion. He recognized it now; all men were submitted to evil influences; he had spoken of it often in his sermons and his prayers—and to himself: "Lead us not into temptation." The temptation was there—why had he not realized it?

When Carolle finally looked up, panic took possession of him. The structure of his past life began to wave and tremble as though supported by pillars of thin paper; the ordered stability of his world: his Bibles, Théodore de Bèze, Socrates' exhortation to live as far as possible in a state of death—all of it drifted away like mist, and he was left standing alone beside the woman he loved. He saw himself bend over and take Carolle Alérac in his arms (I must be insane, he thought), hold her close to his heart—his old heart that was full of experience. He did not dare to kiss her, but he could feel her breast rising and falling against his; her breath mingled with his own. . . . Carolle believed they had both taken leave of their senses, that they had been swept out of this world into the unknown, where there was nothing but death.

Both of them were guilty: she because she remained passively in his arms, and he because he held her there with such determination . . . her eyes were not closed and she saw the expression of tortured rapture upon his face.

He did not speak to her—explanations would come later, or perhaps there would be no explanations. Both of them knew that they were hovering in a hopeless ecstasy and that in hopelessness there is infinite repose.

Naturally there was no mirror in the room, so she stood in front of the clock to put on her toque. He went with her to the front door. From the third step she turned back and held out her hand:

"I came to tell you it was Gottlieb who killed the white hen."

"The white hen? . . ." His voice sounded like the voice of a man emerging from sleep.

He closed the door and stood looking at the umbrella stand which held his two umbrellas, his three sticks, his sister's umbrella and "Jocoton," the lending umbrella. With the clearing of his brain his head began to throb. Fool! Fool! . . . He ached in every joint. What had

he done? In Heaven's name, what had he done? . . .
He could still feel her slender body in his arms and her
quick heart-beats gradually slowing down. He gazed
stupidly at the umbrella stand.

"Is it really as hard as that to choose, silly man? On
a day like this you'd hardly take a stick." His sister
handed him the best of his umbrellas, watched him put
on his coat, take his hat and gloves and run down the
steps. Mlle Huguenin saw him hurrying past her window and thought he had been called to the bedside of
someone who was dying.

PART FOUR

A Surprising Afternoon

CHAPTER ONE

*Y*ou can't see it very well; not in this weather." Guillaume Alérac took the picture to the window. "No, it's too dark, really." There was a note of disinterest in his voice. . . . How lovely the pinks and greys were in the pale afternoon light—that little splash of yellow shone like a cry in the stillness. "Too beautiful for you," thought the old man, "much too beautiful for you, my friend Balagny—no, nothing to be done about it." He quickly replaced the picture on the shadowy wall at the other end of the room. "Another that won't go today!" He felt as though he had rescued a friend; it was just like the time he had offered a horse for sale and had invented imaginary faults to discourage the purchaser at the last moment. It was like that with his pictures too. . . . Oh, well, he couldn't help it; he was born that way.

"I didn't know you were interested in pictures." He came back to his guest. "You've never said so."

"Is this one for sale?" Jérome Balagny pointed to a Van Gogh.

"Everything's for sale." Guillaume Alérac did not

offer his guest a cigar; he looked absently through the window. Then in the silence of that lifeless afternoon he heard:

"I have something else to ask you, sir."

"What is it?"

"Will you honour me with your consent to my marriage with Mademoiselle Carolle Alérac?"

Guillaume Alérac raised his chin—now he knew the reason for this formal appearance: striped trousers, black coat, grey gloves; he might have known that his guest would not dress himself up that way to look at Van Goghs.

"Won't you sit down?" He waved a hand, seated himself in his own chair and punctuated his questions by tapping a paper-knife on the fingers of his left hand.

"Isn't this a rather sudden decision?"

"No, I have been thinking about her for a long time." Jérome Balagny looked at his host intently; Guillaume Alérac crossed his legs, arched his eyebrows —his thin, handsome face had the motionless insistence of a portrait.

"I suppose you know she is only twenty?" There was a cold insolence in the way he said "twenty."

"I want her very much," said Jérome Balagny in a low voice. "I love her. . . ." His hands trembled slightly—slim graceful hands that seemed to have more life in them than the rest of his body. "Perhaps his best point," thought Guillaume Alérac.

"My dear sir, I understand your loving her perfectly. Who could help loving her?" He was surprised at the sharpness of his own words—was he like one of those idiotic fathers who couldn't endure anyone asking to marry their daughters? "Will you tell me what meaning you give the word 'love'? It's been so debased that it no longer signifies very much."

Carolle Alérac's suitor surveyed the long spare body in the leather chair, the unsmiling face; and he began to believe what he had heard of Guillaume Alérac's cruelty.

"Can one analyze these things?" he answered uncomfortably.

"We must do it now or never. . . . You are rich, you bear an honourable name, you say to yourself that her poverty is sufficient to prove the disinterestedness of your motives. And you are right." He stood up quickly. "I offer you my felicitations, but since all this concerns my granddaughter—you will forgive me if I seem brutal —well, I would like to have a different kind of assurance. I don't want to know how much money you are earning, or what your investments yield, and your political opinions don't concern me in the least. I'm an old man," his voice softened, "and I have done a lot of thinking. . . . Will you tell me what you have accomplished in your life?" Guillaume Alérac put down the paper-knife and continued: "I knew your father very well; he was a charming man and I found him most sympathetic. If I were Carolle's father, I would answer you in the usual way. I would tell you (and I would mean it sincerely) that I was honoured by your request and that I would consider it and urge my daughter to say 'Yes.' But I am her grandfather, and grandfathers have the special privilege of having their own ideas. A father wants his daughter to have this or that position in society and he is right to feel that way. . . . I want *happiness* for my granddaughter and that's a difficult thing to obtain. . . . She's such a dear girl!" His expression had changed completely. "I don't say this because she's mine, but because it's true." He looked at Jérome Balagny with troubled eyes. One didn't give one's dog away without a heartache, and this man with a drooping moustache and degenerate hands was asking for Carolle.

The lamps had not been lit and a greyish-white darkness slowly enveloped the two men. The dying fire gleamed faintly upon the books in the lower shelves and from his frame, "The Man with the Falcon" fixed the two dim figures with his malicious stare.

Jérome Balagny sat with his chin in his hand trying

to think what he had done with his life. . . . "He has the look of a gambler, and he's probably a drunkard too," thought Guillaume Alérac; Carolle was not a Sister of Charity, thank God. The very thought of his granddaughter in this man's arms put him in a rage. It was appalling how men could create ridiculous situations simply through not looking at themselves in the mirror. Ugh, that worn face and that look of a homesick bird in his eyes! It took more than a tub and a scrubbing to make a man . . . and what was it he smelt of? Nothing infuriated him more than scented men. He was to give Carolle to this piece of gilded nothingness, was he? The impudence of the fellow pretending to be interested in pictures and wasting his time that way! Guillaume Alérac loathed being made a fool of. Talking about colours and values with that port-drinking nincompoop!

"I suppose my granddaughter knows about this?"

"Oh, I know I'm not a young man. I've not spoken to her yet, but I think I can say that she knows what I feel about her; women are more intuitive than men. You've discovered that, I'm sure."

"If she had been rich, would you have asked me for her?" That anyone should take advantage of his granddaughter's poverty was intolerable; it awakened all his fighting instincts.

"I have told you that I want her very much, sir." A disarming smile spread over his face. "There is nothing sudden about this, I assure you. Will you ask her for me?"

"I shall speak to her, and who knows?—she may be less unreasonable than I am. You never know what a woman's reactions will be."

"Unreasonable?" His lifeless voice hovered above the backs of the chairs.

"I repeat that she is only twenty. She must not be forced into anything."

"If she will have me, can I count on you not to interfere?"

"Can I count on you never to touch another card?" Jérome Balagny did not reply; he seemed not to have heard the question. There was complete darkness in the room now, except for a little circle of dim light in front of the fire.

"Well, you're an honest man, at least," said Guillaume Alérac, holding out his hand.

Jérome Balagny descended the poorly lighted oak staircase. This Alérac house seemed to him like a long ship plunging through the sea at night. There was a smell of death everywhere—who had told him that death had a smell? No, it was cinnamon, rose petals, a touch of orange—those women in the portraits might have just waved their scarves in the darkness. . . . He didn't want to give up Carolle; her sort stirred him too deeply. All this old rubbish could be kept if she would marry him . . . and that old monkey; no, monkey wasn't right—what was he like? He unhitched his horse and decided it was a panther or an okapi he was thinking of . . . a fine head and good strong features—impressive. Of whom did he remind him? Who was it? Of course! That thing in the museum at—at—oh, yes, it was the *Condottiere*. Amazing! . . . Carolle had no father—well, what of it? Parents dead, no scandal. His own were in the cemetery. The okapi was right—at forty-two, one couldn't have everything.

He turned out into the road so sharply that he nearly crushed Catherine against the gate-post, but he noticed nothing. He was thinking that, if he married Carolle, he would order the gate lamps to be kept lighted—he would do things correctly . . . the road was slippery, so he reined in his horse to a walk.

2

Catherine's breath came quickly and her heart was hammering. She had pressed herself flat against the gate-post, but the carriage had barely missed her. Who had visited the Aléracs in such weather? Who was it? Frightened though she had been, the question filled her mind. For years, no carriage had come out of the Aléracs' gate; that, at least, was all over with. No one thought it worth tiring a horse to pay visits there. Who could it have have been?

The sight of the shining harness, the bright wheels and especially the acrid smell of leather had pervaded her and were still probing her senses like quickly search- ing fingers. Why was she breathing so fast? Why did her heart beat so? . . . She let her hands fall from the iron bars of the gate, and they seemed not to be hers at all. She had been so frightened that her body was still not quite her own. She shook the snow from her hair and stood for a moment gazing into the darkness. Who had taken the trouble to harness a horse and come here? Who? And why?

Slowly she walked between the spindle-trees towards the house. All was still. She was overwhelmed by a feel- ing of dreariness that seemed to drag at her shoulders. Was it her engagement? A voice within her said "No."

There was nothing left in the world but the raw scent of the bare trees, the fleeting perfume of blighted asters and the snowflakes coming down slowly, vertically, upon the sodden earth. Her depression reached such a point that she could have fallen at the edge of the drive and lain there like a stone. What had come over her? The

carriage—and the fear that . . . no, worse than fear; a
kind of warning. Suddenly she remembered that she
had had a dream the night before. But what had she
dreamed of? It was all so confused and she tried to re-
construct it as she drew near the house. But it was useless; she was soon engulfed in a mental fog much thicker
than the actual mist that was wetting her hands.

Then out of the depths of her memory, like a rain-
bow sweeping upwards from some dark valley, she
saw the carriage of her dream. Last night—a carriage,
of course. That was her dream. She remembered perfectly now—a stylish carriage with shiny wheels just
like . . . again that anguish of apprehension . . . yes,
it was the very carriage which had so nearly crushed
her against the gate-post. What did it all mean? Why
had she dreamed of that carriage?

She went up the steps, rang the bell and was told
that Mademoiselle had not returned; then the door was
closed quickly.

She could feel her face, her neck, even her shoulders
burning with the shame of it. She wanted to run from
the house, but she was certain that Carolle was there
behind one of the curtains watching her. Carolle must
be there; she was sure of it. . . . With slow, dignified
step, she walked towards the gate . . . her grandfather
too; Masha, Gottlieb, the whole household were laugh-

ing at her—the windows, even the curtains. "Mademoiselle is out." She knew what that meant. There was a
buzzing in her ears; her throat contracted. If she could
only run now, stop up her ears; get away somehow, anywhere; follow someone like a dog. . . . They were not
"at home" to her; they wouldn't receive her.

She could hear Carolle and her friends settling her
fate: "Catherine must not be let in if she comes. We
can't impose her on people. Catherine who? Catherine
what?" . . . Phrases like this arranged themselves in
her mind, words that cut her like knives—there was a
kind of torturing joy in hearing their sounds. Hands
were clutching and squeezing her heart, wringing the
blood out of it. Tears poured down her cheeks and she
caught one with the tip of her tongue, surprised to find
it so absurdly sweet when her life was so bitter.

"Mademoiselle is not at home." Oh, why could no
one see it? She was just as good as the others, even better. Beautiful? Yes; and intelligent, which was still more
important. Clever? Yes; and perhaps a little spiteful.
No one had any idea how far she could go if she were
only given a chance. . . . She gripped hard with her
fingers as though she were holding back a hound that
was pulling at its leash.

After all, everything here was hers. "The ground
she treads is her own." The phrase sounded clearly

through the night; she might have been reading it aloud from a book. Funny to realize that the ground beneath her feet actually belonged to her. Jonathan Graew had purchased her the right to speak aloud of it. . . . She had a momentary vision of that document on his knees the day before, opening and closing its pages like a yellow butterfly.

She looked about her, trying to penetrate the obscurity, but the gently falling snow was all she could see —perhaps it belonged to her too. She held out her palms and they were soon covered with snowflakes; she closed them with a little thrill of pleasure. Perhaps she would take possession of the wind too. . . . She was no longer Catherine, no longer the girl who had stood at the door and asked: "May I see Carolle?" She leaned against one of the maple trees; all her life she would remember the feel of it against her back: the first Alérac tree to know about the new alliance.

It was a strange and impressive ceremony with that great unlit house there among the trees behind her, the snow falling and the north wind beginning to blow through the bare branches. There was something tragic and hopeless about it, but nevertheless it was an important ceremony. She felt the tree at her back, and the wind that came up over the Alérac lands touching her hair with quick fingers. This was life at last! She flung

267

out her arms—who was there to stop her? She knew **it** now; her arms knew it; everything here was really hers!

With a new strength and sureness she walked on slowly towards the gate. It was all right now; she was afraid of no one. . . . The smell of leather and the gleam of carriage wheels (why had they frightened her so?) mingled themselves with her triumphant thoughts. There at the gate, she could almost see it pass her in the snow: an invisible being with the power to shut doors. And her joy dropped from her like a piece of rotten fruit.

Something of vital importance was lacking, and as she realized this a wild look came into her eyes. The snow was going down her neck, but she paid no attention to it. She was walking swiftly now—those box hedges smelt of death—and her footsteps were noiseless, but to her they seemed loud in the darkness. She had come to the granite urn at the corner of the Alérac wall; behind the wall a long shiny box hedge ran all the way back to the gate. There was a hawthorn hedge on the other side of the road and above her the invisible sky. And what awaited her at the end of this tunnel? Nothing. . . . Maman Rose's and Abel's house; then there would be Jonathan Graew; then her wedding and, like a flag waving at the top of a tower, the house of the Aléracs. No! No! That wasn't all there was! No, it couldn't possibly be all! There was something else. She was sure of it. Somewhere in the world there was a different sort of place, a place where there were no Aléracs, no Jonathan Graew, a place where you—where you . . . She stood erect, motionless, in a kind of ecstasy. If the man she loved had seen her face, all would have been well, and their lives would not have been blasted by the calamities that awaited them.

She was no longer troubled by her dream and the absurd anxieties it had evoked; on the contrary she felt her body grow warm with the simple need to hold some-one in her arms, and it was in this mood of repose and deliverance from apprehension that she found herself suddenly face to face with Carolle Alérac.

"Carolle!"

"Kati!"

In both voices there was the same note of joyful relief. Catherine's heart leapt within her: then they hadn't been laughing at her! They hadn't lied to her when they said: "Mademoiselle is not at home." It was the truth! This realization made her want to weep with gratitude, but since it was not possible to explain to Carolle what she had just been through, she cast it all from her like an old coat. And Carolle was so happy to find Catherine at that particular moment; what a day it had been! She took her friend's arm and they walked along together. They did not stop to tap on Mlle Huguenin's windows, though they both thought it would be fun, but turned back towards the Alérac house as though it had never occurred to either of them that they would do anything else, as naturally as the snow fell from the sky.

Catherine was walking on air; the road which had seemed so rough was now as smooth as cream. "Oh, Carolle, doesn't the box smell marvellous?" They both stopped to take deep breaths of it and the odour of the frost-bitten hedge gave them a strange sharp pleasure. They walked on again quickly, very close to one another, thigh touching thigh, two slender bodies; the same height, the same young warm blood, almost breathing the same breath.

What a day it had been for both of them: Catherine engaged to be married and faced with the task of repairing an old needlework chair-back representing a Merovingian king. During her efforts to bring his hand to life with yellow silk he began to look so like Jonathan Graew that it was uncanny. "I have a Merovingian lover!" Then there was Maman Rose bursting into her room every few minutes, full of ideas, darting clumsily this way and that like a huge bee. Catherine's idea that

270

the great Jonathan Graew could look like the king in
that old ragged chair-back made her laugh so hard that
Abel, who that day had chosen to wait for the end of
the world by the kitchen stove, came running in to see
what was the matter with her.

"You can see why I didn't get much done." Of course
she could, and what had she herself accomplished? Nothing. No work on her dress at all. "Were you cold when
you got out of bed this morning? The thought of putting a foot on the cold floor was too much for me—
awful!" Catherine said that it was the same with her,
only of course Maman Rose was not so strict—she didn't
say "as your grandfather," but Carolle knew what she
implied.

"He's never been late to a meal in his life."

"Oh, I can't believe it!"

They were walking up the drive now, and a dim light
shone in one of the windows above the tops of the yews.
"Grandfather's in his study," thought Carolle.

In the enveloping snow and mist they felt as though
all their troubles had fallen from them, melted away in
the darkness. It was like the confessional where someone else took the responsibility for all your sins. That
night, strange things were hovering in the darkness: a
Merovingian fiancé, a dead hen, the Pastor, Noémi
Morédan's plaintive voice asking: "Carolle, do you

271

think a yellow dress would suit me?" Really, Noémi
Morédan was getting crazier every day.

From his study where he was arranging some of his
books and demolishing an invisible Balagny, Guillaume
Alérac heard them clattering up the stairs: the Alérac
centaurs, he had always called them.

Tout—le long—le long—du Missouri . . .

one breathless voice sang; then the other:

Sous les—sous les grands mimosas . . .

and then, through the kitchen door, Gottlieb's falsetto:

Fleuri . . . fleuri . . .

The nearer they came to his door, the softer they
kept their voices, and very little mimosa drifted into
the room where Guillaume Alérac stood with a book
in his hand, smiling at their song. . . . But the fear
that someone might take that beloved child from him
set him to pacing angrily to and fro. He stopped in front
of "The Man with the Falcon" and the two stared at
each other: one holding his pipe in his hand and the
other with his bird perched on his finger. They had
always detested one another, but the picture was such a

fine one that Guillaume Alérac rather enjoyed their mutual hatred.

He heard footsteps on the floor above him, and then Carolle's voice: "Masha! . . . Some tea, please, and bread and rose jam." He could also hear the humming of the cord, as the basket—a labour-saving device of Carolle's—descended precariously through space. He followed the ceremony with his usual apprehension; the cord would certainly break one day and the ancestors in the hall below would be spattered with tea and jam, but the girls had so little fun these days he hadn't the heart to interfere, and Masha was too old for this extra stair-climbing. . . . He went back to *War and Peace*, but his ears were alert for the expected catastrophe.

By the time Natasha entered the Rostovs' drawing-room with Boris and Nicholas, and when the lovely Sonia lay weeping on the old pink quilt, he imagined the girls had long ago finished their tea. . . . What a fool he was to think he could resist this book! Incredible, the power it had over him! . . .

He was on the bridge at Enns with Vaska Denissov and his Bedouin when the Pastor was announced. He put down the book angrily and glared at the door: "What could the man want now? Couldn't he be left alone with his book?"

CHAPTER TWO

THAT room had long been known as the "ice-box," but the two chattering girls on the floor by the fire, eating bread and rose jam and drinking their tea, gave no sign of being cold. Bursts of laughter in the slowly darkening room . . . "Don't mind the dark, do we?" "More tea?" At least a dozen cups had been drunk already. What made them so thirsty? Not the snow, was it? Of course not. They were young, that was all. A book was opened: "Listen to this." Closed. Opened again: "Wait, listen to this."

Cups were emptied—filled and emptied again; home-made bread and rose jam disappeared rapidly. A diet of topazes . . . see, their slender bodies . . .

The fire sent up little green-pointed flames. Carolle's music-stand near the window looked like a yellow iron schoolmistress. Fabian, the violin, was nowhere to be seen, but on the easel a canvas thickly covered with yellows and blues was slowly drying amid exhalations of turpentine and linseed oil. Books lay scattered untidily upon the table, but space had been cleared at one end

274

for a grimly dominating volume: huge, black, and titled in red: Ledger—Alérac Estate.

Catherine was happy there with Carolle that afternoon. The house had its own very special smell of age and weariness—like faded roses in the rain. It was the Alérac smell, emanating from old tapestries and curtains where pink parrots sat among white cherry blossoms; from the old chest against the wall; from the cracks in the parquet floor which contained the dust of a hundred years beneath a shiny patine of wax. Carolle too smelt like faded roses; so did her bed—Catherine had often noticed it when the covers were being turned down at night. Did she have a smell too? She held a hand under her nose: "Not faded roses, but nice." It surprised her to find how good she smelt.

They had endless things to say—mostly monosyllables —as they sat in the firelight poising teacups and pieces of bread and jam:

"Michel?"

"Yes."

"Told him?"

A nod.

"Despair?"

"Yes, he understood.

"You'll never get rid of him."

"Don't I know it?"

"What next?"

Carolle shrugged her shoulders: "Would *you* want to marry him?"

"No. I don't like green ties and striped overcoats." Catherine dug a little cave in her jam. "What are you going to do about him?"

"Don't know. Maybe I'll try the 'Jesuit Method.'"

"Which is?"

"You take a piece of paper and make two lists: for and against; then fold the paper, dividing the two lists. It's called an 'Election.' Weigh the pros and cons carefully. Consider what advantages there would be; what sort of relief—how and when to make use of it. After this, compare the two lists, and, without paying any attention to the admonitions of the flesh, decide which course seems the wiser."

"All right. Let's try it. Give me some paper," and in her graceful handwriting Catherine put this heading at the top of the sheet:

PROPOSED MARRIAGE BETWEEN
CAROLLE ALÉRAC AND MICHEL ROCHEDIEU

and underneath, in smaller letters:

JESUIT METHOD

"Now, dictate to me."

	Favourable	Unfavourable
Height	5 ft. 9	Mother-in-law
Hair	not bad	Hair on his hands
Eyes	ditto	No desire to kiss
Chin	round	him
Moustache	no remarks	Family gatherings
Identifying marks	scar on left arm	on Sundays
Character	absolute integrity	
Total	Dreadful	Dreadful

Conclusion: The Jesuit Method absolutely useless.

Lune, étoile, soleil, tout s'est évanoui . . .

The cups, the bread and butter plate and the remains of the jam had been pushed under a chair. There was dressmaking to be done, for Carolle was going to a dance and her frock, cut out of an old eighteenth century curtain, was not nearly ready. Catherine was on her knees with her mouth full of pins and Carolle turned slowly in front of a tall, dim mirror. " 'Urn," said Catherine (the "t" could not be heard because of

277

the pins), "Too long." "Undo the pleats" . . . "I'm going to baste the hem while it's on you; stand still."

Carolle gazed into the mirror at her slender figure draped in the old material; her bare shoulders drooped a little, her white neck gleamed softly and her eyelashes edged her pale lids so thickly and aggressively that when her eyes were closed her still features retained an extraordinary vividness. Her mouth was lovely but perhaps a little too curved—Spanish—and her nostrils were as sensitive as new grass in the wind. Catherine's hair was almost orange in the firelight as she knelt at work, and her elbows opened and closed like short wings.

"Will the dance be fun?" Carolle shrugged her shoulders. "Don't move or the hem will be spoiled. Put your arm down—the other one too—wait." Catherine looked like a female Buddha kneeling there with one pin in the corner of her mouth, inspecting the hem. "Turn a little—stop; wait, there's something wrong here. . . ." She put the last pin in the hem and tightened the basting thread.

"Catherine, don't work so hard." For a few seconds, Carolle forgot the dress and the crooked hem that was going to produce a very odd-looking skirt. She took the head of orange-coloured hair in both hands and held it tight against her thigh: "Oh, Catherine," there was a note of anxiety in her voice, "tell me that we're always going to be friends. Say it, won't you?"

"It'll be your fault if this dress is ruined; you're wriggling like a snake." Carolle leaned over and kissed the orange hair. She looked at herself again in the mirror: ravishing—oh, yes; there were times when it was marvellous to have a body. She slid her hands over her hips.

Catherine was sitting now with her head against the chimney-breast and the dress lay on her knees like a huge poppy. Carolle had stepped out of the firelight, but one could see her putting on her skirt and pullover and fastening her leather belt. Then she came and sat on the floor with Catherine and began to sew. One was holding the hem, the other the yoke, so that there was a gently curving bridge of silk between them, a yellow hammock filled with big pink and mauve flowers. The mellow, faded colours, fatigued into iridescence by many suns and long months of snow, made one think of flowers in a greenhouse just before sunset.

"Kati?" Carolle spoke quietly, without raising her eyes. "Do you mind very much not going with me tomorrow night?"

"Of course not! What an idea!"

"I'm rather bored at the prospect."

"Why?"

"Oh, I feel dreary—no gloves; and my shoes!" She made a wry face. "All the girls will be with 'papa,' 'mama' or 'my brother'; that upsets me and their new dresses and everything—oh, I don't know—they're all so well-bred."

"Are you out of your mind?"

"No, really! I try not to mind, but they bore me so. I always feel like saying: 'Hurry up, say what you mean.' They're so soft, so insignificant. 'My darling,' says Mama. 'My treasure,' says Papa. 'Isn't she charming?' "

"But what about the dancing? Don't forget that."

"Oh, I like dancing well enough, but . . ." Carolle hesitated, then suddenly looked up from her work with a smile of frustrated arrogance.

"But what?" Catherine asked.

"If I dance three times with Sulivan," she spoke very quickly, "his mother will be furious (you've got no money, Carolle Alérac); four times and she will turn pale; five will give her a syncope; six, and she will leave for England."

"Oh, he's back, then?"

"Yes."

"Will he be there?"

"Yes, and I shall give him every dance."

"Why? Are you in love with him?"

"No, but I'd like to be the death of Madame Sulivan."

280

They both laughed, and while they were still laughing Catherine asked: "Do you know who else will be there?"

If Carolle had looked at Catherine then, she would have noticed a strange expression in her eyes: furtive, narrow—like a thin, green ribbon. But she was working on the yoke of the dress and could not look up; the stitching was so fine that she could scarcely speak, and the names fell one by one from her mouth like little weightless stones: "Morier, Inès, Clair, Perrier-Larive, the Champendals . . ."

"Davoine?"

"Davoine, Faure, Béguin."

The narrow green look seemed to follow each name as it fell.

"No one else?"

"No one, Catherine."

Then the narrow look widened, freed itself, and her body relaxed. She had listened tensely to each name—it would have been so natural to ask Balagny to the dance, for all the mothers were mad about him. But Carolle had said "no one else" and she felt like hugging her . . . however, she wanted to be absolutely certain and made one last casual comment:

"So it's for people under thirty, is it?"

"That's it, Kati"—Carolle was smiling at her—"a cradle dance with nothing but bottles and diapers."

"Well, you must look nice for Madame Sulivan." As she spoke, Catherine's beauty was enhanced for a moment by a look of insolence and fatalism. "I'll come and help you dress tomorrow."

"You'll do nothing of the sort." She spoke almost angrily, for the thought of Catherine not being invited troubled her deeply. Why had they left her out? Why? . . . Of course she knew why it was: the wheels of village society turned in such a tiny space—no bigger than a cotton-spool. She thought of the balance wheels of a watch—the slightest interference and all was thrown into confusion. Everyone knew Catherine; the young men often saw her walking gravely through the streets with her embroidery roll under her arm. Perhaps those prudent mothers thought their young men looked at her too hard: "The poor thing is in an impossible position, simply impossible." Carolle could hear them: "Of course she knew our girls in school; they've often played together." "Well, that's no reason for asking her." "After all, would you let your son marry her?" But that last question would have given the mothers heart failure, so it was never put into words.

Carolle had meant to tell Catherine at once how it

distressed her to go alone, but she was trying to re-arrange one of the pleats and her absorption with that difficulty seemed to prevent her replying till now:

"But, darling, you're not my maid! If I do go," this time she looked straight at Catherine, "if I do go, it will be on Grandfather's account." Then in a lower voice: "He's so anxious for me not to suffer because— oh, you understand." They never spoke of those private difficulties. "You and I," she gazed into the shadows, "we've no place in that world."

"Let me come and help you dress?" Catherine's voice seemed to come from a distance.

"Would you like me to marry Sulivan?"

"Why not?"

"You're wonderful, Kati; is it your own engagement, just twenty-four hours old, that makes you want every-one else to marry? Tell me, do you love your Jonathan? How about it, Queen of the Vale?"

"Wildly," replied Catherine, puffing out her cheeks like a cupid on a fountain. Her gaiety had returned and her needle flew among the big flowers.

A lamp with a green shade was now placed upon one of the chairs, completely changing the aspect of the room; the windows looked like six pieces of the night, cut out and hung around the walls. Here and there an occasional object gleamed outside the enchanted circle formed around the two girls by the lamplight: the little gilt lettering to the left of the mirror read "Bourbon —Island of Delight," but the print itself was shrouded in darkness. The long soft pleated dress grew gradually under their hands.

To Guillaume Alérac, as he entered the room, they seemed like two bouquets of lilies of the valley.

"Well, Catherine, what about the engagement? Are you happy?" The first bouquet inclined its young head.

"And you, my dear?" He looked down at Carolle. "Nothing to tell me?" The second bouquet got up and curtsied:

"Indeed I have, Grandfather! I am promised to Prince Marcassin, who plays the German flute to perfection and hunts with unbelievable daring."

Gottlieb's falsetto was heard in the hall below, reminding them that there was chocolate *soufflé* for dinner, and they vanished down the staircase with the speed of wings.

The abandoned dress lay open at the neck; two armholes gaped and in the glow from the embers Guillaume Alérac thought he saw two hands. He stood for a moment with the idea of some grim tragedy in his mind: "death of a young girl. . . ." Then taking up the lamp he quickly left the room. On the stairs he thought of his wife, Ishbell Alérac, who had brought him no happiness.

CHAPTER THREE

ÉCILE DE LA TOUR was waiting for her
brother: the strangest man—a real saint,
but with certain faults, thank Heaven. For instance
he couldn't endure things with cheese in them. Such a
clean, nourishing food. She had often told him so:
"After all, it's only milk and you like milk; you drink it
every day. If you'd just remember that, you wouldn't
mind a little cheese in the soup?" She looked round the
room with obvious satisfaction—oh, yes, her brother was
an exquisite person.

The black-gowned ancestress in the oval frame seemed
to raise her eyes: "How could anyone descended from
us help being exquisite?"

Mlle de la Tour smiled knowingly: "Of course! . . .
and what power he had over human souls! He spoke so
wonderfully; at first one found his voice monotonous,
but suddenly it would flare up, vibrate with passion. She
remembered one of his Easter sermons on the text:
"Thou art the Christ, the Son of the living God." The
words had gone through the church like a knife cutting
some large soft piece of fruit: "Thou art the Christ,

the Son of the living God," and they had all sat with mouths open and their spines tingling with emotion. The voice rose and fell, hovered above them, touching them with the quickness and lightness of a weasel's foot, then rang out triumphantly: "The Son of the living God!" Yes, it had been wonderful—so moving that she had forgotten all about the harmonium and the postman had had to lead the hymn without it.

She looked through the window at the pale sky. . . . Why, with gifts like that, did her brother insist on staying here in this little country parish? Why would he never let her change a single piece of the furniture in what they called his "reception room"? Was this an inherited trait or just an oddity of his own? Probably inherited, but from whom? The de la Tours or the Lavergnes? She consulted the oval frame. It was hard to decide; still—that stubborn forehead. Yes, the Lavergnes were to blame.

"Don't you agree, Dolly?" The "Girl with the Muff" opposite the mirror seemed to shrug her shoulders. Absurd to think that a Pastor, Mlle de la Tour and the Aléracs (all were related through her) could have sprung from that slender girl in crimson velvet with brown curls about her neck, one slim hand hidden in her muff and the other holding a shepherd's crook with a blue ribbon on it! Her way of holding her muff and her crook and her sidelong indolent glance at one gave her a delightful appearance of frivolity. "Wheedler," said Mlle de la Tour softly as she walked over to take a closer look at her great-grandmother: "Alas, I've got nothing of you in me. What could one have of you in these days? Your muff? Hardly. Your crook? No, darling; we live in the mountains among the rocks; and who would buy us chinchilla muffs?" She turned away from the portrait, her eyebrows arching sadly. "With what money?" The spotted gilt of the furniture, the chipped panelling and a threadbare pheasant on a chairback answered her.

What a world she lived in! More caustic lips would have said, "What a cemetery!" The dead were gathered there in various guises: Aunt Constance appeared as a Louis XV armchair—an excellent survival; Uncle Agénor, as a pair of tongs exactly like him; that spindly chair represented an Alérac lost at sea, poor fellow! Cousin Lois had left a pair of earrings and two "poufs"; and that group—she was looking at an arrangement of four chairs and a sofa—that group came from the brother —the grandfather. . . . "No, I'm all wrong," she said aloud. But it was really quite simple to keep straight; her mother had always said: "Frills, ribbons and little cushioned chairs from my side; the heavy pieces from your father's." So the figures in those needlework seats and backs were Lavergnes. . . . At that moment the cousin who lived in the clock struck three: "Three o'clock and Bertrand not home yet!" Mlle de la Tour laid her hand upon the curving arm of the Louis XV chair: "Dear Aunt Constance . . ." and for a moment that lady in her stiff silk dress walked into living memory.

Cécile de la Tour continued her discreet resurrection of the dead. Cousin Lucien looked up at her from the second page of a green album. How slowly the afternoon was going! The minutes seemed to stick as though one had put bird lime on their feet — heavens, why bother to catch birds of that kind?

She closed the album, straightened a bunch of flowers —a charming figure in that quiet room: drooping eyelids hovering over eyes that did not seem to belong to her at all. To look into them was like opening a box of new pastels and glancing along the row from yellow to blue, past pinks so faint that they seemed to have no colour, but of course they had. Cécile de la Tour's eyes were like that—*she* would tell you they were Catholic eyes in a Protestant face.

With her foot she pushed one of Cousin Lois's poufs gently towards the window and, bringing over a gilt chair that had come from a relative with bad taste, she busied herself with her white wool again. What dreadful weather! The snow was coming down so hard that it somehow lost its whiteness—black snow, but who would believe it? "If I told Bertrand the snow was black, he . . ." She smiled indulgently at his probable incredulity; how blind some men were, poor dears!

She realized that the "Girl with the Muff" was looking at her again; that cunning sidelong glance of hers was very persistent. Strange how uneasy and harassed the life of a portrait could be—just like one's own. Raising her eyes and pressing her cheek lightly against the silk cushion of the chair, she gazed back thoughtfully: "Certainly the one more like Dolly than any of us was Alexandrine Alérac. What an adorable creature!"

She counted her stitches: 13 . . . 18 . . . 24; decrease at 24. Her gaze drifted to Aunt Constance's armchair; then to a goblet full of meadow-saffron. "I wonder—I wonder . . ." but she did not complete her thought. What she meant was: "I wonder if Bertrand still thinks about Alexandrine Alérac?" The movement of her slippered foot answered "Yes," for the satin toe tapped the air in an affirmative rhythm: "Yes, he still loves her; his never mentioning her name proves it." For her brother's sake she tried to banish the ghost of Alexandrine Alérac, but what could one do about ghosts? One never discovered why they appeared or what would drive them away. She moved a graceful hand impatiently. "It's amazing," she said aloud, "that one cannot bear her any ill-will; amazing too, that one should always think of her as a girl and never as one who loved and bore a child."

A fixed expression seemed for a moment to alienate Mlle de la Tour's features from her body; then her delicately curved lips parted: "What a tragedy!" A sigh was heard by the sofas and the fire-tongs that no person would ever hear: "I can't deny it, he was—yes, he was really irresistible." She slid her emerald out to the tip of her finger (Aunt Olympe's emerald); her feelings were so confused that she could only sigh again: "Poor Bertrand!"

A luxurious melancholy hovered about her mouth and her passionate contemplation of her ghosts became a little more remote. At half-past four she jumped up, furious with herself for having spent the whole afternoon with Alexandrine Alérac. What disloyalty to her brother! She bit her lip. She must always stand by Bertrand; there was no question about that. Naturally she would stand by Bertrand, but where on earth was he? Why did he leave her alone for a whole afternoon in a ghost-ridden house that creaked like an old ship? And the snow was so depressing too!

She began to feel peevish: "Very well, my dear, your punishment for neglecting me will be braised veal and macaroni with cheese for dinner." Then she looked boldly into the oval frame.

The thought of her brother hesitating in front of the umbrella-stand that morning softened her revengeful feelings. Poor silly man! She had had to get out his umbrella for him. Plans for a coffee soufflé soon took her attention; it was his favourite dessert and he would need coddling after his struggle with the snow and wind. Small pleasures were not to be scorned even if one *were* privileged to enjoy the larger blessings of life, or so it seemed to her. "In this vale of tears," as Mme Vauthier would say . . . the thought of Mme Vauthier made her smile. She was fond of her brother's parishioners, well—pretty fond of them; not so devoted as he was. She had no vocation for it, though she felt it required a certain devotion to knit all day long for the poor and to have to use that dreadful charity wool. All she could do was to get the softest there was, and white—for the girl-mothers.

She was greatly beloved by the parishioners, who thought it was wonderful the way she overlooked the things that drove her brother crazy. She would carry a ribboned stick and wear her jade necklace when visiting the farmers (one should always show one's love for beautiful things), and of all her brother's teachings, she seemed to remember only: "Consider the lilies of the field . . ." Her pleasure in everything was marvellous and she was so gentle when she held a sick person's hand and said with a smile: "God doesn't want you to suffer," and then that note of confidence: "You'll be better soon," as though she had added: "now that I've come to help you." Her brother and his Bible had a difficult task compared with hers.

CHAPTER FOUR

THE PASTOR had flung himself out into the snowstorm. As he hurried along over the cottony surface of the road, looking straight ahead of him, dwarf-like figures, which turned into men as they came up to him, raised their hats, and he raised his in reply. Fortunately, he was able to smile at them. What more could he do? Nothing—absolutely nothing! He felt empty and desolate—a branch slapped across his face—no, he could not speak to anyone now, he hadn't the courage to stop, even for a minute, to ask how they were. What a mercy that Jonathan Graew seemed just as preoccupied as he was himself! Something was wrong with that man, and he ought—yes, he ought indeed to have spoken to him . . . She had said something about a hen. What could a hen have to do with it? What had she meant? Poor little thing! At that moment he passed Mlle Huguenin's house. "A pastor has no life of his own at all," she thought. "Look at him now, tearing along the road, racing with death."

. . . She had come to ask him something, but what? He racked his brains, but could not think what it was.

. . . "Yes, Samuel? Oh, certainly; come to the Parsonage tomorrow." . . . She had asked for something— what had he given her? . . . He thought of the early part of the morning: it was like searching through memories of a remote past. Could that peace and order in his life ever be established again? How calm those morning hours in his study had been! He had just written down the word "Bèze" when she had opened the door. "Until then everything was in order." He spoke aloud, but it didn't matter because he had come to the Alérac wall and there was no one to hear him. He saw the long box hedge reaching to the carriage entrance, through which carriages no longer passed, and imagined the big quiet house among its snow-covered trees.

. . . Until then everything was in order . . . there was snow on her fur jacket—naturally, since it was snowing; but it had surprised him nevertheless and he had held his hand over his eyes for a moment. On taking it away he had noticed Carolle's white face—then she had begun to weep. He had gone to her, then to the window; he could still feel the pressure of the window frame on his forehead, could still see the snowflakes whirling down upon the garden. Then Théodore de Bèze had looked up at him from the desk, a cold piercing look. "It cuts like a knife," he had said to himself, even after he had started to talk to Carolle. Perhaps

Théodore de Bèze was to blame for what he had done. A piercing look like that could discover things inside one that had long been hidden.

He leaned against a tree by the roadside and watched the snow falling. Everything was supernaturally calm, white and still. The trees behind him all looked the same; not really like trees at all. The earth seemed deprived of life; there was not even the soft beating of a strayed bird's wings.

He had walked on again without realizing it and was soon obliged to speak to Mlle Grandjean and the two Bellards. After a word to each of them, he began to wonder what had made him take the road into the town . . . more people passed him now; it was noon and men were coming out of the factories and workshops, and he continued his self-examination among raised caps and smiles that had to be acknowledged, or interrupted it completely when he saw a tired, worried face . . . he would have given all he possessed to get into a train, sink down on a seat and be carried off, no matter where.

He went into a men's clothing shop to buy a black tie, but the saleswoman kept telling him he would have a larger choice among the fancy ones, that black was not being much worn that year, and she insisted upon dragging out flimsy, bright-coloured things that looked like dolls in silk dresses (suddenly he thought of one of the boys in the parish who had died because of an unhappy love affair. What comfort had he been able to give him?), and while the saleswoman wrapped neckties round her wrist for him to see, all the shallow, mechanical things he had done in his rôle of pastor, all the meaningless words he had spoken, all the empty handclasps, all the artificiality passed before him like a procession of grey phantoms. "What right had he to call himself a saver of souls?"

It seemed to him that instead of warm capable hands he had been offering damp sponges to those who came to him for help; he saw now that he had journeyed through life over a rubber road, momentarily taking the impress of his feet, but retaining no mark of his passage. Had he ever done anyone a real or lasting service? . . . He pointed to a dark grosgrain necktie. "That's what I want, Mademoiselle; something dark, no pattern at all." He was speaking abstractedly, and at that moment peace entered his soul as simply and naturally as a drop of water might fall upon a leaf. It happened so suddenly that he felt almost dizzy; he wanted to ask the silly girl for a chair and sit for a while in that odd world of braces and socks which had so inexplicably restored his tranquillity. He was a pastor no longer; he didn't love Carolle Alérac—that was all over. He was merely a man, who had bought a black silk necktie, waiting for his change.

But when he was outside again in the snow, walking in the now empty street, his peace of mind vanished crumb by crumb, like Tom Thumb's piece of bread. In Sagne and Viot's window, forty clocks and two hundred watches showed what time it was. The apothecary waved at him from behind his glass door: the parish apothecary was rich. "Generous? Not very—he never pays his tithe." In the seedsman's window across the street, bundles of raffia were hanging like yellow horses' tails. Over another door he read a doctor's sign: "Diagnostician and Pulmonary Specialist," and there was a bell too, as if one could ring it and be cured. But he did not ring.

He crossed the empty market square, and as he stood under the Carderas's yellow boot, looking at rubber heels and metal supports for tender feet, the fear that Carolle would never come to the Parsonage again swept over him and the memory of his old love clutched at his heart. He stared blindly at the silk slippers in the window and read for the tenth time: "Repairs done promptly and carefully." A poster in the next window shouted: "Drink Byrrh!" . . . Then his whole body

what was going to happen—she didn't think he knew himself what was going to happen; he said he was going to be married in the spring, and if she was set on living in the Alérac house—of course The Vale wasn't good enough for her—well, there wasn't any use in giving money to the doctor to cure her knee because she would rather be in her grave than live to see Catherine Graew move into that house—that would be her name, wouldn't it? Catherine Graew . . . she repeated it several times.

The gas was lit now in the bookstore, and the thin golden ladder glowed faintly. . . . Catherine Graew! . . . Mme Vauthier's hands closed angrily on the handle of the umbrella which formed a dark canopy over her head. Despite her solidly planted feet, the firm grasp of her hands, and the unconquerable expression upon her face, one could tell from the slight trembling of her lips that there was despair in her heart. . . . "Some men have no more sense than bottle-fed calves—oh, Pastor, if you were only ten years younger (yes, I know what I'm saying) Carolle Alérac could marry one of her own kith and kin and you'd have a real wife and not a flighty good-for-nothing you could never depend on. . . ."

Her words made him feel twenty years older instead of ten years younger; he saw himself a dried-up old man, perhaps as well preserved as Guillaume Alérac, and he knew that he needed Carolle for those few years of grace as urgently and as desperately as a person bitten by a mad dog needs vaccine.

2

He went back by way of the gas works, through a part of the town where he knew he would find evidences of poverty, suffering and death; he felt the necessity to renew his acquaintance with it all, and in that dreary quarter he found what he was seeking. Even the names of the streets suggested destitution, and when he came to the dreariest of all, which lost itself in a horror of dilapidation, its name was the rue des Fleurs—where were the flowers?—and he stood looking at a half-burnt house: windowless holes in a blackened wall and a red eider-down quilt scattering its grey feathers on the white snow. A chimney rose bleakly over the ruins and a row of large casks against a wall exhaled a sour smell of fermentation. Farther on, over the low door of a hideous brown house, he read in gothic letters: "Germino Baths." Who could wash in that place? He could imagine the tubs, towels and sponges, but he did not have to imagine the steam, for it poured from ventholes into the street, filling it with the smell of soap and beer.

The snow-gloved leaves on a frost-bitten sunflower in a deserted garden hung down like the limp hands of a degenerate. The yellow stalk looked as though it had experienced everything and knew the world to be nothing but a chaos of bottles, stones and broken china. "The poor ye have with you always. . . ." He had forgotten Alexandrine Alérac; he was no longer in anguish; that anyone could be playing Couperin's *Bavolets Flottants* seemed to him comic—almost tragic, but he looked at his watch and knew that his sister was sitting at her piano at that moment. Suddenly and quite inexplicably he thought of Aunt Constance's armchair; why did this bring tears to his eyes?

At the end of the street he saw the bulging gas tanks and as he looked at them he quailed again at the thought of that morning's happenings. Perhaps they had meant very little; perhaps something terrific. He no longer seemed able to judge. What right had he to lead others when he was so uncertain of his own path? . . . He was conscious of the soft radiance of the "yellow dress" on his left, but Carolle Alérac's gravely smiling face on his right seemed to be a part of some remotely obscure destiny. . . . At the next corner he heard circus music and looking up the street he saw the wagons being emptied. The horses were unharnessed and tied to hitching posts; they gazed fixedly at the snow with weary indifference to their surroundings. The flag lay upon a pile of tarpaulins. Tomorrow it would flutter proudly from the top of its pole, but now it was only a dirty red rag.

He had found the people he had been seeking, but could not understand where their courage came from. Slowly the circus took shape; a group of little boys watched the snake-woman wandering about in green tights among the piles of rope and canvas. . . . Where did their courage come from?

Every hammer stroke, every rope that was tightened seemed to cry out—even the woman in a black spangled bodice sitting at the ticket window seemed horribly pathetic to him: sterile old age, through with love, and probably, beneath that crafty smile, as stupid as a talking doll. "The poor ye have with you always." What were they waiting for? What?

From town to town they went, setting up the circus, jumping through hoops, putting on tights, beating a march on the big drum, counting the money, showing the bear or the seal with its balloon; then everything down, horses hitched to the wagons—begin all over again in the next town. . . . What did they expect? What had they the right to expect?

"This drop of blood have I shed for thee. . . ." He

tried to imagine Pascal there in that place of blaring trumpets, tarpaulins and sweat. What would the snake-woman say? How could one talk to them? How understand them? Dead mouths of men who had been corpses too long. . . . He would have liked to take everything—the tinsel trappings, the people, the whole earth—under his wing as a hen takes her chickens, but he remembered the reason: "You never wanted to." And he wondered whether they would want him to.

He walked behind the gas works towards the cemetery. What a sinister sight, that long building sprawling under the grey sky! The smell of corpses seemed to follow him persistently. At last he came to the open country; on his left, thorny underbrush and bare twigs, then fields—relentless desolation. This time he was sure he would meet no one. He didn't feel like going home yet, didn't want to hear Couperin or see his sister. And he certainly could not endure that piercing look of Théodore de Bèze! . . . His soaking shoes went cl . . . cl . . . cl . . . as he made his way, a solitary black figure under the low-hanging sky. When he came to Mlle Huguenin's door he realized that what he did want was to go in somewhere and sit for a while, turning things over in his mind. So he lifted the knocker, let it fall, and was soon standing in the hallway.

3

She thought it perfectly natural that the Pastor should pay her a visit, though he was soaking wet and covered with snow and looked more like a wood-cutter than a pastor. He took a chair near the fire, and before he had noticed the pools of water forming round his feet she left him, saying she would get tea. In the hall she found what she wanted. After all she knew what to do about men's clothes; she spent her life cutting out and sewing them. The Pastor's overcoat was heavy. "It's wet —right through to the lining, and his umbrella looks like a walking-stick coated with sugar." Why on earth hadn't he opened it? Why carry a closed umbrella on a day like this? (She was the second woman to ask that question.) In order to get rid of the snow on the umbrella she opened the window so abruptly that the birds took flight from the maple tree and a gust of cold air blew into the kitchen. Then she put on the water to boil and got out her yellow cups. For the hundredth time she decided they were pretty ones—and they were. She took elaborate pains to keep the Pastor's hat from losing its shape, and while her iron was heating and her hands smoothing out the brim under some sheets of tissue paper she wondered how she should go about cleaning his shoes. He could not possibly go home like that—and of course she also wondered what he could have been doing. . . . Her curiosity was so intense that the iron trembled in her hand as she held it poised above the hat. She imagined every possible explanation and then, conscious of her absurdity, began all over again. What a blessing it was that her theories exploded quietly! Otherwise the noise would have betrayed her. She finally reached the conclusion that it was useless to guess. . . . The coat hung over a drying-rack, the open umbrella was like a huge black mushroom darkening a corner of the kitchen, and the hat was perched like a crow on an earthenware jug, slowly coming out of its limp torpor. . . . Strange, but there was something comic in people's most romantic afflictions—she looked from the mushroom to the crow—clearly the Pastor's afflictions were romantic; she had noticed that immediately. He had been through something, and oh, she wanted so badly to know what it was!

The cat sniffed the hat, the umbrella, and the coat, reprovingly. "I suppose you know all, where I know nothing," she said, leaning over to give it a little slice of cake.

4

When she had gone to the kitchen, he straightened his necktie. His hair was wet and when he looked at his shoes he realized that it was a dreadful thing to be in love at fifty. He wiped his face with his handkerchief.

How peaceful it was in that room! He felt as Jonathan Graew had felt the day before: as though someone had wrapped him in a warm sheet; and he needed this kind of care. "I think I'm going to be ill, but I can't be till after Christmas; there's too much work to be done." He tried to smooth out the creases in his coat, stretched the lapels, and then looked at his shoes. What a state they were in! He glanced over his shoulder and saw the tracks he had made across the room . . . mad, all of them, with their passion for shiny floors; his sister too. Clean up the mess he had made? What was there to do it with? . . . He appreciated the tactfulness of that faint rattle of spoons and cups coming from the kitchen which seemed to say: "You have time to relax a little; we won't come bursting in upon you; tea can't be made quickly."

He took a stick of wood from the basket and set himself to picking the caked snow and leaves out of his heels. "Dirty white—just like me," he thought. He raised his head and, seeing himself in the mirror, realized that something had changed within him. Almost without his knowing it, the final decision had been made: when he left Mlle Huguenin he would go to Guillaume Alérac and ask him for Carolle. He would be refused and that would be extremely difficult for everybody, but he would ask just the same. . . . What an appalling thing his conscience was! . . . That girl must not be allowed to think for an instant that he had taken advantage of her loneliness; it would be better if she were to smile at his ridiculous request, though that would wound him deeply. However, it would be very unlike her to treat him in such a way; she had proved herself incapable of that. What he wanted her to say was: "He's asking me to marry him because he loves me," and not: "Men never come near me, not even the Pastor, without trying to kiss me." No, never that! The only thing he desired now was that she should think of him without disgust. . . . Yes, he would go.

He pushed the last scrap of mud into the embers with his foot, put the stick back in the basket and wiped his fingers with his handkerchief. It was surprising how well he had been able to clean his shoes with a piece of wood. . . . He looked into the mirror again, examining himself with a certain hostility.

Mlle Huguenin found him sitting with a book in his lap.

"Ah, you're fond of that one too?" She was smiling like a little girl. "It's true—one never forgets them."

"Yes, I always come back to it." He seemed slightly embarrassed as he replaced the volume on the children's shelf.

When she set down the tea-tray she noticed that the problem of his dirty shoes had been solved. Wondering if he had used the poker, she glanced at the fireplace and then realized that the faint bitter smell in the room came from his having blown up the fire so that the muddy leaves would burn. She lit the lamp and the jar of raspberry jelly glowed among the heavy silver spoons and the yellow cups like a big crimson eye.

They drew close to the table and their hands touched now and then as they helped themselves to sugar, lemon or a buttered roll. They talked of parish affairs, the poor, and Alice Nicolet's dropsy.

"She was so pretty. I hope they haven't left a mirror in her room. Someone should tell the attendant—she's so changed now."

"Nothing can be done for her. That particular kind of despair is very difficult to deal with." He sighed. "A doctor ought to be able to do something: injections, morphine, I don't know. What could I do about that part of it? And her soul? What peace can I bring her? You know she was under my instruction before her baptism, and now I feel utterly useless." He lifted a hand and let it fall hopelessly.

Mlle Huguenin knew that he was wrong. He had brought peace to every one of the poor souls who had died in his arms. He had taken their burdens on his shoulders, always sacrificing his own peace of mind for theirs. But no, he assured her that he had much to learn about human suffering. No doubt a pastor should not feel that way; it was perhaps illogical, but it was true. The parish was a heavy responsibility—all those houses on his shoulders. What a weight of tiles and bricks! The Vuillemins were in a bad way; Mlle Huguenin must speak to the wife and he would have a talk with the husband—perhaps it could be patched up somehow. Her reluctance annoyed him a little: did he think it would be worth the trouble, since they didn't really want to live together any longer? But he reminded her that there were the children to be considered, and he spoke with all his old conviction.

Did she think funds could be raised for a Christmas Fair? Difficult, with so much unemployment. He had seen the Perrochets and could get nothing more from them. No. Something different would be better, something that would interest the whole parish. Perhaps they could put on a mystery play and take it from village to village—that might be just the thing. It could be given on Sunday afternoons. She would have to undertake the costumes, with his sister's help, and of course she would play one of the parts herself.

"Don't be absurd!" she exclaimed. "I'm speechless even in front of ten people."

"I won't hear of your not being in it."

"Carolle Alérac too?"

"Of course." His tone changed slightly. "By the way, I met Mme Vauthier this afternoon." Then he told her of Jonathan Graew's engagement.

She lifted her eyes, put down her cup and wondered if his paleness meant that he had wanted Catherine himself. But no, that was impossible; he could never care for a girl like that.

So completely can people conceal their private concerns that she never for an instant suspected his love for Carolle Alérac, nor did he, sitting there at her tea-table, have the slightest idea how terrible for her was the news he had just imparted . . . the objects in the room gave one the impression that they knew everything and would preserve a discreet silence.

When they stood together on the doorstep, Mlle Huguenin had an uncomfortable feeling that she had failed in some way; there was something she had not given him, something essential—but what? . . . And she seemed older to him; he noticed a drawn look on her face. He too felt there was something he would have liked to do for her, but what was it? They had lost their keys to each other, and they parted with silent, searching looks. Their friendship meant a great deal to him—in some ways there was no one to whom he was more devoted . . . his hat again resembled a pastor's hat and his coat looked as it should have looked: dark and heavy. Yes, she had sent him off properly.

5

His black figure moved past her windows and she heard his footsteps for a while in the darkness; then all was still. Turning the key in the cupboard door, she opened it and a sharp odour rushed out at her. She closed her eyes and coughed—she knew she used too much camphor; people were right to tease her for it, but in these old houses, the moths . . . Her mind was in confusion and she stood there with trembling legs while the Pastor's words cut their way into her brain. Finally the words formed a sentence and she could read, as though in a telegram she had just opened, the announcement of Jonathan Graew's engagement. She remembered how it was now: she had put down her cup and eaten a piece of bread and jelly, and between that mouthful and putting down her cup she had heard it. Now she was in the nethermost hell. Oh, the hours she had spent wondering what the dreaded moment would be like! She had imagined everything: how it would affect her and what she would say. She had thought herself ready, and now—she shrugged her shoulders—it had come, and it had been so different. Worse than she had anticipated, except that she had sat still and (how did they put it?) "borne the blow" in silence. Something was tearing at her heart, torturing her, and she did not realize what it was, for she knew nothing of hatred; even the word meant little to her.

Her hands reached into the cupboard—how had they got the strength to do it?—lifted up the tweeds, pushed aside the cheviots. The lamp-light glowed faintly upon a wisp of hair escaped from the bottom of her chignon, and her breathing could be heard in the quiet room. She turned away from the cupboard holding a thin parcel clasped to her breast; her eyes were lowered and her face was devoid of expression. Putting the parcel down on the table under the lamp, she took out two pins; the parcel had been wrapped and unwrapped so often that the paper, always creased in the same place, fell open like a piece of cloth. Along one edge, "Model for hunting waistcoat" had been written hastily.

She flattened out the paper and for a moment the

waistcoat looked as though it had been cut from a thin slab of damp earth; the pockets were edged with leather and the buttons shaped like mushrooms. Her customer had desired it that way, and she had often imagined herself bending over some wet path in the woods with tape and scissors, cutting from the earth a waistcoat that would smell of mushrooms and hares.

She took the waistcoat, held it at arm's length and a strange light came into her eyes, changing her expression completely. An unaccountable exhilaration took possession of her; she who had always been by nature on the side of the hunted appeared now, inexplicably, to have joined in the chase. She was torn between the joy of pursuit and the horror of the kill. Now there was a gun in her hands with shot and powder in it; then she saw herself, a little pulsating thing lying among the leaves. Her nostrils trembled; an almost suffocating joy possessed her, and then it was over—someone seemed to be holding her: a rustle of leaves, a shot, the smell of gunpowder. . . . After long minutes she was back in the peaceful room, standing at her table in the lamp-light, her hands trembling.

There was no arm to support her and she was so tired now; all her joints ached. For the hundredth time she thought of what the Bible said about adultery: "Ye have heard that it was said by them of old time . . .

But I say unto you . . ." She knew perfectly well that she had not heeded the warning; she did not need to recall the text for that. To no human being could she ever confide what it was she experienced when she held that waistcoat in her hands; and one thing was certain: she would never denounce any woman again.

Her thoughts returned to the uncompromising words of the text: ". . . hath committed . . ." and there was a hopeless look in her eyes: "What else can one do, if one is in love?" These words which, to her sense, condemned her, also showed what a tiny share she had had of this world's happiness. Never anything else, never! But this, yes: adultery with him in her heart.

She laid the waistcoat back in its wrapping; then she folded the paper and pinned the ends: "Model for hunting waistcoat." After the word "waistcoat" came a dot which had made a hole. Her pen had trembled there so long that it had gone right through the paper. Had she the right to mark the parcel simply: "Model for hunting waistcoat," or should she have been absolutely honest with herself and written: "Model for hunting waistcoat for Jonathan Graew"? The hole in the paper represented her debate.

She slipped the parcel back among the dark-coloured tweeds and cheviots, and in obedience to her passion for neatness which controlled her even during the most difficult moments she straightened the piles and smoothed out wrinkled surfaces with the palm of her hand. Then she closed the cupboard and, since the odour of camphor and naphthaline was still hanging in the room, she opened the window and let in the cold night air.

CHAPTER FIVE

$\mathcal{G}$UILLAUME ALÉRAC got up suddenly, went over to his desk and began to push some papers about with his ivory paper-knife. What a day it had been—people were really fantastic! Graew this morning; Balagny at three o'clock; and now . . . he glanced keenly at the Pastor out of the corner of his eye and put the paper-knife down gently.

The two men looked at one another; Bertrand de la Tour crossed his legs and clasped his hands round his right knee. His words sounded like those of a sick man:

"It's a mad idea, isn't it?"

Guillaume Alérac gazed into the embers without replying, and they sat for a moment in the silence of the old house. It was an extraordinary atmosphere: one felt the presence of a host one could not see, but whose anxious, though rather abstracted breathing was perfectly audible.

A young woman in a yellow dress looked down at them from an old frame over the desk. There was a touch of scorn in her smile: "You see, I'm here." What thoughts lay behind those drooping eyelids? . . . Guillaume Alérac looked up as though he had heard her speak and Bertrand de la Tour's eyes followed his. The soft yellow radiance of her dress enveloped them both. Did the lovely shoulders go up just a little and then fall again?

The room was full of shadows now, but the lamp-light found its way to the white teeth in the portrait and made the crystal bird upon its invisible table glitter like spring-water. Bertrand de la Tour's weary voice was heard:

"There's nothing I've forgotten. Nothing. You must know that."

"Yes, I've lived long enough to understand." Guillaume Alérac picked up a tortoise-shell snuff box and put it down again; his firm chin moved nervously. "You don't have much luck with us, Bertrand de la Tour." He laid a hand upon the Pastor's shoulder. "No. Don't protest. We bring people bad luck; I know it only too well." He was standing in the shadow, but one could see that he was trying to control the restlessness of his hands. He went over to the portrait again. The girl in the yellow dress looked at him eagerly, expectantly.

"She suffered too," he said simply.

The pile of papers on the desk was grey and white in the lamp-light and the rest of the room was strangely unreal. It had the aspect of a little country station at night with several passengers waiting for a train that did not come.

They were silent now, but each knew that the other was thinking of that April morning (how easily the door opens upon tragic events) when she had entered the room with a bunch of jonquils in her hand, brilliant acid yellow—the first ones of the season. She had come towards them and, at a sign from Guillaume Alérac, Bertrand de la Tour had taken the bouquet and her hands in his own. It had all started that way—yellow and green—a sharp, stinging, intoxicating happiness. The house was in a turmoil because of the arrival of a visitor from the Antilles, a guest who had sent marvellous gifts ahead of him. Servants were hurrying everywhere, down to the cellar, up to the attic; curtains were shaken out, muslins were starched; spring perfumes came in at the windows and the odour of sizzling butter and brown pie-crust rose up from Masha's busy kitchen.

Guillaume Alérac spoke now as if he were sure they had both reached the same point in their painful memories:

"She was the most beautiful thing I possessed, and I gave her to you."

Bertrand de la Tour grasped his hand:

"And I still have reason to thank you, even now; and

to thank her," he added in a lower voice, "for I have never been alone even for a day. And I am not alone now." Then, as though he had discovered the real cause of his torment, "Perhaps it is because she looks so like her?"

"No," said Guillaume Alérac vigorously, "it is because you need to live, and I sympathize with you. . . . You know what my answer is," his smile supplied the gentleness that was lacking in his voice, "but I will speak to her—I will do that for you. Whatever happens, please remember, won't you, that I once gave you my dearest possession?" He went over to the lamp and turned up the slowly diminishing flame, "Don't hold this against me!" He stood by Bertrand de la Tour's chair again: "If you really love her, you must desire her happiness. Well . . ." he looked at him with the directness of a doctor stating an opinion, "at fifty one cannot make a young girl happy."

The lamp wick began to make a forlorn little hissing sound: "This lamp is empty; I must go and ring for more petroleum." But the Pastor preceded him into the hall and Guillaume Alérac laid a hand on his shoulder. The tenderness of the gesture convinced him that the older man had penetrated to the most secret recesses of his suffering, that upon the barren road he must now follow there would be another figure preceding him—someone who understood everything.

They descended the staircase, and Guillaume Alérac did not withdraw his hand from the Pastor's shoulder until they came to the front door. A flurry of snowflakes blew into the hall and he said: "Don't forget that I did choose you once." Then he lowered his voice, "Work is the best thing after all; the rest is far away from us." He closed the door and went slowly upstairs to the room where he was to find the two bouquets of lilies of the valley. . . . "I am promised to Prince Marcassin, who plays exquisitely on the German flute. . . ." Guillaume Alérac stifled a sigh and turned his attention to scratching a little spot on the lapel of his coat. . . . Well—it was an odd world.

2

When dinner was over, Guillaume Alérac pushed back his chair, put down his napkin and went up to his study. Carolle concealed her astonishment at what seemed to her very much like an escape and cracked the shell of the almond she had in her hand:

"Look! A philippina!" Catherine took one of the kernels.

"When is it to be?"

322

"After the sermon on Sunday."

"What forfeit?"

"Gloves," said Carolle, knowing she would lose.

Guillaume Alérac's slow, muffled footsteps in the room above them were so suggestive of anxious expectancy that they swallowed up all the other noises in the house. Catherine thought again of the shiny black carriage making thin lines in the new snow. The footsteps began to frighten her; they seemed to be connected in some way with the carriage, and she herself was involved in it all. She did not understand how, but she knew there was something brewing that was going to hurt her and she drew her shoulders together.

"Oh, please don't go yet," Carolle protested when she asked for her cloak.

"Yes, I must. Maman Rose and Abel will be expecting me—Jonathan Graew too. After all, when one is engaged . . ." She puffed out her cheeks again. "I'll come and help you dress for the dance."

"No—please."

"Yes, I will; that's settled."

Gottlieb appeared with the lantern and, led by Carolle, they crossed the hall like three phantoms. The ancestors looked down from the walls and the muffled footsteps above them sounded through the lonely house, now rapid, now hesitant, then stopping altogether

(Carolle knew he was standing at the window); then they were off again; then a longer look out of the window. She thought Catherine would never get her things on and stood waiting silently, her head humming with all that had been happening. Would that dialogue up there between the soles of his shoes and the threadbare carpet never finish? What answer could there be to that endless questioning? Then Catherine said she could only find one of her gloves, and Carolle knelt down to grope for it under the chairs, but she could feel nothing but the cold floor—no glove. She seemed to see the antiquary's face bending over her, with that little mirthless chuckle that left his lips caught above his teeth. "For very little—in the event of dispossession." Oh, those footsteps! She would cry out if they didn't stop, or else she would be sick there in the hall.

She too believed herself to be involved, caught in the rhythm of that angry treading. But how? Bertrand de la Tour? She had spoken to no one about it and she never would. No, it couldn't be that. The whole day passed in review before her. Now she was at the Morédans', and she heard herself talking of securities. . . . Why couldn't Gottlieb stop waving the lantern? No gloves could be found that way, and those huge leaping shadows made her feel dizzy. . . . And that expression on Constance Morédan's face when Carolle had taken her grandmother's emerald out of her hand-bag (Ishbell Alérac's engagement ring) and the way she had grasped it in her hand and agreed immediately to lend her the money! It was true, she supposed, that Constance Morédan had been madly in love with her grandfather; that she had copied all Mme Ishbell's dresses, even their materials and colours; that she had refused to marry anyone else and, when Mme Ishbell was dead, had bloomed like a bush of white roses in June. Was it all true? Then Noémi's question, asked with trembling lips and rapture in her eyes: "Do you think a yellow dress would suit me?" Did some women really go out of their minds if they remained old maids? . . . Her hand touched Catherine's under one of the chairs and in spite of the footsteps they both laughed. Gottlieb's lantern waved and waved; no one could stop him. A lace-frilled hand would leave its frame for a second, only to be quickly withdrawn; or a stag's antlers would make fantastic rushes at them through the shadows. Then Catherine said she had lost her beret. "It's on your head, silly." And it was. . . . Every time the footsteps came to a halt, the house seemed to be struggling to get its breath, like someone very ill lying under heavy bed-clothes.

"Don't bother to hunt any more; you can give it to me tomorrow."

"Here's the glove," said Gottlieb in a thin, rasping voice.

At last they opened the door and Catherine's slender figure went down the steps. Gottlieb followed and the snowflakes plunged at his lantern like flies crazed by the light.

Carolle closed the door and stood in the cold dark hall. How quiet everything was, suddenly. "The time has come," she thought, "but for what?" The whole house seemed to be whispering: "The time has come. Hurry. Go upstairs; you'll see."

The walls above her and the portraits on them exhaled a faint mouldy smell like dead leaves; not unpleasant. . . . Then her thoughts returned to the Morédans; she saw the heavy ring again and Constance Morédan's clutching fingers. That hand seemed to have been waiting all its life for that ring. The silence accompanying her gesture had been like the great whirling bowls of silence in Bach's music.

She stopped for a second on the stair-landing; the day had really exhausted her; she scarcely knew whether she had legs and feet or not, and she had only walked for an hour. She saw the squirrel again, the gentian's pointing finger, and the dainty little weasel tracks in the snow; but when she thought of Bertrand de la Tour the candle in her hands began to tremble and she sat down on the chest. It was all so confusing. There had been no beginning to that story and there would be no end to it. She had been flung into the midst of a terrible situation. . . . But what marvellous features he had! She would have liked to take his handsome head in her hands: "Don't look at me, don't look at me that way! I'm not equal to this love."

The thin flame of her candle cut through the enveloping shadows, and above the handrail she saw the ancestor whose sweet, cruel smile was so like Guillaume Alérac's. She held her candle out towards the portrait. Yes, he was very like her grandfather: the nostrils, the line of the left eyebrow and the shape of the mouth were identical. As she withdrew the candle the expression changed; the smile became oblique, furtive. She had an uncomfortable feeling that it was following her up the stairs and turned instinctively to look again, but she saw only her own hand on the rail and a yellow gleam on the bottom step.

3

Her grandfather did not look up when she pushed open the study door, and she was sure from the expression on his face that Bertrand de la Tour had been there. Now she would have to face what she dreaded more than anything in the world: his judgment and his condemnation.

His gaze pierced her as it had pierced the fustian musketeer that morning in the schoolhouse, and she found herself looking down at one of his narrow shiny pumps on the carpet.

"How long . . ." As he spoke, a cloud gathered before her eyes; she looked up at "The Man with the Falcon" and he seemed grey and lifeless under his wide-brimmed hat. "How long have you known Balagny?"

"Balagny?" Her voice sounded like Bertrand's, that morning on the staircase, when he had asked: "Did you say 'a white hen'?"

"Yes. Jérome Balagny. When a man asks for my consent to his marriage with my granddaughter, I conclude that he has met her once or twice. Where was it?"

He left his chair and paced up and down the room; he was not angry with Carolle, but with himself for not being able to deal impartially with the situation, and the more he blamed himself the more exasperated he became. He had worked himself into the kind of fury that, in the case of a woman, would terminate in hysterical weeping, and for most men in a storm of cursing. What had he to offer this child he loved so dearly? A man of forty-two who owned the factories that poisoned the town with smoke, and a pastor, a

REDWOOD LIBRARY
NEWPORT, R. I.

splendid upright man—the best in the world—but fifty
years old. Who was to blame for it? What was wrong?
. . . He stood for a second before the yellow portrait
and Carolle saw that his mouth was trembling; then
he came towards her.

"I've had an offer of marriage for you. Yes, this afternoon at three o'clock. The gentleman pretended to be
interested in my pictures, and then asked for you. That's
what happened, dear." His voice was gentle now. "What
answer do you want me to give this gentleman of forty-
two? . . . He seems to find you attractive." He turned
from her and spoke harshly again: "What if he does?
It means nothing. Find me someone in this world who
would not think you attractive!" He touched her cheek
with the back of his hand.

Then he told her, in much the same way, of the
Pastor's request: "To him I said 'No,' and I'm sorry I
had to say it." He picked up the poker, carefully arranged the glowing logs, and, in a voice she had never
heard him use before, added: "We've done him enough
harm already, quite enough." He raised his eyes to the
yellow portrait and the lines round his mouth deep-
ened.

"The Man with the Falcon" was smiling slyly; he
looked as though he had won an important game, re-
quiring great skill. A dark spot on the breast of the

crystal bird was like the hole made by a bullet from a noiseless gun. A deep silence pervaded the room. Carolle sat with her head bent over; she seemed to be stirring her offers of marriage round with the tip of one of her fingers.

"Forty-two years old," Guillaume Alérac continued; "hands all right, well-bred; but the eyes of a gambler." He opened his own very wide to emphasize the point, but Carolle did not look up. "And his motives are of the best." He walked to the window and pulled the curtain aside angrily. The idea that no man who was not completely disinterested would marry this child infuriated him. "His motives are absolutely unselfish," he said, coming back to Carolle's chair; and when she made no sign, he continued: "Absolutely unselfish, my dear, and you're not likely to find another of that sort." He spoke as calmly as he could; he was trying to be fair.

"And now you must tell me what answer to give this man of forty-two." He emphasized the "forty-two" as though disclosing the fact that her suitor was a leper or even worse.

"You can tell him that I am too young to decide now, that I must have time to think it over." Her voice trailed off into a whisper.

"You'd send him packing if you didn't have your old grandfather to consider? Isn't that it? And all these pictures." He flung an arm out towards the shadowy walls. " 'No man putteth new wine into old bottles,' dear; or 'a piece of new cloth unto an old garment.' And those are not my words; I'm not the one who brought light into the world. . . . Run along now and think it over." But he stopped her at the door and said with a pathetic smile: "If I were young and had my life to live over again, and if I were able to find you, your name would be Madame Guillaume Alérac." Then with a gay twinkle in his eye he added gallantly: "And I wouldn't let them ship me off to England; I'd refuse to go."

She knew what he was alluding to and the colour mounted slowly into her cheeks. Her shy, embarrassed smile was irresistible.

"Flirt with Sulivan all you like, my dear," he was the indulgent grandfather now, "it's the privilege of youth. But I can't help wondering what you see in that vapid young man."

The mere thought of Carolle calling Esther Sulivan "mother" enraged him. Esther Sulivan's husband had a personality like a cake of soap and they had produced exactly what one would expect of a magpie and a cake of soap: a young man with girlish hands who danced like an angel.

"Don't take him, dear. I don't want my child to

marry into a finicky family like that who would tolerate her with pursed lips."

Having thus demolished the third suitor, Guillaume Alérac settled down again to *War and Peace*.

4

Carolle put her candle on the mantelpiece and sank into a chair. These proposals had made her feel as though she were going to be ill: her head was hot and aching, her joints were sore, and when she crossed her legs they seemed heavy and somehow not her legs at all. She looked at the thin flame of her candle, burning steadily and silently, and rested a foot on one of the fire-dogs; but she felt no warmth, for the fire was dead. It was colder when one moved about, so she kept as still as possible. If one of her legs stirred the least bit, little shivers ran up and down under her stockings. She was longing for sleep, but lacked the strength to get into bed. There was such a lot to do: brush her hair, clean her teeth, pull off her stockings—she usually did it all quickly and untidily, with a kind of sleight-of-hand— dress, stockings, petticoat, everything flew this way and that. Then when she was about to jump into bed: "What about thunderstorms, my child?"—and she would scurry round in her night-dress, bare feet on the cold floor, picking them up. She was terribly afraid of fires in the country, where water was so scarce, and Masha's orders had to be obeyed, so she would fold her clothes and pile them neatly on a chair in the order in which she would put them on in case of a calamity: stockings on top, not one above the other but side by side like two harmless black snakes.

Feeling that few people would have the courage to undress after two offers of marriage, she lay there with her legs crossed, half asleep in her chair. First Balagny's face bent over her, then Bertrand de la Tour's, and on opening her eyes for a moment she saw part of the sleeve of her new dress in the dim candle-light, and a piece of the icon reflected in the mirror; nothing more. Odd how little she could see of the icon: none of the foreground, but the crowded gilt roofs were there: Holy Jerusalem moving along in the night. There was something almost magical about the icon; as she looked at it, a great happiness welled up in her and tears came into her eyes. When one is young and very tired, sometimes the most ordinary things are suddenly filled with meaning; one sees signs and portents everywhere. It was strange that *Revelation* had not been written by a young girl!

She was cold now up to her knees and her shoulders were drawn together. The tiniest motion of her head sent shivers down her neck. But she was really all right: happy, and only a little sad. Jerusalem glowed in the darkness; the candle burned steadily. Nothing was settled. A man had taken her in his arms; her dress was not finished. Anything might happen.

She took off her clothes slowly, got into bed and was soon asleep. Then she dreamed that Catherine was looking at her with cold, unfriendly eyes. She was asking her a question. But what was that question? Catherine's voice had been low—almost a whisper; she had scarcely been able to hear it, so of course she couldn't remember. It seemed to her that she had spent the whole night trying to remember Catherine's words, and now she was so tired! She had hunted everywhere for them: down between the sheets, under the pillows, out in the darkness of the room; but her searching fingers did not find them, and Catherine's unfriendly eyes were on her all the time.

In the early morning she sat up wearily in bed and the words came to her: "Are you sure Balagny will not be at the dance?" How absurd! Balagny? Catherine had never even mentioned his name to her!

She sank back among the pillows and fell asleep again.

bw. Sa2582

SEVEN DAYS

JUN 9   '36
JUN 11   '36   APR 20 '37
JUN 15   '36   APR 23 '37
JUN 24   '36   MAY 24 '37
JUL 1   '36   JUN 15 '37
                JUL 6   '37
JUL 10   '36
JUL 17   '36   JUL 13 '37
JUL 24   '36   JUL 23 '37
JUL 28   '36
                JUL 31
AUG 3   '36   WITHDRAWN
                AUG 23 '37
AUG 28   '36
SEP 8   '36   SEP 2 '37
SEP 19   '36   FEB 27 1943
SEP 21   '36   MAR 13 1943
OCT 1   '36
OCT 17   '36   FEB 8   1944
                MAR 5   1946
OCT 23   '36   DEC 19 1964
NOV 6   '36
NOV 16   '36   OCT 24 1968
NOV 20   '36   NOV 4 1972
FEB 17   '37
MAR 4   '37
APR 7   '37